Down Here In
The Dream Quarter

by *Barry N. Malzberg*

OVERLAY
THE FALLING ASTRONAUTS
IN THE ENCLOSURE
UNDERLAY
THE DESTRUCTION OF THE TEMPLE
PHASE IV
THE SODOM AND GOMORRAH BUSINESS
BEYOND APOLLO
HEROVIT'S WORLD
THE GAMESMAN
REVELATIONS
GUERNICA NIGHT
CONVERSATIONS
THE DAY OF THE BURNING
TACTICS OF CONQUEST
GALAXIES
SCOP
THE MEN INSIDE
ON A PLANET ALIEN
OUT FROM GANYMEDE (collection)
THE BEST OF BARRY N. MALZBERG (collection)
THE MANY WORLDS OF BARRY MALZBERG (collection)
DOWN HERE IN THE DREAM QUARTER (collection)

as *K. M. O'Donnell*

THE EMPTY PEOPLE
DWELLERS OF THE DEEP
GATHER IN THE HALL OF THE PLANETS
UNIVERSE DAY
FINAL WAR & OTHER FANTASIES (collection)
IN THE POCKET AND OTHER S-F STORIES (collection)

with *Bill Pronzini*
THE RUNNING OF BEASTS

Down Here In The Dream Quarter

BARRY N. MALZBERG

DOUBLEDAY & COMPANY, INC.

GARDEN CITY, NEW YORK, 1976

2/1979
(signature)

All of the characters in the book
are fictitious, and any resemblance
to actual persons, living or dead,
is purely coincidental.

Library of Congress Cataloging in Publication Data

Malzberg, Barry N
Down here in the dream quarter.

1. Science fiction, American.   I. Title.
PZ4.M2615Do [PS3563.A434]   813'.5'4
ISBN 0-385-12268-3
Library of Congress Catalog Card Number 76-14706

Copyright Information

INTRODUCTION: A SHORT ONE FOR THE BOYS IN THE BACK ROOM copyright ©
1976, 1977, by Barry N. Malzberg.
A GALAXY CALLED ROME copyright © 1975 by Mercury Publications, Inc. Pub-
lished in FANTASY & SCIENCE FICTION, July 1975.
THIRTY-SEVEN NORTHWEST copyright © 1977 by Barry N. Malzberg.
SEDAN DEVILLE copyright © 1974 by Mercury Publications, Inc. Published in
FANTASY & SCIENCE FICTION, December 1974.
STATE OF THE ART copyright © 1974 by Robert Silverberg. Published in NEW
DIMENSIONS IV.
ISAIAH copyright © 1973 by Ultimate Publications Inc. Published in FANTASTIC,
September 1973.
ON THE CAMPAIGN TRAIL copyright © 1975 by Roger Elwood. Published in FU-
TURE CORRUPTION.

Again for the Editors:

Ben Bova
Roger Elwood
Edward L. Ferman
David Gerrold
Harry M. Harrison
Robert Hoskins
Adele Leone Hull
Ben Pesta
Robert Silverberg
Ted White
and
Sharon Jarvis

Contents

DOWN HERE IN THE DREAM QUARTER
INTRODUCTION: A SHORT ONE FOR THE BOYS IN THE BACK ROOM

About a year ago, looking for another way to contend with the famous and well-known mid-life crisis, I took to going to the local library and taking out at random authors' biographies. Ross and Tom and John and Ernest and James and John again and Sinclair; like that. It was interesting at the start but the reason that I have returned to the Calais coupé and 1952 ASFs for bedtime reading can best be summarized by what I told my wife after biography number nine or perhaps ten, "It's the same book, it's the same *life*. Different names, different dates, maybe different life-styles but oh my God it's one book about all these people. Childhood rejection, early struggles, itinerant employment, first publication, first wife, initial success, social drinking, second wife, huge success, private drinking, blue period, green period, paranoia, sullenness, withdrawal, separation, burnout, bottle, collapse, oblivion. This is not," I concluded, "recreational reading."

Country squire John (*New Yorker* John) and vigorous Ernest; witty Thurber and Kaufman and spectacular Ross and Tom, it was all the same book and these, by all the saints of heaven, were the biggies, the icons, the most successful of their time. If it was one book for all of them, how much shorter and more dismal a book for people like your faithful undersigned, genre writers, that is to say, writers who—let us be honest about this—may possess skills, some of them, to the level of the best of their generation but who have little chance to be the subjects of biographies; writers who do their work for the popular markets in the context of entertainment and are thus limned by the present. One of the lesser insights of my venture into the basement of the library was that for all of us it is pretty much the same although genre writers are forced, occasionally, to make sauterne or scuffling affairs serve the function of scotch and faithful wife number three.

Therefore, therefore, in this introduction to this sixth and possibly last of my short-story collections (there may be more but they will include work no later than this in point of time since I have ceased like a drunk pounding helplessly at a luncheonette window in the cold to write science fiction) let me spare the reader, gentle and ungentle alike. I would locate myself, standard biographywise, somewhere between the Blue Period and the Green but now and then at 5 A.M. I think about the Burnout while not disremembering the Early Achievements. Put me roughly in mid-life, in mid-career, at that point where most male American writers give up and find something else to do while a stubborn and admirable few break through to their best work. Leave precise placement to the biographers who, if my luck holds, will neglect to get at me.

I thought I would talk a bit instead about the Early Struggles. Periods Blue and Green appear differently to every writer (some even call them Yellow) whereas Early Struggles are more or less the same and of more universal appeal. How did I get started writing this stuff, anyway? What brought me into the room? What did I think I was getting into and, hey, if so much of your stuff appears to be anti-science fictional, anti-technological anyway why did you come in to bother us? Why didn't you go into the goddamned *Partisan Review* or maybe men's magazines?

Why, indeed? More and more I think about this; if one is ever going to become contemplative in a productive way, mid-life or mid-career is the proper time. It is only in the past year that I have, as a matter of fact, tried to evaluate my career and its origins in any systematized way. I was writing so fast, struggling so hard, moving on so quickly that for many years I literally had no *time* to think. (Now I may have too much.) I sold my first science fiction story on January 11, 1967, and my first science fiction novel about two years later, by which time I had sold another dozen short stories. By 1972 I had sold thirteen science fiction novels and about eighty short stories; by the end of 1974 I had sold twenty-four and in excess of a hundred and fifty. Still not ten years from that first sale I have produced a body of work which quantitatively (quality judgments are not within my province) will compare, I think, to the most prolific writers in a genre whose history has been filled with prolificity; this is a field historically so ill-paying that one had to write a great deal to make even a modest living and a year's output by an industrious and disciplined full-time professional hereabouts would be a

respectable career by the standards of the academy, and no wonder. Even in this company, however, I have been unusually prolific.
I have, you see, been so damned *busy* that for a long time it never
occurred to me to ask myself what I was doing here.

What the hell. I was just here to try and sell a few literary short
stories, that was all, except that I got lucky and found that I had a
feeling for the stuff and could do novel length too and from then on
it was just a matter of going as far as my productivity and talent
would take me. I never intended to make a career as an sf writer;
back in 1965 Christopher Anvil or R. C. Fitzpatrick looked pretty
good to me by career standards. Sell a few short stories a year,
make a few hundred dollars, get my name in print, buy a kind of
marginal recognition. Every success, every step was a bit of a
surprise. I never expected to be a major science fiction writer let
alone the figure I have become. (Which if not "major" is certainly
that in terms of visibility as best symbol of a certain kind of writing
in my field in my country just as J. G. Ballard occupies the same
role in England.) Don't bother your modest correspondent, folks:
he just found that he could first take and then not resist the next
step and the next . . .

My uncle, a very successful man, died of a terrible cancer at the
age of sixty-three many years ago. I think his sister was quite right
in saying that what killed him was ambition. It is ambition which is
the undoing of many of us. Wanting to be the new Christopher
Anvil was fine, no harm in it; wanting to sell a novel for the sake of
selling a single novel wasn't fatal either . . . but step by step by
rung by rung ambition was going with me, walloping me in the
behind and finally catching up in 1971 or so and I think it is possible to say that if my career as a science fiction writer is over today
it is a career whose epitaph must read KILLED BY AMBITION: HE
WANTED TO CHANGE THE FIELD AND MAKE IT ANEW. And all of it,
seen in retrospect a fine inevitability. It could have been no other
way. Sorrow, sorrow. Still, the work is done and some of it has
value.

How did I get here? I think I was asking. Well, I used to read a
lot of this stuff in prepubescence. Every science fiction writer who
ever was until, say, about 1970 (when for other reasons the game
changed; many of the newer writers are transplanted littérateurs
who discovered the field out of the necessity to find some living
market for fiction). It is the only generality which for amost fifty

years bound together all of us, ladies and gents, pulp writers and artistes, good and bad alike: we had all read it at a certain stage of life when it intersected crucially with our own difficult perceptions of helplessness* and had made it part of our psychic landscape. Most science fiction writers go right on reading it, moving in their later teens to their attempts to reproduce, first stumbling, later (which may take very little time) not so stumbling and finally successful until the transition from reader to writer looks in retrospect merely like an inevitable rite of passage. Indeed, most of the well-known science fiction writers of the generation right up to mine had a record of published correspondence in the magazines, articles in the fan magazines, attendance at conventions . . . they fell into the field at pubescence and in one sense never got out. I do not mean this pejoratively.

A far greater percentage do. Get out, that is to say. It would be ridiculous to contend that every prepubescent who reads science fiction moves on to try and write it; as a matter of fact only an insignificant fraction do. The great majority, perhaps upward of 90 per cent, put science fiction away in middle to late adolescence when they find more accessible outlets for their feelings of helplessness and do not read it or read it only occasionally for the rest of their lives. A certain number return and become heavy readers of it again in their twenties . . . but I would contend that I am the only member of this large group who ever came back to be a *writer* let alone have a significant career in the genre.

Because I did give it up of course. Almost completely. In fact, I denied science fiction in my later teens the way certain well-known professionals now deny their published correspondence in fan magazines, their activities at conventions. Between the ages of fourteen and twenty-five I cannot remember *ever* reading a science fiction novel. Oh, maybe *More than Human, The Stars My Destination, Gladiator-at-Law,* but, uh, those weren't really science fiction, they were, um, *good.* Science fiction was escapist stuff for kids and kiddish adults; I did not even consider science fiction writers to be writers, not real, writer-type writers anyway.† Anybody a twelve-

---

* Effortlessly the famous response to a famous questionnaire puts it: "the golden age of science fiction is thirteen."
† I learned far better of course and were this not in the confessional mode I would never put this down. But I do so to point out to my most loathing critics that they cannot possibly do to me what have versions of my earlier self, or, as my mother once pointed out, citing a Russian proverb, "A hundred Cossacks on their horses cannot hurt you as you can hurt yourself."

year-old Malzberg could believe in was obviously no friend of mine.

How dark my sin; dark, darker than desire. At twenty-five I was a burnt-out case, the author of about a million unpublished words, about 100,000 of them (I felt then and agree now) of some literary quality. The *Hudson Review* thought I was promising but not quite right for them, *The Atlantic* took a special interest in my manuscripts but not *that* special. *Esquire* would appreciate my enclosing a stamped self-addressed envelope in the future and *Kenyon* was particularly sorry to send back work of high literary quality which, nevertheless, the volume of submissions forced them to do.

I think I would have given up. (And how I wish in the 5 A.M. over and again that I had!) But I went job hunting and the first job offered was as an employee of a large literary agency and I was in no spirit to turn down anything in June of 1965 and after hanging around the agency just a bit it occurred to me that Christopher Anvil and Mack Reynolds didn't have it so bad after all. They didn't have to contend with the Guggenheim committees much less the editorial board of the *Hudson Review* for one thing, and for another they were knocking down four cents a word on acceptance as opposed to two and half cents a word (if that) on publication. Burnt-out cases, if they do not go for the bottle, inevitably go for the money. (Read the literary biographies for verification.) "I used to read this stuff," I thought, "I know I have a feeling for it; maybe I can do it again."

I tried. What did I have to lose? (My virginity if that is the word I am looking for was already gone; I sold my first story to a tenth-rate men's magazine on 11/19/65. I remember almost nothing about it except that it dealt with a prostitute who had, save me, "round orgasms.") My first piece, written in 12/65, was a murky and awful three-thousand-worder called "Full Circle," something about apocalypse which Fred Pohl failed to receive and which my growing market sense told me almost immediately was not at all salable. My second, whose title falls from memory, written three months later, had to do with modern social chaos as being caused by disruptive alien patrol; Campbell rejected that and although my suspicion of JWC was already fully formed—I had been catching up frantically on the field during all this time, you see—I saw his point as well. My third sf piece, written in September, was a parody of a round dozen of the greats which I could tell on rereading could not possibly be offered; my fourth, a pastiche of the Kuttner Gallegher stories, was written in 11/66 and although Campbell rejected it it is the only one of the early stories of which I am actually fond; I caught Gallegher's drunken lunacy and the narcissism of Joe the Can Opener if only by clumsily welding them to a standard EQMM-type plot. Campbell told my agent he didn't think I was the equal of Hank Kuttner; I hadn't thought then (or now) that I ever pretended to be.

In 12/66 I wrote in one sitting in circumstances explained elsewhere a twelve-hundred-word piece "We're Coming Through the Windows" framed in an epistolary fashion to Fred Pohl and submitted immediately to him. My agent's phone call on 1/11/67 telling me that Pohl was buying the piece for $36 gave me, and I know my wife and children are listening and I know they will understand, the single happiest moment of my life. During the next nine months I was still trying to find the range in a sequence of short-shorts, one or two of which I sold in years following, all of which are negligible and forgotten.

Then, in May of 1967, sitting in the living room of our apartment at 102 West Seventy-fifth Street, breathing in great draughts of reeking Amsterdam and Columbus Avenue air while trying to figure out a mindless plot I could try for AHMM, I was stricken with an inspiration. In my trunk I had a twelve-thousand-word piece, "Shoe a Troop of Horse," about an endless war in an ambiguous time fought for no reason. (People later took it to be about Vietnam and it became about as famous as any story in our little category can be but I did not have Vietnam at all in mind when I wrote the story in 2/65. I didn't even know at that time what a "teach-in" was except it was something that no proper writer should be attending. Silence, exile, cunning.) Why not give it a science fictional title and see if I could sneak it through? It had come as close to selling the literary markets as anything I had written when I wanted to be a literary writer; maybe the ambiguity would appear, to a science fiction editor, as extrapolation.

I was, by that time, twenty-eight years old and not without a certain low cunning. I retitled the story "Final War," retyped the first page and sent it off to Campbell, who promptly rejected it with a form slip. Fred Pohl turned it back as non-science fiction (Fred Pohl was no fool) but said that it reinforced his feeling about the writer's talent and he wanted to be kept on the list. (What list he did not specify.) Damon Knight for *Orbit* thought it a great literary accomplishment but entirely out of category. Edward L. Ferman, with his father, Joseph Wolfe, took it on 10/1/67 for *Fantasy & Science Fiction* and paid me $250 and changed my life. Even before it was published I sold a second literary story, "Death to the Keeper," to them and one piece to Harry Harrison at *Amazing*. "Final War" was published in March 1968 and subsequently was anthologized seven times in the United States alone and was the basis of my first book sale, a collection to Ace.

I was on my way. Where I would not know for several years and why I am not sure I know even now . . . but I was on my way.

January 21, 1976, 10:30 P.M. Six inches of snow on the ground. Two million published words of science fiction on the shelves around me. Down here; down here in the dream quarter.

New Jersey: January 1976

Down Here In
The Dream Quarter

A Galaxy Called Rome

IN MEMORY OF JOHN W. CAMPBELL

I

This is not a novelette but a series of notes. The novelette cannot be truly written because it partakes of its time, which is distant and could be perceived only through the idiom and devices of that era.

Thus the piece, by virtue of these reasons and others too personal even for this variety of True Confession, is little more than a set of constructions toward something less substantial . . . and, like the author, it cannot be completed.

II

The novelette would lean heavily upon two articles by the late John Campbell, for thirty-three years the editor of *Astounding/Analog*, which were written shortly before his death untimely on July 11, 1971, and appeared as editorials in his magazine later that year, the second being perhaps the last piece which will ever bear his byline. They imagine a black galaxy which would result from the implosion of a neutron star, an implosion so mighty that gravitational forces unleashed would contain not only light itself but space and time; and *A Galaxy Called Rome* is his title, not mine, since he envisions a spacecraft that might be trapped within such a black galaxy and be unable to get out . . . because escape velocity would have to exceed the speed of light. All paths of travel would lead to this galaxy, then, none away. A galaxy called Rome.

III

Conceive then of a faster-than-light spaceship which would tumble into the black galaxy and would be unable to leave. Tumbling would be easy, or at least inevitable, since one of the characteristics of the black galaxy would be its *invisibility,* and there the ship would be. The story would then pivot on the efforts of the crew to get out. The ship is named *Skipstone.* It was completed in 3892. Five hundred people died so that it might fly, but in this age life is held even more cheaply than it is today.

Left to my own devices, I might be less interested in the escape problem than that of adjustment. Light housekeeping in an anterior sector of the universe; submission to the elements, a fine, ironic literary despair. This is not science fiction however. Science fiction was created by Hugo Gernsback to show us the ways out of technological impasse. So be it.

IV

As interesting as the material was, I quailed even at this series of notes, let alone a polished, completed work. My personal life is my black hole, I felt like pointing out (who would listen?); my daughters provide more correct and sticky implosion than any neutron star, and the sound of the pulsars is as nothing to the music of the paddock area at Aqueduct racetrack in Ozone Park, Queens, on a clear summer Tuesday. "Enough of these breathtaking concepts, infinite distances, quasar leaps, binding messages amidst the arms of the spiral nebula," I could have pointed out. "I know that there are those who find an ultimate truth there, but I am not one of them. I would rather dedicate the years of life remaining (my melodramatic streak) to an understanding of the agonies of this middle-class town in northern New Jersey; until I can deal with those, how can I comprehend Ridgefield Park, to say nothing of the extension of fission to include progressively heavier gases?" Indeed, I almost abided to this until it occurred to me that Ridgefield Park would forever be as mysterious as the stars and that one could not deny infinity merely to pursue a particular that would be impenetrable until the day of one's death.

So I decided to try the novelette, at least as this series of notes, although with some trepidation, but trepidation did not unsettle me, nor did I grieve, for my life is merely a set of notes for a life, and Ridgefield Park merely a rough working model of Trenton, in which, nevertheless, several thousand people live who cannot discern their right hands from their left, and also much cattle.

V

It is 3895. The spacecraft *Skipstone*, on an exploratory flight through the major and minor galaxies surrounding the Milky Way, falls into the black galaxy of a neutron star and is lost forever. The captain of this ship, the only living consciousness of it, is its commander, Lena Thomas. True, the hold of the ship carries five hundred and fifteen of the dead sealed in gelatinous fix who will absorb unshielded gamma rays. True, these rays will at some time in the future hasten their reconstitution. True, again, that another part of the hold contains the prosthesis of seven skilled engineers, male and female, who could be switched on at only slight inconvenience and would provide Lena not only with answers to any technical problems which would arise but with companionship to while away the long and grave hours of the *Skipstone*'s flight.

Lena, however, does not use the prosthesis, nor does she feel the necessity to. She is highly skilled and competent, at least in relation to the routine tasks of this testing flight, and she feels that to call for outside help would only be an admission of weakness, would be reported back to the Bureau and lessen her potential for promotion. (She is right; the Bureau has monitored every cubicle of this ship, both visually and biologically; she can see or do nothing which does not trace to a printout; they would not think well of her if she was dependent upon outside assistance.) Toward the embalmed she feels somewhat more; her condition rattling in the hold of the ship as it moves on tachyonic drive seems to approximate theirs: although they are deprived of consciousness, that quality seems to be almost irrelevant to the condition of hyperspace; and if there were any way that she could bridge their mystery, she might well address them. As it is, she must settle for imaginary dialogues and for long, quiescent periods when she will watch the monitors, watch the rainbow of hyperspace, the collision of the spectrum, and say nothing whatsoever.

Saying nothing will not do, however, and the fact is that Lena talks incessantly at times, if only to herself. This is good because the story should have much dialogue; dramatic incident is best impelled through straightforward characterization, and Lena's compulsive need, now and then, to state her condition and its relation to the spaces she occupies will satisfy this need.

In her conversation, of course, she often addresses the embalmed. "Consider," she says to them, some of them dead eight hundred years, others dead weeks, all of them stacked in the hold in relation to their status in life and their ability to hoard assets to pay for the process that will return them their lives, "Consider what's going on here," pointing through the hold, the colors gleaming through the portholes onto her wrist, colors dancing in the air, her eyes quite full and maddened in this light, which does not indicate that she is mad but only that the condition of hyperspace itself is insane, the Michelson-Morley effect having a psychological as well as physical reality here. "Why it could be *me* dead and in the hold and all of you here in the dock watching the colors spin, it's all the same, all the same faster than light," and indeed the twisting and sliding effects of the tachyonic drive are such that at the moment of speech what Lena says is true.

The dead live; the living are dead, all slides and becomes jumbled together as she has noted; and were it not that their objective poles of consciousness were fixed by years of training and discipline, just as hers are transfixed by a different kind of training and discipline, she would press the levers to eject the dead one-by-one into the larger coffin of space, something which is indicated only as an emergency procedure under the gravest of terms and which would result in her removal from the Bureau immediately upon her return. The dead are precious cargo; they are, in essence, paying for the experiments and must be handled with the greatest delicacy. "I will handle you with the greatest delicacy," Lena says in hyperspace, "and I will never let you go, little packages in my little prison," and so on, singing and chanting as the ship moves on somewhat in excess of one million miles per second, always accelerating; and yet, except for the colors, the nausea, the disorienting swing, her own mounting insanity, the terms of this story, she might be in the IRT Lenox Avenue local at rush hour, moving slowly uptown as circles of illness move through the fainting car in the bowels of summer.

VI

She is twenty-eight years old. Almost two thousand years in the future, when man has established colonies on forty planets in the Milky Way, has fully populated the solar system, is working in the faster-than-light experiments as quickly as he can to move through other galaxies, the medical science of that day is not notably superior to that of our own, and the human lifespan has not been significantly extended, nor have the diseases of mankind which are now known as congenital been eradicated. Most of the embalmed were in their eighties or nineties; a few of them, the more recent deaths, were nearly a hundred, but the average lifespan still hangs somewhat short of eighty, and most of these have died from cancer, heart attacks, renal failure, cerebral blowout, and the like. There is some irony in the fact that man can have at least established a toehold in his galaxy, can have solved the mysteries of the FTL drive, and yet finds the fact of his own biology as stupefying as he has throughout history, but every sociologist understands that those who live in a culture are least qualified to criticize it (because they have fully assimilated the codes of the culture, even as to criticism), and Lena does not see this irony any more than the reader will have to in order to appreciate the deeper and more metaphysical irony of the story, which is this: that greater speed, greater space, greater progress, greater sensation has not resulted in any definable expansion of the limits of consciousness and personality and all that the FTL drive is to Lena is an increasing entrapment.

It is important to understand that she is merely a technician; that although she is highly skilled and has been trained through the Bureau for many years for her job as pilot, she really does not need to possess the technical knowledge of any graduate scientists of our own time . . . that her job, which is essentially a probe-and-ferrying, could be done by an adolescent; and that all of her training has afforded her no protection against the boredom and depression of her assignment.

When she is done with this latest probe, she will return to Uranus and be granted a six-month leave. She is looking forward to that. She appreciates the opportunity. She is only twenty-eight, and she is tired of being sent with the dead to tumble through the spectrum for weeks at a time, and what she would very much like to be, at least for a while, is a young woman. She would like to be at peace. She would like to be loved. She would like to have sex.

VII

Something must be made of the element of sex in this story, if only because it deals with a female protagonist (where asepsis will not work); and in the tradition of modern literary science fiction, where some credence is given to the whole range of human needs and behaviors, it would be clumsy and amateurish to ignore the issue. Certainly the easy scenes can be written and to great effect: Lena masturbating as she stares through the port at the colored levels of hyperspace; Lena dreaming thickly of intercourse as she unconsciously massages her nipples, the ship plunging deeper and deeper (as she does not yet know) toward the Black Galaxy; the Black Galaxy itself as some ultimate vaginal symbol of absorption whose Freudian overcast will not be ignored in the imagery of this story . . . indeed, one can envision Lena stumbling toward the Evictors at the depths of her panic in the Black Galaxy to bring out one of the embalmed, her grim and necrophiliac fantasies as the body is slowly moved upwards on its glistening slab, the way that her eyes will look as she comes to consciousness and realizes what she has become . . . oh, this would be a very powerful scene indeed, almost anything to do with sex in space is powerful (one must also conjure with the effects of hyperspace upon the orgasm; would it be the orgasm which all of us know and love so well or something entirely different, perhaps detumescence, perhaps exaltation?), and I would face the issue squarely, if only I could, and in line with the very real need of the story to have powerful and effective dialogue.

"For God's sake," Lena would say at the end, the music of her entrapment squeezing her, coming over her, blotting her toward extinction, "for God's sake, all we ever needed was a screw, that's all that sent us out into space, that's all that it ever meant to us, I've got to have it, got to have it, do you understand?" jamming her fingers in and out of her aqueous surfaces—

—But of course this would not work, at last in the story which I am trying to conceptualize. Space *is* aseptic; that is the secret of science fiction for forty-five years; it is not deceit or its adolescent audience or the publication codes which have deprived most of the literature of the range of human sexuality but the fact that in the clean and abysmal spaces between the stars sex, that demonstration of our perverse and irreplaceable humanity, would have no role at all. Not for nothing did the astronauts return to tell us their vision of otherworldliness, not for nothing did they stagger in their thick landing gear as they walked toward the colonels' salute, not for nothing did all of those marriages, all of those wonderful kids undergo such terrible strains. There is simply no room for it. It does not fit. Lena would understand this. "I never thought of sex," she would say, "never thought of it once, not even at the end when everything was around me and I was dancing."

VIII

Therefore it will be necessary to characterize Lena in some other way, and that opportunity will only come through the moment of crisis, the moment at which the *Skipstone* is drawn into the Black Galaxy of the neutron star. This moment will occur fairly early into the story, perhaps five or six hundred words deep (her previous life on the ship and impressions of hyperspace will come in expository chunks interwoven between sections of ongoing action), and her only indication of what has happened will be when there is a deep, lurching shiver in the gut of the ship where the embalmed lay and then she feels herself falling.

To explain this sensation it is important to explain normal hyperspace, the skip-drive which is merely to draw the curtains and to be in a cubicle. There is no sensation of motion in hyperspace, there could not be, the drive taking the *Skipstone* past any concepts of sound or light and into an area where there is no language to encompass nor glands to register. Were she to draw the curtains (curiously similar in their frills and pastels to what we might see hanging today in lower-middle-class homes of the kind I inhabit), she would be deprived of any sensation, but of course she cannot; she must open them to the portholes, and through them she can see the song of the colors to which I have previously alluded. Inside, there is a deep and grievous wretchedness, a feeling of terrible loss (which may explain why Lena thinks of exhuming the dead) that may be ascribed to the affects of hyperspace upon the corpus; but these sensations can be shielded, are not visible from the outside, and can be completely controlled by the phlegmatic types who comprise most of the pilots of these experimental flights. (Lena is rather phlegmatic herself. She reacts more to stress than some of her counterparts but well within the normal range prescribed by the Bureau, which admittedly does a superficial check.)

The effects of falling into the Black Galaxy are entirely different however, and it is here where Lena's emotional equipment becomes completely unstuck.

IX

At this point in the story great gobs of physics, astronomical and mathematical data would have to be incorporated, hopefully in a way which would furnish the hard-science basis of the story without repelling the reader.

Of course one should not worry so much about the repulsion of the reader; most who read science fiction do so in pursuit of exactly this kind of hard speculation (most often they are disappointed, but then most often they are after a time unable to tell the difference), and they would sit still much longer for a lecture than would, say, readers of the fictions of John Cheever, who could hardly bear sociological diatribes wedged into the everlasting vision of Gehenna which is Cheever's gift to his admirers. Thus it would be possible without awkwardness to make the following facts known, and these facts could indeed be set off from the body of the story and simply told like this:

It is posited that in other galaxies there are such as neutron stars, stars of four or five hundred times the size of our own or "normal" suns, which in their continuing nuclear process, burning and burning to maintain their light, will collapse in a mere ten to fifteen thousand years of difficult existence, their hydrogen fusing to helium then nitrogen and then to even heavier elements until with an implosion of terrific force, hungering for power which is no longer there, they collapse upon one another and bring disaster.

Disaster not only to themselves but possibly to the entire galaxy which they inhabit, for the gravitational force created by the implosion would be so vast as to literally seal in light. Not only light but sound and properties of all the stars in that great tube of force . . . so that the galaxy itself would be sucked into the funnel of gravitation created by the collapse and be absorbed into the flickering and desperate heart of the extinguished star.

It is possible to make several extrapolations from the fact of the neutron stars—and of the neutron stars themselves we have no doubt; many nova and supernova are now known to have been created by exactly this effect, not *ex-* but *im-*plosion—and some of them are these:

(a) The gravitational forces created, like great spokes wheeling out from the star, would drag in all parts of the galaxy within their compass; and because of the force of that gravitation, the galaxy would be invisible . . . these forces would, as has been said, literally contain light.

(b) The neutron star, functioning like a cosmic vacuum cleaner, might literally destroy the universe. Indeed, the universe may be in the slow process at this moment of being destroyed as hundreds of millions of its suns and planets are being inexorably drawn toward these great vortexes. The process would be *slow*, of course, but it is seemingly inexorable. One neutron star, theoretically, could absorb the universe. There are many more than one.

(c) The universe may have, obversely, been *created* by such an implosion, throwing out enormous cosmic filaments that, in a flickering instant of time which is as eons to us but an instant to the cosmologists, are now being drawn back in. The universe may be an accident.

(d) Cosmology aside, a ship trapped in such a vortex, such a "black," or invisible, galaxy, drawn toward the deadly source of the neutron star would be unable to leave it through normal faster-than-light drive . . . because the gravitation would absorb light, it would be impossible to build up any level of acceleration (which would at some point not exceed the speed of light) to permit escape. If it were possible to emerge from the field, it could only be done by an immediate switch to tachyonic drive without accelerative buildup . . . a process which could drive the occupant insane and which would, in any case, have no clear destination. The black hole of the dead star is a literal vacuum in space . . . one could fall through the hole, but where, then, would one go?

(e) The actual process of being in the field of the dead star might well drive one insane.

For all of these reasons Lena does not know that she has fallen into the Galaxy Called Rome until the ship simply does so.
And she would instantly and irreparably become insane.

X

The technological data having been stated, the crisis of the story —the collapse into the Galaxy—having occurred early on, it would now be the obligation of the writer to describe the actual sensations involved in falling into the Black Galaxy. Since little or nothing is known of what these sensations would be—other than that it is clear that the gravitation would suspend almost all physical laws and might well suspend time itself, time only being a function of physics—it would be easy to lurch into a surrealistic mode here; Lena could see monsters slithering on the walls, two-dimensional monsters that is, little cut-outs of her past; she could re-enact her life *in full consciousness* from birth until death; she could literally be turned inside-out anatomically and perform in her imagination or in the flesh gross physical acts upon herself; she could live and die a thousand times in the lightless, timeless expanse of the pit . . . all of this could be done within the confines of the story, and it would doubtless lead to some very powerful material. One could do it picaresque fashion, one perversity or lunacy to a chapter—that is to say, the chapters spliced together with more data on the gravitational excesses and the fact that neutron stars (this is interesting) are probably the pulsars which we have identified, stars which can be detected through sound but not by sight from unimaginable distances. The author could do this kind of thing, and do it very well indeed; he has done it literally hundreds of times before, but this, perhaps, would be in disregard of Lena. She has needs more imperative than those of the author, or even those of the editors. She is in terrible pain. She is suffering.

Falling, she sees the dead; falling, she hears the dead; the dead address her from the hold, and they are screaming, "Release us, release us, we are alive, we are in pain, we are in torment"; in their gelatinous flux, their distended limbs sutured finger and toe to the membranes which hold them, their decay has been reversed as the warp into which they have fallen has reversed time; and they are begging Lena from a torment which they cannot phrase, so profound is it; their voices are in her head, pealing and banging like oddly shaped bells, "Release us!" they scream; "we are no longer dead, the trumpet has sounded!" and so on and so forth, but Lena literally does not know what to do. She is merely the ferryman on this dread passage; she is not a medical specialist; she knows nothing of prophylaxis or restoration, and any movement she made to release them from the gelatin which holds them would surely destroy their biology, no matter what the state of their minds.

But even if this were not so, even if she could by releasing them give them peace, she cannot because she is succumbing to her own responses. In the black hole, if the dead are risen, then the risen are certainly the dead; she dies in this space, Lena does; she dies a thousand times over a period of seventy thousand years (because there is no objective time here, chronology is controlled only by the psyche, and Lena has a thousand full lives and a thousand full deaths), and it is terrible, of course, but it is also interesting because for every cycle of death there is a life, seventy years in which she can meditate upon her condition in solitude; and by the two hundredth year or more (or less, each of the lives is individual, some of them long, others short), Lena has come to an understanding of exactly where she is and what has happened to her. That it has taken her fourteen thousand years to reach this understanding is in one way incredible, and yet it is a kind of miracle as well because in an infinite universe with infinite possibilities, all of them reconstituted for her, it is highly unlikely that even in fourteen thousand years she would stumble upon the answer, had it not been for the fact that she is unusually strong-willed and that some of the personalities through which she has lived are highly creative and controlled and have been able to do some serious thinking. Also there is a carry-over from life to life, even with the differing personalities, so that she is able to make use of preceding knowledge.

Most of the personalities are weak, of course, and not a few are insane, and almost all are cowardly, but there is a little residue; even in the worst of them there is enough residue to carry forth the knowledge, and so it is in the fourteen-thousandth year, when the truth of it has finally come upon her and she realizes what has happened to her and what is going on and what she must do to get out of there, and so it is [then] that she summons all of the strength and will which are left to her, and stumbling to the console (she is in her sixty-eighth year of this life and in the personality of an old, sniveling, whining man, an exferryman himself), she summons one of the prostheses, the master engineer, the controller. All of this time the dead have been shrieking and clanging in her ears, fourteen thousand years of agony billowing from the hold and surrounding her in sheets like iron; and as the master engineer, exactly as he was when she last saw him fourteen thousand years and two weeks ago emerges from the console, the machinery whirring slickly, she gasps in relief, too weak to even respond with pleasure to the fact that in this condition of antitime, antilight, anticausality the machinery still works. But then it would. The machinery always works, even in this final and most terrible of all the hard-science stories. It is not the machinery which fails but its operators or, in extreme cases, the cosmos.

"What's the matter?" the master engineer says.

The stupidity of this question, its naivete and irrelevance in the midst of the hell she has occupied, stuns Lena, but she realizes even through the haze that the master engineer would, of course, come without memory of circumstances and would have to be apprised of background. This is inevitable. Whining and sniveling, she tells him in her old man's voice what has happened.

"Why that's terrible!" the master engineer says. "That's really terrible," and lumbering to a porthole, he looks out at the Black Galaxy, the Galaxy Called Rome, and one look at it causes him to lock into position and then disintegrate, not because the machinery has failed (the machinery never fails, not ultimately) but because it has merely recreated a human substance which could not possibly come to grips with what has been seen outside that porthole.

Lena is left alone again, then, with the shouts of the dead carrying forward.

Realizing instantly what has happened to her—fourteen thousand years of perception can lead to a quicker reaction time, if nothing else—she addresses the console again, uses the switches and produces three more prostheses, all of them engineers barely subsidiary to the one she has already addressed. (Their resemblance to the three comforters of Job will not be ignored here, and there will be an opportunity to squeeze in some quick religious allegory, which is always useful to give an ambitious story yet another level of meaning.) Although they are not quite as qualified or definitive in their opinions as the original engineer, they are bright enough by far to absorb her explanation, and, this time, her warnings not to go to the portholes, not to look upon the galaxy, are heeded. Instead, they stand there in rigid and curiously mortified postures, as if waiting for Lena to speak.

"So you see," she says finally, as if concluding a long and difficult conversation, which in fact she has, "as far as I can see, the only way to get out of this black galaxy is to go directly into tachyonic drive. Without any accelerative build-up at all."

The three comforters nod slowly, bleakly. They do not quite

know what she is talking about, but then again, they have not had fourteen thousand years to ponder this point. "Unless you can see anything else," Lena says, "unless you can think of anything different. Otherwise, it's going to be infinity in here, and I can't take much more of this, really. Fourteen thousand years is enough."

"Perhaps," the first comforter suggests softly, "perhaps it is your fate and your destiny to spend infinity in this black hole. Perhaps in some way you are determining the fate of the universe. After all, it was you who said that it all might be a gigantic accident, eh? Perhaps your suffering gives it purpose."

"And then too," the second lisps, "you've got to consider the deads down there. This isn't very easy for them, you know, what with being jolted alive and all that, and an immediate vault into tachyonic would probably destroy them for good. The Bureau wouldn't like that, and you'd be liable for some pretty stiff damages. No, if I were you I'd stay with the dead," the second concludes, and a clamorous murmur seems to arise from the hold at this, although whether it is one of approval or of terrible pain is difficult to tell. The dead are not very expressive.

"Anyway," the third says, brushing a forelock out of his eyes, averting his glance from the omnipresent and dreadful portholes, "there's little enough to be done about this situation. You've fallen into a neutron star, a black funnel. It is utterly beyond the puny capacities and possibilities of man. I'd accept my fate if I were you." His model was a senior scientist working on quasar theory, but in reality he appears to be a metaphysician. "There are corners of experience into which man cannot stray without being severely penalized."

"That's very easy for you to say," Lena says bitterly, her whine breaking into clear glissando, "but you haven't suffered as I have. Also, there's at least a theoretical possibility that I'll get out of here if I do the build-up without acceleration."

"But where will you land?" the third says, waving a trembling forefinger. "And when? All rules of space and time have been destroyed here; only gravity persists. You can fall through the center of this sun, but you do not know where you will come out or at what period of time. It is inconceivable that you would emerge into normal space in the time you think of as contemporary."

"No," the second says, "I wouldn't do that. You and the dead are joined together now; it is truly your fate to remain with them. What is death? What is life? In the Galaxy Called Rome all roads lead to the same, you see; you have ample time to consider these questions, and I'm sure that you will come up with something truly viable, of much interest."

"Ah, well," the first says, looking at Lena, "if you must know, I think that it would be much nobler of you to remain here; for all we know, your condition gives substance and viability to the universe. Perhaps you *are* the universe. But you're not going to listen anyway, and so I won't argue the point. I really won't," he says rather petulantly and then makes a gesture to the other two; the three of them quite deliberately march to a porthole, push a curtain aside and look out upon it. Before Lena can stop them—not that she is sure she would, not that she is sure that this is not exactly what she has willed—they have been reduced to ash.

And she is left alone with the screams of the dead.

XI

It can be seen that the satiric aspects of the scene above can be milked for great implication, and unless a very skillful controlling hand is kept upon the material, the piece could easily degenerate into farce at this moment. It is possible, as almost any comedian knows, to reduce (or elevate) the starkest and most terrible issues to scatology or farce simply by particularizing them; and it will be hard not to use this scene for a kind of needed comic relief in what is, after all, an extremely depressing tale, the more depressing because it has used the largest possible canvas on which to imprint its messages that man is irretrievably dwarfed by the cosmos. (At least, that is the message which it would be easiest to wring out of the material; actually I have other things in mind, but how many will be able to detect them?)

What will save the scene and the story itself, around this point, will be the lush physical descriptions of the Black Galaxy, the neutron star, the altering effects they have had upon perceived reality. Every rhetorical trick, every typographical device, every nuance of language and memory which the writer has to call upon will be utilized in this section describing the appearance of the black hole and its effects upon Lena's (admittedly distorted) consciousness. It will be a bleak vision, of course, but not necessarily a hopeless one; it will demonstrate that our concepts of "beauty" or "ugliness" or "evil" or "good" or "love" or "death" are little more than metaphors, semantically limited, framed-in by the poor receiving equipment in our heads; and it will be suggested that, rather than showing us a different or alternative reality, the black hole may only be showing us the only reality we know, but *extended,* infinitely extended so that the story may give us, as good science fiction often does, at this point some glimpse of possibilities beyond ourselves, possibilities not to be contained in word rates or the problems of editorial qualification. And also at this point of the story it might be worthwhile to characterize Lena in a "warmer" and more "sympathetic" fashion so that the reader can see her as a distinct and admirable human being, quite plucky in the face of all her disasters and fourteen thousand years, two hundred lives. This can be done through conventional fictional technique: individuation through defining idiosyncrasy, tricks of speech, habits, mannerisms, and so on. In common everyday fiction we could give her an affecting stutter, a dimple on her left breast, a love of policemen, fear of red convertibles, and leave it at that; in this story, because of its considerably extended theme, it will be necessary to do better than that, to find originalities of idiosyncrasy which will, in their wonder and suggestion of panoramic possibility, approximate the black hole . . . but no matter. No matter. This can be done; the section interweaving Lena and her vision of the black hole will be the flashiest and most admired but in truth the easiest section of the story to write, and I am sure that I would have no trouble with it whatsoever if, as I said much earlier, this were a story instead of a series of notes for a story, the story itself being unutterably beyond our time and space and devices and to be glimpsed only in empty little flickers of light much as Lena can glimpse the black hole, much as she knows the gravity of the neutron star. These notes are as close to the vision of the story as Lena herself would ever get.

As this section ends, it is clear that Lena has made her decision to attempt to leave the Black Galaxy by automatic boost to tachyonic drive. She does not know where she will emerge or how, but she does know that she can bear this no longer.

She prepares to set the controls, but before this it is necessary to write the dialogue with the dead.

XII

One of them presumably will appoint himself as the spokesman of the many and will appear before Lena in this newspace as if in a dream. "Listen here," this dead would say, one born in 3361, dead in 3401, waiting eight centuries for exhumation to a society that can rid his body of leukemia (he is bound to be disappointed), "you've got to face the facts of the situation here. We can't just leave in this way. Better the death we know than the death you will give us."

"The decision is made," Lena says, her fingers straight on the controls. "There will be no turning back."

"We are dead now," the leukemic says. "At least let this death continue. At least in the bowels of this galaxy where there is no time we have a kind of life or at least that nonexistence of which we have always dreamed. I could tell you many of the things we have learned during these fourteen thousand years, but they would make little sense to you, of course. We have learned resignation. We have had great insights. Of course all of this would go beyond you."

"Nothing goes beyond me. Nothing at all. But it does not matter."

"Everything matters. Even here there is consequence, causality, a sense of humanness, one of responsibility. You can suspend physical laws, you can suspend life itself, but you cannot separate the moral imperatives of humanity. There are absolutes. It would be apostasy to try and leave."

"Man must leave," Lena says, "man must struggle, man must attempt to control his conditions. Even if he goes from worse to obliteration, that is still his destiny." Perhaps the dialogue is a little florid here. Nevertheless, this will be the thrust of it. It is to be noted that putting this conventional viewpoint in the character of a woman will give another of those necessary levels of irony with which the story must abound if it is to be anything other than a freak show, a cascade of sleazy wonders shown shamefully behind a tent . . . but irony will give it legitimacy. "I don't care about the dead," Lena says. "I only care about the living."

"Then care about the universe," the dead man says, "care about that, if nothing else. By trying to come out through the center of the black hole, you may rupture the seamless fabric of time and space itself. You may destroy everything. Past and present and future. The explosion may extend the funnel of gravitational force to infinite size, and all of the universe will be driven into the hole." Lena shakes her head. She knows that the dead is merely another one of her tempters in a more cunning and cadaverous guise. "You are lying to me," she says. "This is merely another effect of the Galaxy Called Rome. I am responsible to myself, only to myself. The universe is not at issue."

"That's a rationalization," the leukemic says, seeing her hesitation, sensing his victory, "and you know it as well as I do. You can't be an utter solipsist. You aren't God, there is no God, not here, but if there was it wouldn't be you. You must measure the universe about yourself."

Lena looks at the dead and the dead looks at her; and in that confrontation, in the shade of his eyes as they pass through the dull lusters of the neutron star effect, she sees that they are close to a communion so terrible that it will become a weld, become a connection . . . that if she listens to the dead for more than another instant, she will collapse within those eyes as the *Skipstone* has collapsed into the black hole; and she cannot bear this, it cannot be . . . she must hold to the belief, that there is some separation between the living and the dead and that there is dignity in that separation, that life is not death but something else because, if she cannot accept that, she denies herself . . . and quickly then, quickly before she can consider further, she hits the controls that will convert the ship instantly past the power of light; and then in the explosion of many suns that might only be her heart she hides her head in her arms and screams.

And the dead screams with her, and it is not a scream of joy but not of terror either . . . it is the true natal cry suspended between the moments of limbo, life and expiration, and their shrieks entwine in the womb of the *Skipstone* as it pours through into the redeemed light.

XIII

The story is open-ended, of course.

Perhaps Lena emerges into her own time and space once more, all of this having been a sheath over the greater reality. Perhaps she emerges into an otherness. Then again, she may never get out of the black hole at all but remains and lives there, the *Skipstone* a planet in the tubular universe of the neutron star, the first or last of a series of planets collapsing toward their deadened sun. If the story is done correctly, if the ambiguities are prepared right, if the technological data is stated well, if the material is properly visualized . . . well, it does not matter then what happens to Lena, her *Skipstone* and her dead. Any ending will do. Any would suffice and be emotionally satisfying to the reader.

Still, there is an inevitable ending.

It seems clear to the writer, who will not, cannot write this story, but if he did he would drive it through to this one conclusion, the conclusion clear, implied really from the first and bound, bound utterly, into the text.

So let the author have it.

XIV

In the infinity of time and space, all is possible, and as they are vomited from that great black hole, spilled from this anus of a neutron star (I will not miss a single Freudian implication if I can), Lena and her dead take on this infinity, partake of the vast canvas of possibility. Now they are in the Antares Cluster flickering like a bulb; here they are at the heart of Sirius the Dog Star five hundred screams from the hold; here again in ancient Rome watching Jesus trudge up carrying the Cross of Calvary . . . and then again in another unimaginable galaxy dead across from the Milky Way a billion light-years in span with a hundred thousand habitable planets, each of them with their Calvary . . . and they are not, they are not yet satisfied.

They cannot, being human, partake of infinity; they can partake of only what they know. They cannot, being created from the consciousness of the writer, partake of what he does not know but what is only close to him. Trapped within the consciousness of the writer, the penitentiary of his being, as the writer is himself trapped in the *Skipstone* of his mortality, Lena and her dead emerge in the year 1975 to the town of Ridgefield Park, New Jersey, and there they inhabit the bodies of its fifteen thousand souls, and there they are, there they are yet, dwelling amidst the refineries, strolling on Main Street, sitting in the Rialto theatre, shopping in the supermarkets, pairing off and clutching one another in the imploded stars of their beds on this very night at this very moment, as that accident, the author, himself one of them, has conceived them.

It is unimaginable that they would come, Lena and the dead, from the heart of the Galaxy Called Rome to tenant Ridgefield Park, New Jersey . . . but more unimaginable still that from all the Ridgefield Parks of our time we will come and assemble and build the great engines which will take us to the stars and some of the stars will bring us death and some bring life and some will bring nothing at all but the engines will go on and on and so—after a fashion, in our fashion—will we.

AFTERWORD TO A GALAXY CALLED ROME

This story, probably the longest and most ambitious I ever attempted for science fiction short of novel length was commissioned by the co-editors of an anthology called *Faster than Light* published about a year ago. They rejected the piece as lacking rigorous hard science content and fudging on its extrapolation by being "literary." This turndown angered me—even unto this moment—as has no other through the years.

I claim that "A Galaxy Called Rome," whatever its other flaws, is a serious and extended effort which represents a viable statement of one way in which the hard science story can hold some version of literary merit. Furthermore, the science checks out pretty well too, at least in terms of those who have seen it subsequently. If the introductions to short-story collections are, for genre writers, like memoirs to literary writers—i.e., a place to pay off old enemies and make a few new ones—then you may take this as being a minor example of the form.

Still, editorial prerogative is supposed to be just that (at least that is what the editors say and writers have no recourse other than to become editors themselves and humiliate other writers, which very often they do) and the gentlemen were kind in furnishing the articles incorporated as research material and generous on rejection in releasing the exclusive right to use of that material.

Here I address an old (maybe oldest) question in our tortured category which will never be resolved: *what is science fiction?* And, if we can ever define it, does it "mean" anything in the sense that commercial and literary fiction which deals with objective, verifiable fact can be said to "mean" if not precisely "be"? Is science fiction merely another slightly distorted paradigm of common reality or is it something else which, at its best, can mysteriously assume the reality of a future we will never have?

Difficult questions but I think that some tentative answers are here. I believe that good fiction can unfold its truths only on its own terms, that it cannot be paraphrased in terms other than its own and that the answers cannot be summarized. But perhaps there are given some suggestions.

Thirty-seven Northwest

Now. I was not supposed to prowl Jupiter alone. The original plan was that there were to be the three of us: Nala, Tim and myself, electronically linked to share our observations and compare our impressions before the findings were transmitted to base. Not alone; no. It was their promise that I would be but one of three.

But Nala left the unit on sudden transfer and I do not know where she is and just last evening something happened to Tim, none of us know what. When the preparations for the Jupiter descent began at the beginning of this shift he was not there and it was only me in the dock.

It was made clear to me that I could not be forced to go alone. "Under the statutes, a landing team of three is the basic unit of exploration," they said, "and it is your option whether you will go with less and if you refuse we cannot make you. All that we can tell you and this is true is that it will go much better with you and be to your future credit if you *are* willing to go. We need this information very badly and cannot wait to assemble another team. We think that you will be perfectly safe on the surface and without companions the expedition will go even more rapidly. But this is merely a request and you are advised that we cannot compel you to go even though it is very much to your advantage to do so and things will go easier for you in the long run if you do so. Now it is your decision, Thomas. You must make it quickly."

So I decided to go alone. When all of the brief calculations were finished it came to this: I knew that it would indeed be easier for me if I submitted and the dangers of the expedition on my own were far outweighed by the dangers of refusal. They would refuse me privileges in return. They would exile me from the unit. They might even make of me what I fear they have made of Nala.

II

So I go into the dock and submit to the preparations: the disinfectant, the tapes of knowledge, the gear and the centrifuge and in time am placed in a capsule and sent unconscious on a long, swinging descent, coming out of coma to find the hatch open and the purple gases of Jupiter coming into the capsule to touch me in threads of greeting. Shielded by sixty pounds of gear I am impermeable to all poisonous effects but it is nevertheless frightening to think that all of this death swirls around me, the utter foreignness of this planet which I have studied but never seen. Coming from the hatch I feel the terrific pull of the gravity, like grappling ropes thrust around me, and even insulated by layers of hydraulic gear as I am I have a feeling of *immensity*, it is the only way that I can describe this realization that I now weigh over a ton and without the highly complicated equipment surrounding me would be lying huddled amidst the methane gases like one of those helpless animals we see in the Hall of Artifacts.

But there is no time to meditate upon my condition; what I must do is to strike out and be done. Accordingly responding to the programmed instructions, my hands moving in response to the tape running through the gear, I set up the equipment, prepare the visual checks, turn on the gyroscopes. As I cut in the switches I hear a satisfied sound pouring through the amplifier; now base is in visual contact with Jupiter and can see what I see, more in fact, since they are not distracted as I am by the realization that I am in terrible, terrible danger. "That's good," base says, "you're doing very good. Could you move around a little? Face toward the west? We'd like to get a look at that mound over there."

To my vantage point, shielded by the gear, vision now blocked by the sweat pouring across my eyes, it is impossible to conceive of any mound whatsoever but turning I see what base has referred to, a stack of gases, deeper blue than those surrounding, swinging in an open space surrounded by phosphorescence; the impression through the visuals certainly would be of a solid mound or elevation. "That's it," base says, "just stand like that for a while if you will. We want to investigate this more closely."

Obediently I hold position. While I do so, listening to the hydraulics groan as they work to sustain me, some true apprehension of my position comes through: here I am on the surface of Jupiter acting as sole referent for base and if the gear would fail I would be exposed to a horrid kind of death indeed; it would be a gigantic foot coming from somewhere beyond the atmosphere, pressing me deeper into the gases which would swim through and then, through my failing gear, poison. "That's it," base says calmly, "now if you'd turn a little bit toward the east, ten or fifteen degrees we'd say, toward two o'clock and begin to walk slowly we'd like to have a look at something else."

"You know," I find myself saying, "this is not fair. It's not fair to send people out like this. Jupiter is very dangerous. I shouldn't be alone here."

"You're doing fine," base says. "Turn now please and start walking."

"It shouldn't be a requirement. There should be another way of having this done, a way that wouldn't make people go onto a place like this, risk themselves—"

"You're just overreacting to a new situation. Please begin walking and move your head slowly from left to right as you do so. We wish to obtain some close-ups."

"What if I didn't?" I say. "What if I refused to cooperate with you? What if I wouldn't go walking so that you could see your mounds and your purple gases and just stood here?"

"Why then," base says so matter-of-factly that it is as if the answer is so obvious I should have always known it and indeed, indeed I have, "then we would simply wait until you got over being difficult and cooperated with us."

"And how long would that be?"

"Why," base says with a little astonishment, "as long as you wanted, of course."

III

Tim is the liveliest of us and would have been keeping up chatter about the Jovian landscape, Nala is much quieter but in her way far more passionate and would have been relaying impressions of color and landscape beyond the rest of us, but I can neither chatter like Tim nor perceive like Nala, so I keep my further thoughts to myself and stride through the gases with the aid of hydraulics, reduced to numbness now, only interested in cooperating with base as quickly as I can so that this will be brought to an end and I will be back in the chute of the conveyor. I turn left, turn right, look east, look west, bend and stretch, lie full-length in an arc of nitrogen so that certain effects of solar refraction can be studied. Base is quiet except to issue additional orders which sometimes come quite quickly; other times many moments elapse before anything is said and it is during those moments that I have the terror of being abandoned, the fear that transmission link has somehow failed and I will be left on the surface of this deadly planet unable to return, capable only of witnessing my own death when the air supply runs out, the hydraulics' charge fails and I perish. Once I scream out frantically and base, irritated, tells me to stop this: they are concentrating on their observations, any override merely sets them back; once, against my will I start a long monologue in which I talk about the unfairness of it, the unfairness of all of this, Tim and Nala have been excused from exploration and I have been bullied into it against my will even though the statutes provide that no one needs to go on an expedition by himself. "Shut up," base says finally, "we're not going to ask you this again. There will be plenty of time to discuss this later and I'm sure that everyone will be interested in your ideas but right now we are concentrating on metering. Any additional speeches will be considered obstruction of research and you will be dealt with harshly. Move north four strides please and angle thirty-seven degrees west."

I do so, astonished at their callousness. But the astonishment oozes away and it occurs to me, for the very first time, that there is no reason to be surprised: they are conducting research, they are using me as their conduit and there is absolutely no reason why a conduit should be allowed to interfere with its own purposes.

IV

At length they tell me that the observations and experiments are approaching an end and that I may shortly return to the conveyor. It seems, by then, to have been a very long time but I have lost all sense of chronology, since my insight about how little I truly matter to them my mind has been far away from there, I have been thinking dully of Tim and Nala but only in terms of images, flicker-flashes, no words, not even feeling. I wonder why they are not with me and whether they refused the expedition for a different reason, one which I am only now beginning to understand but not very well. "There is one last experiment we wish to perform," base says, "and then you may return. Remove your helmet, please."

"What? What is that?"

"There is a detachable screw which you will find at the base joint, just at your neck, rather prominently exposed to a projection of four centimeters. If you will put your right hand to that screw and begin to work it in a counterclockwise direction it will come off in seven complete revolutions and then, by putting both hands underneath your helmet, you will find yourself able to raise it fully. Please do this now."

"Now wait," I say, "just wait." Something appears to have happened which is beyond my comprehension but I am trying to be sensible about this even though my respiration is suddenly shallow and rapid. I turn slightly from the filtered rays coming from the solar refractor which I have placed for them and say, "I can't do this. I can't remove my helmet."

"Of course you can. You have just been given full instructions."

"But you don't understand. You don't understand any of this. If I do so I'll breathe in this atmosphere. It's poisonous."

"Do so please."

"But it's poisonous!" I say. My voice has broken slightly. "I'll inhale it and die."

"That is not for you to worry about," base says. "We have asked you before please do not concern yourself with unnecessary speculations. Just loosen the screw. The helmet will come off quite easily and you will respire deeply five times at an inclination of forty-five degrees from the ground."

"It's poisonous!" I say frantically. "I told you, if I breathe it, I'll die!"

"Why don't you leave these concerns to us?" base says. "Don't you think that we're perfectly aware of the range of experimentation, of the limits of the observations we wish to make? Release the helmet."

"I can't do that," I say. "I just can't." I shake my head emphatically although I know in the monitors I am merely a grotesque form hobbling through the obscuring gases; they can see nothing of me except a blob. "I don't want to die."

Base seems exasperated and when it becomes this way it takes on an exaggerated tone of patience. I have observed this before in the simulator experiments. "Now listen," it says, "the time factor is important here and if these findings are not made quite promptly they will be worthless to us. Please obey instructions. Please remove the helmet. Don't you think we know what we're doing?"

I think about this for a moment. I have always trusted base, of course; it is ingrained within us very deeply. If it were not for base the colony itself on Ganymede would not exist; base is our sole sustenance. Nevertheless I can calculate the situation when I see it whole. "Yes," I say after a long pause, "I think you know what you're doing. But what you're doing will kill me."

"Do you think we want to kill you? Do you think that's the purpose of this?"

I shake my head. "I don't know," I say, "I can't answer that. I can't decide. I don't know whether you want to kill me or not. I just know that you *will*."

"All right," base says, "this is the last time. If you do not cooperate now, if you do not assist our experimentation right now we will abandon you. We will leave you on Jupiter. We will not assist you back to the conveyor. The conveyor will be deactivated."

There is nothing to say. I look into the purple surrounding and it is as if I see my own blood, swirling poisonously in the veins. I always knew that it would be this way. Somewhere, at some level, I understand now that it could have been no different.

"Take off the helmet," base says, "take it off right now. Forget the proper angling." Its voice takes on stridency. "It's too late for that. Just get it off right now!" The voice breaks on the *get*, gasps into the *now*. "Now," it says again, somewhat more steadily.

Slowly I raise my hand to the place where the screw is and begin to work it counterclockwise. There is simply nothing else to do.

V

In the moment that I am turning the screw, in the moment before I lift off the helmet, in that moment as the helmet comes off me and I see clearly the surfaces of Jupiter, I remember what Nala had said to me a long time ago and which I had forgotten until this instant. "No," she had said, "no, I won't go, they're not here to help us, they tell us that they're here for that and merely our servants but I don't trust them, I don't trust any of them. Why should I trust them? Why should I trust anything they say? Why aren't there adults here?" she said. "Why is it only us? Explain that," she said and I could not. I could not answer but at the time it seemed pointless, of course, one of Nala's silly mysteries which she would often play with just as Tim would play with the concept of Jupiter and what it might mean if Jupiter did not really exist, if there was nothing outside of Ganymede at all but the stars and all of it a fraud. "Explain something, anything," she had said but I had told her nothing. Nothing to say and then it had been forgotten until the time we were notified that the expedition itself was to begin, base saying that the three would go and then I had remembered what Nala had said, that she would never cooperate with them, never go . . . but that was after, long after I had committed myself and was on the surface.

Too late.

Too late, too late: the helmet is off now, my eyes are staring and as the ropes of color move I see for the first time the aspect of Jupiter as it truly overwhelms me and in my ears a sound which might be base laughing or crying, shouting or saying the mass of redemption. Does it make any difference? Does it make any difference *what* they say over us?

Just look at what they have done.

New Jersey: 1973

AFTERWORD TO THIRTY-SEVEN NORTHWEST

What all post-technological cultures share is the absolute brutality with which they treat their children, all their children. (I don't think most other cultures were or are any better but it is this one I know well enough to generalize.) "Thirty-seven Northwest" uses the devices of science fiction to make this point but it is no more a science fiction story than *Lord of the Flies* is a fantasy.

The only science fiction writer ever to have done a body of work on this point is the underrated Kris Neville. In works like "Betty-ann," "Overture," "In the Government Printing Office" and others he has articulated the brutality with visionary skill. He deserves a much wider audience and greater recognition within the field, to say nothing of without.

Sedan Deville

Dear Sir:

Big coupe de ville Deora custom option on it; she say put all this together explain your case. I say to coupe de ville no this is not way to do it but she say fantastic big car power antenna power door locks power seats power windows power trunk release FM-radio and signal seek she say you state your case to them just like I state mine to yours. Gaskets loose I fix, I think. Kurt Delvecchio take advice.

I published writer Kurt Delvecchio. Eight months ago I send short story based on true life experiences with Cadillac cars to editor *Terrific Science Fiction* he ask if I ever publish before and say will clean up grammar but buy story because it unusual. I write second story also based on true life experience and editor take this one too and then I write another story which he take and then I write still one more just like other three based on life experience of Cadillac car and editor reject saying stories amusing and original at first but all pretty much in same key. Then I get letter from publisher saying magazine going out of business except for last issue enclosed with my first story and also check and also other two stories not publishing. They say tight market.

Reading story in magazine discourage because cleaning up grammar seem to have taken out heart but as editor explain readership of science-fiction magazines wants good grammar and so he does this for me because I have fine idea at first and what he call "instinctual feel." So this is situation right now: one story publish two stories would be publish but return with no money one story rejected no good and one story half finished because of news I receive. White coupe de ville say I put this very good you not misunderstand.

I understand that you are agent. That your job as agent is to sell stories of writers and deduct ten percent (10%) of sale price after sale. I ask you to sell this story I send with letter; it is the second (2nd) story I wrote which he would have bought had it not been for accident. Once you sell story you get next story to sell then next then I finish up fifth and so on. I have much to tell as you see also true and real message which must be explained now.

I also enclose copy of publish story in magazine so that you can see I am publish writer.

Dear Sir:

In answer to your question I engine mechanic in Cadillac dealership in Paramus New Jersey eight miles from the Washington Bridge this is how I got material for story and how I got what you call "convincing portrait of Cadillac car." Cadillac overhead valve V-8 fantastic big engine four hundred and seventy-five cubic inches since nineteen seventy-one standard, five hundred cc in Eldorado convertible and coupe both turning two hundred and seventy-five horsepower. Engine was once big and simple but now is big and complicated due to intake manifolds complex carburetor attachments high-temperature condensers and other technical things to meet new emission control requirements. Working on overhead valve V-8 all day most jobs relating to poor carburetion with underhood temperatures near one thousand degrees fahrenheit enables man to understand workings of Cadillac car.

Cadillac car is a simple and elegant tool and engines last forever. Know from transmission and electrical system men in shop that in Cadillacs these go all the time fuses popping bands slipping but even in auto graveyard on Pennsylvania Avenue Cadillac engine still turns over, still works; engine is heart of car and will not die. Transmissions and electrical not so good also front wheel alignment terrible very hard to wheels balance but not this department. Working under hoods of Cadillac vehicles gives me good understanding of cars and I put this understanding in my stories which Mr. Walter Thomas complimented me upon and published one would have published two others in his magazine.

You ask why second story also about Cadillac do I not have range? I do not know what you mean by "range" I tell you only Cadillac car is like a woman great in its mysteries and not exhausted not even in twenty-five stories. Second story takes different point of view like woman would to two different men and I surprise you not see this.

I do not understand what you mean either by reading fee for

unpublished writers; I am not unpublished writer as issue of magazine I sent to you makes quite clear but published writer once two other stories accepted. Wages at dealership are union scale plus overtime; take home to wife one hundred and sixty-three dollars and twenty cents last week which was typical week less sick benefits union dues taxes and so on. I can not afford to pay fee for reading or sending around stories. I began writing stories to make more money to add to wages. I enclose third story also accepted story by Mr. Walter Thomas which I hope you like and will sell for me.

Dear Sir:

Boss mechanic very pleased by idea Kurt Delvecchio is published writer; pass magazine around in shop. Some make jokes about what Cadillac mechanic doing writing for comic-book type magazine but they over in Fleetwood department working on series seventy-five chassis and do not speak English most of them quite stupid. Salesmen also very impressed: sometimes they take customers and point out me, Kurt Delvecchio, the "writing mechanic."

I do not understand your remark about third story; third story about Cadillac just as second and first were because all I write about is Cadillacs because I heard you must write what you know and that is what I know . . . Cadillac sedan de ville, Cadillac coupe de ville, Cadillac calais and Fleetwood, Eldorado Coupe and Convertible, flower cars and commercial chassis for ambulance and hearses. That is what I know and working on overhead valve V-8 plugs and points singing to me at idle speed two thousand rpm true when well tuned it is like car is alive and speaking to me. All I do is put down words that car speaks car is real and alive I merely its messenger at times like these. Other times I just like other mechanics although have ambitions which most do not. I no pay a reading or marketing fee to circulate one (1) story of published writer and send you this fourth story which Mr. Walter Thomas reject because he say it too different in scope and style while still being too much like in others. I hope you read and send this one out for me as due to recent crisis which you must know and read about I mean so-called "energy crisis" business in dealership down eighty per cent business in shop down twenty-seven per cent junior men being laid off and although Kurt Delvecchio has some seniority I wish to find another source of income just in case.

Dear Sir:

Story told from point of view of see-through hood ornament (option extra cost twenty dollars $20.00) because that is what I feel when wrote it; the way see-through hood ornament on coupe de ville would feel as being driven around Paramus Route 4 and Route 17 intersection also Bergen Mall. If had not felt it would not have written it Cadillac car is a real thing even though "energy crisis" going to destroy it is just as real as "aliens" or "Terrans" and other things in Mr. Walter Thomas's magazines (which I have read) and you wrong to say that it not salable also to say that this is positively last time you will react to story without fee I must pay fee of thirty dollars ($30) in future. This show no understanding also no realization that Kurt Delvecchio is not amateur but true professional writer who combine love and knowledge of Cadillac car with stories that make Cadillac car *real* for first time in universe it give it side of story.

Very angry at you for this treatment white coupe de ville on which I worked today (only car in shop) also very mad despite defective ignition and dropped gaskets which have drenched oil pan and suspension system. White coupe de ville and I agree will not deal with you any more.

Instead to prove that Kurt Delvecchio is no fool and that he know how to sell to science-fiction magazines or anywhere else for that matter coupe de ville and I (it is '72 coupe de ville with customized Cabriolet roof and Deora option on portholes) are going to send copies of my letters to you copies which I very cleverly keep at advice of Mr. Walter Thomas who encouraging new author tells him always to keep copies of letters he writes to publishers or editors or agents and white coupe de ville and I send out story *together* story being copies of these letters to next science-fiction magazine on list.

When next science-fiction magazine publishes letters *proving* that Kurt Delvecchio has something of great interest to say you will be sorry! but I will give you no percentage because of the many insults you have heaped on me in your own letters. White cabriolet coupe de ville stay overnight in shop tonight; tomorrow morning early I finish gaskets and it go away and I cry when it leave shop because shop then empty Kurt Delvecchio being one of only three (3) mechanics left but that is life as Mr. Walter Thomas would have said. If you do not think that these cars are alive or that evil men are killing them you not understand what is happening or what real meaning of stories is is what Deora and I we say to you. *"Energy crisis" a plot to kill deora.*

AFTERWORD TO SEDAN DEVILLE

One of my worst-kept secrets (do I have any closely held?) is my nearly metaphysical affection for the four hundred and seventy-two-cubic-inch, turbo-hydramatic-transmissioned product of the Cadillac Motor Division. At least (as Harry Harrison pointed out) my sin at two and a half tons is highly visible, on permanent display. No dissemblance here. I think that the Cadillac motor vehicle embodies all that is corrupt and sinister in American life but one of its most engaging facets is that it works no better than anything else on the continent. So much for corruption and sin. The good guys do not have a corner on the incompetence mart and this is reassuring.

I have owned three Cadillacs in my time; a seven-year-old coupé which I loved dearly (and of which mention in a fan magazine article caused an enraged commentator to list me near the top of the Exploiting Class) and which dropped her transmission sickeningly on the FDR Drive north, a lovely eight-year-old convertible which experienced total ignition failure in my driveway, and the present occupant, a four-year-old Calais coupé bought new in 1973 which, for a long time, was the pride of my life. When the manipulated "energy crisis" and gasoline shortage descended upon us in the gray winter of 1974 I wrote this story as an ode to *temps perdu* which happily at 58.9 cents a gallon became *temps reconnaissant* only a few months later.

I have no idea whether "Sedan Deville" possesses enduring merit; probably it does not. I am convinced, however, that as the only science fiction story about Cadillacs ever to find the mass markets it will occupy a very unique place in the literature and will be a rich find for archaeologists someday. Harry Harrison did a short story about an unspecified gas eater only a few months after this was published and *Brave New World* was, of course, really about Fords, but who else in the fifty-year history of a form whose development closely parallels that of the modern merchandising history of the automobile has written a story of the Cadillac?

State of the Art

Here we all are, at this elegant sidewalk café perched on the edges of what appears to be a ruined Paris. Hard to tell; outside of this circle of brightness, much is opaque. Originally we were supposed to gather in the Algonquin, but that hotel was demolished seventeen years ago to make way for Intervalley Seven. "Disgusting," Dostoevski says, thudding his heavy tumbler against the table, "the ruination of the environment, the nature of man to impress his internal corruption upon the landscape. I tell you, we are fast approaching the end of time."

Dostoevski is gloomy. The twenty years in Siberia have warped his soul and given him a somewhat grimmer outlook on humanity than, perhaps, events will justify. Nevertheless he must be attended to. All of us attend to one another with extreme courtesy, but Dostoevski deserves our good wishes. He contributed many important works to the literature and besides the change has discombobulated him. Siberia was not good for his personality; I must concede that. "Of course," I say gently, draining the last sparkling dregs, "but still, technology is not an absolute. A neutral quality like sex can be turned in any direction; so can machinery. Watch; the environment may change but it will also become more pleasant." I signal for a waiter. The service is abominable in this café, but then they have not been on the main line for years. Something about deliveries being undependable; the impossibility of getting good staff. A waiter shuffles over, his clothing glistening with dirt, and shrugs as I give him the order. Another mug for Dostoevski, an apéritif for Gertrude Stein, a little more wine for myself. Hemingway will pass this round. Shakespeare is now in the men's room having more difficulty with his bowels; perhaps a little cheese and crackers. The others, another round as previously. We make quite a group hunched around this small table, blocking the aisles, giving the café a reputation for seediness and disruption even beyond its wont, but we are customers, and the waiter, grumbling, goes off to the kitchen. "But you've certainly got a point, Fyodor," I add pleasantly, "and you're entitled to your opinion. I *defend* your opinion."

"The hell with all of it," Hemingway says. He stands, tucks his writing pad under his arm, heads toward an exit. "I have listened to the merde. All this afternoon I have been possessed by nothing but merde. Now it is time to go off and do good things. To feel richly, to know greatly. To conquer feeling with hope." He is in one of his sulks again. Really, despite all our efforts, we have been able to do very little with him. The man is simply not companionable. "I am off for sunlight," he says and staggers through the aisles, leaving us with his share of the check as usual, and stepping off into the Rue de la Paix is hit by a passing streetcar which dismembers him thoroughly and leaves him in small pieces on the sidewalk.

Gertrude Stein giggles a little and raises a napkin to her lips, fondling Alice Toklas' hands. "Ernest never did have any taste," she says, "and all his gestures fail as gestures." She shakes her head, puts the napkin down, leans over toward Alice's ear and disappears into some intense conversation as pedestrians and gendarmes outside gather around the ruins of Ernest. The streetcar has stopped and from its windows, faces look out incuriously, mumbling. "Like petals on a wet, black bough," Ezra says, speaking for the first time this afternoon, and goes back to his jottings. Now the crowd covers Ernest and it is difficult to see what is going on. I assume that in due time they will put him into one of the conveyors for reprocessing. It hardly matters. None of this matters. My relationship with Ernest has not been a happy one, and although I am embarrassed to admit this, I am not entirely sorry to think that he is dead.

Shakespeare returns from the men's room simultaneously with the appearance of the waiter carrying our glasses, and they almost collide. "Bloody fool!" Bill says, collapsing into a chair. "You stink up everything!" And the waiter, with the air of a man who has suffered greatly and has now passed tested limits, balances the tray on one hand, takes off a glass of wine and throws it into Bill's face. "Bastard!" Shakespeare says, but his expression does not change, his eyes revolving flat and dead above his cheekbones. Incontestably, the man is drunk. In any other condition he would knock the waiter unconscious.

But nothing will happen this afternoon. The moment of tension passes, the waiter looks toward the sky and, recovering his control after a moment, puts the glasses before us. As he bends near me, I ask him quietly for the check. The waiter's face suffuses with rage, but somehow I am able to convince him that I mean no insult and he says that he will go off to the kitchen and see what he can do. Truly, I am the only one of us who is able to deal with the common, ordinary realities of the afternoon, the others being abstracted into their private roles or sorrows, but in all honesty I am getting somewhat tired of this and for the first time it occurs to me that I am becoming bored with my companions and our afternoon routine and that I may bring it to a halt. I would hardly be missed if I did not appear at the table at one o'clock. But if I did not, I wonder, who would order the drinks?

I think about all this, looking out idly toward the street where, even though only a few moments have passed, there is no sign of Ernest's recent tragedy. Pedestrians whisk by quickly, automobiles honk their scattered way past, a fat patrolman with a cheerful expression paces in front of the café, hands on hips, looking at the sun. The one conveyor clanking its way on the street-edge is clean and empty; Ernest is already gone. It is depressing to think that for all of his bombast his death has had so little effect upon the world, but then, as most of my companions would advise me, it is very difficult to make any kind of permanent change in the landscape. Technology has done this to us, and also the alienation effect which progressively separates men from the consequences of their acts, the products of their labor.

As if catching my thoughts, which have taken a rather stricken and metaphysical turn, Dostoevski looks up at me and winks. "It is difficult, is it not, my friend," he says, "to see so much and do so little, eh? The Czars would have had a word for this kind of condition, but I call it refractory."

"He's just pouting," Gertrude Stein says. "He thinks he's sufficient when he is really insufficient, is that not so, Alice?" Beaming Alice nods; the two old lesbians clasp hands again and recommence their incessant laughter. Really, I cannot stand them—their presence at the table is a constant embarrassment and most of the waiter's hostility, I know, is directed toward them—but what can I do? Paris was their idea, after all, and a good suggestion it was. If we had not gone to Paris we might have ended up meeting in New York or Berlin and with the Algonquin demolished, how many places are there left which are really good for our discussions? I nod judiciously and turn my gaze from them. It is better at most times not to see too deeply, as my friends have advised me, and with some difficulty, I have made progress with this advice.

"I believe," Shakespeare says heavily, "I believe that I am suddenly very ill, oh you fools," and to our astonished gaze—Bill never complains; he has always been the heartiest of the lot—stands swaying in the dense little spaces of the café, his skin turned a sudden vigorous orange color. "It must be the wine, the heat, the afternoon, the pain oh my friends," he says, "oh let me unbutton here," and tugs at his waistcoat; in the midst of his struggles, however, a spasm of some violent kind hits him and he collapses heavily over the table, bringing it to the floor in an incandescence of cups, saucers, glasses, beer, wines, liqueurs. Into the middle of this he plunges, and rolling once on the floor lies still.

Standing, Fyodor eyes him with disgust and then takes a large watch out of his pocket. "I believe the old bastard has died," he says, checking the time, "but if you will excuse me, I really have had enough of this. There is a great deal of work to be done and I hope to conclude an important subsidiary deal on *Crime and Punishment* before sunset." He turns to leave.

I am offended by his coldness, by the total lack of regard which it is now clear was his only true feeling about our afternoons, but before I can ponder this further or remonstrate with him, the waiter has appeared flanked by two police and a large angry man who must be the owner of the café and who looks at Shakespeare's corpse with revulsion. The waiter whispers desperately into the owner's ear; he seems to be trying to explain that he had nothing whatsoever to do with this occurrence. The owner shrugs him off. "I'm quite sorry," he says to us as the police stare solemnly, "but we cannot allow this anymore. You have been stinking and drinking up my café, the last café of Paris, for many weeks now and the disgrace is intolerable. My staff is at their wits' end and my wife threatens to leave me." He kicks the corpse. "You are all impounded for further investigation," he says.

"This is disgraceful," says Gertrude. "Alice, help me!" And Fyodor, with the ancient cunning of the prison camps, tries to slink toward the exit, but the police are efficient and determined in the way that even post-technological gendarmes can be and before I can quite grasp what has happened we are all in handcuffs. Fyodor too, and being led away.

"We will give you a full report," one of the police says to the owner, "we can give you our assurances of that."

"This is an outrage," Fyodor says. "You can slap chains upon us and your machinery but you will never, never, imprison the free, lunging, human soul," and flings himself at the nearest police but is knocked unconscious by one mild blow—Fyodor is quite frail for all of his bombast—and topples to the floor, dragging all of us with him. We seem to be hooked on the same chain.

I feel Shakespeare's corpse, already cooling underneath me, to the left and right I absorb the struggles and kicks of Alice and Gertrude, I raise my head to see that old Count Leo too, just returning from a brisk walk, has somehow been hooked and chained, but my gaze passes through and then beyond all of them; looking upon the street I see with precision I have never had before the movement of the conveyor and then, as the mass around me begins to roll in that direction, I understand that in the absence of proper police procedures, we are all going to be taken there instantly, and it is with relief—how I always knew in the deepest of my Fyodor's aspects that it would be with relief!—that I feel Gertrude's dark kiss upon me and in that way we are all carried out.

AFTERWORD TO STATE OF THE ART

This, not a characteristic story, is a deliberate pastiche of Robert Silverberg's admirable "Good News from the Vatican" which won an SFWA Nebula Award and no surprise in 1972. Sidewalk cafe, decadence, stormy and cataclysmic events refracted through superficial chatter. It was written for Silverberg's *New Dimensions IV* and sold very easily. About a year ago I pointed out the facts above to Silverberg and he said that he had failed to notice the similarity and in fact did not notice it even when called to his attention. You go and figure it out: I cannot.

Originally I had wanted to set this in the old Algonquin and substituted for the present cast people like Kaufman, Woollcott, Dorothy Parker and so on but I found myself absolutely convinced that the story would not work that way. I am not quite sure why this is so but here is a guess: the Algonquin Round table was essentially frivolous and populated by frivolous, although very brilliant, people. One cannot impose absurdity upon triviality to any satiric effect. The characters of *this* setting are not only dead serious but entirely dead and if you think this is a light piece you have missed the point.

Isaiah

So I take myself to the Lubavitcher Congregation in Williamsburg, Brooklyn. Williamsburg is still the largest reservoir of Chasidism in the Western world although things have hardly been so brisk since the Lubavitcher rabbi himself died and many in the community, strangulated by urban pressures, moved to bucolic New City or points even farther north. "I need to discuss the issue with someone who speaks a good English," I say hopefully to the few depressed Chasidim, a bare minyan who are chanting over prayer books in the vestry. My command of Hebrew or Yiddish is really almost nil. It is disgraceful for someone in my position to have almost no grasp of tongues but what can I do? It is all that I can manage to keep up with the research aspects.

"My English is acceptable," a middle-aged Chasid says, standing and beckoning me into the room. "What do you want?" He gestures toward a rack in the corner on which tallises are hung, prayer books perched. "You may join us, certainly."

"I don't want to join you," I say and then realizing that this sounds discourteous add, "I'm not a practicing Jew."

"All Jews must practice," the middle-aged man says wisely enough. The others nod somnolently, return to their chanting. "In fact," he whispers, "practice makes perfect."

"It's not that," I say.

Very ill at ease I sit convulsively upon a near chair, take out a handkerchief and wipe my face in little streaks as the Chasid moves over to join me. "Perhaps after the services," he says, "after the afternoon prayers we can talk."

Afternoon prayers. Evening prayers, morning prayers, prayers upon arising and eating. They live their lives within a network of prayer; not, of course, that this can be said to have done them any real good. On the other hand, who am I to judge? The only prayers which I have ever attempted were not within the framework of really organized religion. "Not good enough," I croak, "we must talk now. I have so little time—"

The Chasid shrugs. "Time is a contradiction," he says. "It is self-willed, self-created." A bit of a metaphysician. The others have dropped out of our discussion. They are immersed in their prayers, each at a different rate in a different way. Voices mesh and part. This is the essence of Chasidic ritual I am given to understand, the individuality of worship, but actually I know very little of forms. "Perhaps you're in the wrong place?" the Chasid says kindly. "Are you looking for someone?"

"No!" I shout convulsively. Faces turn, chairs scatter, eyes look at me with great interest. With a few shattered breaths I regain control of myself. "I am not looking for anyone," I say. "No person. I am looking for information."

"What information?"

"Judaism is a messianic religion, is that not so? You believe that the Messiah has not yet come to earth but that he will and that when he does, peace and justice will reign. Unlike the Christians who hold that the Messiah already came and went, will return for the second coming, you believe that he has yet to appear. Am I right?"

"It is slightly more complex than that," my new friend says, wincing at his prayer book. "There are various levels of meaning."

"But is that not so?"

"You are discussing an entire religion, my friend. It cannot be summed up in a few words. There are some Jews who believe that the Messiah will come but there are others who are not so sure, who believe that Judaism exists only to bear witness that he will never come. Since the great purges and sufferings of the twentieth century, in fact—"

"All right," I say breathing excitedly. "That's true. I understand that part of it. Hitler and the exterminations made it impossible for many Jews to accept a messianic version of religion; the Messiah would not allow such things to come to pass without intervention if he existed. But messianism is built deeply into the religion. All of the rituals, all of the prayers, as far as I know are built upon an acceptance, a belief, a waiting . . ."

"I have had enough of this," the Chasid says, standing. "Doubtless this is of great interest to you but you ought to seek a rabbi, a scholar, perhaps someone at the theological institute with whom you could discuss all of this. This however is a place of worship."

"But what are you worshiping if you won't even talk about the basis?"

The Chasid as if from a great height gives me a penetrating look and tucks his prayer book under his arm. "If you must equate worship and understanding," he says, "you are missing the point entirely." He walks away. The minyan continues to drone but obviously I have been dismissed and after a while I leave the Lubavitcher vestry quietly, trying to hold myself against a scream or an explosion.

So I take myself to a Reform congregation in Teaneck, New Jersey, and there on a dull Monday afternoon meet and speak with the student rabbi, a young man with round eyes and a distracted expression. "Of course it's a messianic religion," he says. "Judaism is structured on the coming of the Messiah." He looks at a wall; actually it is not his office but that of the rabbi himself, who is presently visiting students of the congregation families at northeastern colleges but has no objection to giving his assistant use of the office in his absence and even the opportunity to conduct Friday evening services. "But I'm afraid that I can't solve your problem otherwise. No one knows when the Messiah will come and this sense of mystery is built deeply into the religion. It is a religion without answers of almost any sort."

He is trying hard. Obviously there is no hypocrisy in my student rabbi. Really, he is trying very hard and he is also relatively learned. Nevertheless a sense of woe overtakes me, a feeling of disengaged purposes and weariness, and so I stand, looking over his shoulder at some religious emblem on the wall. "It's hopeless," I say, "it's hopeless."

"What's hopeless?" the rabbi says without much interest. Really, they have enough trouble in Teaneck: zoning, taxation, infusion of Orthodox into certain sections draining the public schools, a rising crime rate and great transient population, to say nothing of the student rabbi's more specific problem, which is to find a congregation somewhere. I feel sympathy for him. Really, this is not his problem.

"There's just no clear framework," I say rather pointlessly and leave him. In the parking lot I have a stab of regret: I really should return and apologize for my abruptness but I decide that it would only be a gesture. Truly now: the young rabbi's problems, much as my own, would only be unduly complicated by the coming of the

Messiah on top of everything else and now I feel a blade of panic. My options are running out.

So I take myself to a Thursday night discussion meeting of the Ethical Culture Society, a large proportion of which is composed of intellectual, questioning, alienated Jews. There is some problem filling in the gaps between these encounters but I do the best I can and limbo is not particularly unpleasant if one keeps expectations low. "I think we have to discard the messianic approach in toto," the discussion leader says when I politely raise my question. People stare: a newcomer, particularly a conversational newcomer, is always interesting. "It is best to think of messianism as a metaphor for that mysterious exaltation which can come from keeping ritual. Ritual equals religion equals ecstasy in some sects. The vitality of the Chasids demonstrates this, I'd think."

I see little vitality in the Chasids but politely say instead, "Then you say there is no messianic underlay any more."

"Not any more than there are physiological reasons for the dietary laws," the discussion leader says. "I think we should get off this topic, however. Judaism is of marginal interest to most of us and we try to look at the world more eclectically, bonding together many religions, many ways of life. Not that Judaism isn't a *worthy* subject of discussion, of course," he concludes, perhaps reacting to some felt disapproval, "but we try to take the best from the best and reassemble. Messianism is deleterious since we know in post-technological America that the solution to our problems must lie within ourselves, that we must change the world as we see it and that our lives consist of what is known on this earth and nowhere else."

He nods somewhat emphatically and the faces turn from me back toward the podium. There are several unescorted girls for whom I feel a certain distant attraction but it would be rankest hypocrisy to stay, my business now concluded, on that basis. I leave the lecture hall quietly and try to get to a neighborhood synagogue for meditation and prayer but neighborhood synagogues are closed and locked (vandalism abounds) on Thursday nights and Williamsburg too far to travel on the dangerous underground.

So I return and explain the situation as best I can and apologize for my lapses and make clear my efforts and he listens quietly, hearing me through to the end patiently as is his wont, smoking a cigarette down to the end and then putting it absently underneath the throne, unextinguished, the faint residue of smoke surrounding like incense. "I don't know what to say," I conclude. "There are no easy answers."

"That is true," he says. He shrugs. He lights another cigarette. He sits back. After waiting for so long he has cultivated nothing if not patience and his attitude betrays no restlessness. "Still, we have to come to some kind of a decision on this."

"It's not my decision," I say quietly, not in an offensive or disagreeable way but firmly enough so that my position is clear. "I just can't make that decision; it isn't my right."

"I understand," he says. He sighs, shrugs again, extinguishes this cigarette under his foot and stands heavily, using his hands to wedge himself from the throne. He grunts. He has, after all, been inert for so long. "I might as well," he says finally. "I've been waiting for so long hoping that things would just work themselves out but your Ethical Culture man was quite right, wasn't he? You have to make your own way." He ventures a signal and from the haze where they have been waiting for seven thousand years the Ten Priests emerge, whispering.

"I should have accepted that a long time ago," he says and gestures again. The birds are free now, the Great Snake itself, muttering, wraps in a coil around the heavens and dimly the darkness and the light descend.

Watching this I do not know if I am happy or sad but it is good after so long to see him back at work again, doing what he always did best. The Chasids would be gratified. Teaneck is another story.

AFTERWORD TO ISAIAH

"Isaiah" was written for Jack Dann's anthology of Jewish science fiction* *Wandering Stars;* he asked me for a two-thousand-word piece. It was rejected as somehow "not satisfying" and he told me a year later that the real reason for the rejection was that he had

---

* I still think that this sounds like the punchline of a bad joke and I'm a *practicing* Jew.

hoped for something longer from me. When I reminded him that the two-thousand-words had been to *his* commission he shook his head and said, "Yes, I guess I should have bought it." You go fight the world. As was the case with so much of my ambitious, off-trail stuff that could not quite catch with the one or two four-cent markets available, I was happy to sell it to Ted White's *Fantastic* and happy enough to see it in print. It has a second chance here and a first in hardcover; maybe someone will actually note this time around that it is struggling (not necessarily successfully) with an idea which is anything but slight and ends on the single most dazzlingly pessimistic note I ever achieved in a career filled with cheerless, unforward-looking stories.

In the *Fantastic* version the Reform synagogue was in Massapequa, but Teaneck, a town in Bergen County, New Jersey, which I selected purely at random in substitute, does even better. I think.

On the Campaign Trail

At Fargo another assassination attempt. Small, pockmarked man three or four feet from us in huddle of autograph-seekers was seized by private guards (national security is worthless; the Federals, I believe, are functioning only as spies), taken hurriedly into local shop, Happy Hosiery & Underwear, where under rough frisking he gave up: one thirty-eight-caliber Smith & Wesson revolver, two hunting knives, one small needle. Disclaimed any interest in hurting the candidate. Said that he simply went around with such implements because of dangerous times, etc., but at our insistence was booked reluctantly by local police. Candidate shielded from this flurry of activity although when he came to door of Happy Hosiery & Underwear he looked at me peculiarly for a moment or two. "Something wrong? How are you doing?" he said. "Nothing," I said, "nothing." "Something seems to be wrong," he said while shaking hands of three women customers (hosiery). I believe that he suspects something amiss but is too courteous to force the issue.

Good crowd in Hastings, brought to their feet three times by fighting speech pretested in survey areas but never used in exactly this frame. "New tomorrow, a new vision, a destruction of the forces of evil, the need for purgation and return to our older values," and so on. One woman became hysterical and had to be helped from auditorium, a dismaying moment, since we thought she might be a plant from the administration. Given first aid in ladies' room she turned out to be harmless, having hundreds of photographs of the candidate in her purse; scraps of unfinished letters to him, etc. Later at reception raised several thousand dollars in new pledges. Candidate somewhat distracted and wearied from the pace of last few weeks. Became inebriated after several cocktails and began to discuss sex with mayor but we were able to get him out of there without further difficulty. Thank God.

c.

Fire in the motel this morning, choking vapors, sparks flying, three wagon companies called, etc. Candidate slept through all of this in rear wing, unaware, but four were overcome by smoke in the east palisade and a busy morning was spent by all checking them into hospitals, dealing with the press, shielding candidate from the seriousness of the incident and so on. Some espionage is suspected but it would be very difficult to prove and since all in hospital are expected to recover with or without ill effects, state police have suggested that we treat it as an unfortunate accident, act of God, so on. Reports that assassin in Fargo has tested sane on preliminary investigation and thus we may be faced with a decision: do we proceed with the formal charges or allow him to be released? It was made clear that this must be our decision. I opt for release despite the risks.

d.

Fire bomb in Huntsville went off during candidate's speech, enormous crowd packed solidly, some panic, the hall vacated as quickly as possible and so on. Local police continuing investigation. Local police conditioned to advise against quick arrest. Candidate motioned me to come over to him while surrounded by press asking for his opinion; ordered me to see him in his room that night. Quite nervous about this (how can I be held responsible?) but no way around it. Afterward, while waiting for new arrangements to clear, had a few ecstatic moments with Mary in a vacated prefabricated classroom behind the senior high school. "I think that someone is trying to disrupt this campaign," she said. I asked her how she could possibly weave together a fire bomb, a fire, an assassination attempt and a disturbance in Happy Hosiery & Underwear into an intricate network of menace. She had no reply. She is an attractive girl and one of the few solaces of the difficult campaign for me but she is rather paranoid.

e.

"These incidents must stop," the candidate said to me, hitting his fist into palm (the other palm) in that abruptly forceful gesture which the media have already so exploited. "I don't know if these are unhappy coincidences or a genuine attempt on the part of the opposition to destroy me but it is intolerable to continue in such circumstances. I want it stopped! I want better security," and he pounded that abused palm yet again but in his eyes I saw a certain bleakness and uncertainty, a hint of genuine fear. Is it possible that he is concerned about his own safety? The thought had never before occurred to me. I would certainly think less of him if he were a physical coward, although he was right in adding that a person holding the office for which we are campaigning need not be an expert in self-defense.

f.

Alone with Mary in Wellington for a brief, dry coupling on the unchanged sheets of her motel room, then off to the amphitheater alone for a rally. Candidate at his best tonight although sweating heavily behind the makeup and his voice cracked twice during last phases of speech. Later at reception I found him leaning against a wall, a hand stroking a potted palm, whispering, "I can't stand it any more, I can't stand it any more," but I put this down to a temporary neurasthenic episode and brought him back to the center of the room where several shook his hand and pledged further new contributions. There is money in this.

g.

Back to Fargo, a collective decision. Unfortunate assassination attempt will not prevent us from campaigning throughout the nation; we will not be frightened away, etc. Candidate strangely distracted on the plane, but then the decision was not his. At Fargo, debarking, was pulled aside by Mary, who said that she is going home. "I can't take the pressure any more," she said and then, "Besides, I feel that you're just using me." Tried to tell her that this was not the case, felt a genuine and sincere regard for her, etc., but she was adamant. Showed me plane ticket indicating that she was booked on next eastbound flight.

"What can I say?" I said. "You misunderstand the stump situation." She pulled me into some recess of the arrival building and kissed me desperately, her mouth uncoiling in a moistness which beneath she had never shown (at least for me) but even as I responded longingly, seeking her with my abused but hidden genitals, she was gone, running at high speed down the slick corridors and toward an exit gate. I stood looking after her for a while thinking about the profound similarity of sexuality and politics. Or difference.

h.

Candidate assassinated during rally, apparently by the same man detained by local police during our first visit. Hard to be sure; things, needless to say, are rather confused. Four shots crossing from hip to temple, the last opening up his face disastrously in resemblance to pulped fruit. He fell very quietly behind the rostrum. Lay there kicking. Local police, ambulance corps, medical personnel and so on responded promptly and the candidate was taken to hospital within five minutes of incident where he died at 12:17 A.M. of massive cerebral damage. The accused assailant is in the hands of police. A further statement is expected shortly.

i.

Good crowd at Sea Girt, large enthusiastic audience which applauded everything new candidate had to say and which remained quite cheerful despite the presence of police with drawn guns, security forces everywhere, etc. Candidate now just hitting his stride after hesitant opening hours. Campaign gathering momentum.

New candidate rather distracted at reception but this is to be expected; the strain is understandable and rumors of assassins continue. Four militants seized by police, accused of having plotted an attempt which might have succeeded except for sudden change of candidates.

Later called Mary to bring her up to date. Initially hostile she became warmer as we talked and when I replaced the receiver it was damp with little beads of sweat and spit that clung to it like aphids.

AFTERWORD TO ON THE CAMPAIGN TRAIL

Here is another of the schematics, done very quickly and off-handedly in the fall of 1972, which turned out, to the surprise of the writer, to be a reasonable paradigm of a future which lay not hundreds of years but only three or four ahead. Needless to say, this anticipatory thrust had no effect at the time it was written nor was it recognized as being so when one Gerald Ford began to take to the hustings. The writer in America functions in obscurity; how much more obscure the domain and audience of the science fiction writer, who, the more serious he becomes, the more resistant he finds the audience.

I did a lot of these political stories over the years, of which "Vox Populi" and this one in the present collection are typical, if abbreviated, examples. I have been interested in politics for a very long time but only with a bystander's concern; I am, in short, a fan of politics and politicians the way that I was once a fan of the New York Giants, baseball division. The fan's lightheartedness began to fade when he realized ten years ago that these people were, just incidentally you understand, killing us, but the fan's notes persist even though the only two worthwhile national figures in American political life in my time have, I feel, totally betrayed me and all of us.

Report to Headquarters

Gentlemen: With considerable difficulty I have managed to compile the following primitive glossary of the X'Thi. Working under great pressure and in difficult circumstances as I have been, this was not an easy job and may be riddled with inaccuracy. Nevertheless, considering that I was able to assemble it within two cycles and *under exceedingly embarrassing personal situations* I think that it is a job of some quality.

Conditions here remain as stated in previous reports, and I hope that the rescue party is continuing with all due haste. I do not know how much longer I can hold out in these circumstances irretrievably alien, although they are, of course, trying to do everything to make me comfortable. Mooning season is approaching, however, I am warned by the X'Thi, and with it their apparent "decampment" (I think that this is the equivalent I am seeking) and they cannot take me with them. What am I supposed to do then, gentlemen? Stay here with diminishing supplies and die? You can understand my problem. You must render me help.

AZAPLI: The act of triring or having just trired, the retraction of tentacles; the tendency of tentacles to constrict the blood vessels when extended, leading to vascular suffering and, in extreme cases, sudden death. For this reason the X'Thi trire as little as possible, although triring is inevitable during Hok, a metaphysical situation. They are trying to reduce Hok, however.

BLOLOMITE: The principal substance of reduction, that substance which appears to be a metaphor for the Cosmic Jolt which, the X'Thi believe, resulted in the creation of the universe and their own central, crucial role in it. Blolomite can neither be seen, touched, tasted, heard nor felt but it is the major source of all energy. During Hok, Blolomite may be seen for brief flashes in the light of the paralleled moons.

COSMIC JOLT: That central, lurching force with which the X'Thi believe that the universe began; alternatively, that C.L.F. (I am using abbreviations in order to save transmission time and costs and hope that you appreciate this gesture) with which the universe will end; their conception of the known universe, and all of time for that matter, as being a loop or thread suspended between the poles of Cosmic Jolts. The interval between the first Cosmic Jolt and the second appears to be calculated, as neatly as I can manage this, as being in reductions of sixty to seventy trires.

A panic appears to have been created by the landing of the vehicle upon Coul's Planet; the impact sprang up little filaments of Blolomite and many of the X'Thi took this to be the second and the more jarring of the Cosmic Jolts. It may have been for this reason, the impact and the panic, the assault of the X'Thi upon the vehicle, which caused me to use the reactor. I regret this very much. I have communicated this regret to the X'Thi. They have accepted my apology. I do not believe that they will seek retaliatory action since they are a gentle and spiritual people, but cannot guarantee this.

COUL'S PLANET: I do not believe that there is any megalomania in my referring to this rather bucolic if gaseous world as the above. As *Coul's Planet.* The naming of territory after its discoverer has an old and honorable tradition dating back to the maritime industry and also from the early days of interplanetary survey. Coul's Planet, along with the remainder of the universe, was, as stated by the X'Thi, formed from the Cosmic Jolt an unimaginable interval ago and will similarly terminate in another. In another Cosmic Jolt. In the meantime it is composed of a series of noxious gases suspended by light gravity above a liquefied core: methane, hydrogen and nitrous oxide in equal parts circulate rather energetically around the unseen core. Here at the heart of Coul's Planet I reside, surrounded by the friendly steel and metal alloy bulkheads of this ship which protect me from the environment and which also through an intricate series of viewscope devices permit me to remain in contact with the X'Thi, the lords of this planet. I am located, to the best of my knowledge, some twenty-five hundred miles north of the equator, rather near to one of the snow-capped poles. The X'Thi have no name for their own planet. The stupid creatures! They say that its name is ineffable, known only to the Creator of the universe. Therefore I have given it its proper name.

DECAMPMENT: Shift of Coul's Planet in the cosmos which, according to the X'Thi, results in a necessary redistribution of gaseous materials which would otherwise become stagnant. Forming waste. Reconstitution of Blolomite during the decampment renders the planet safe until the next period, but grave shocks to the environment force the X'Thi into their annual rite of displacement which takes them to the northern pole through this period of readjustment. They cannot take me with them and that is why recovery efforts must be accelerated and why you must do everything within your power to save me from the horrors of unreconstituted Blolomite, slowly encircling this little craft in their dread dread tentacles which *I cannot retract.*

DISPLACEMENT, RITE OF: See DECAMPMENT.

E: That cosmic sound (emanating of course from the Cosmic Jolt) with which all creation began. According to myth of the X'The, "E:" was the shout of the Creator as, in his anguish, he caused Coul's Planet to be.

HOK: Apparently a religious festival preceding decampment. (See DECAMPMENT, DISPLACEMENT.) Alterations in the eco/geological balance signaling the advent of decampment cause physical changes in the environment. Blolomite appears in dull flashes of energy, suddenly revealed to the naked eye. One can, during Hok, reach out and physically touch the Blolomite or endure the illusion that it can be touched as seen in the vibrating, varying light swinging from the equator to the poles, revealing the substance in all its dull luster, recapitulating as it were the appearance of the planet as it might have been during the Cosmic Jolt. During Hok the normally tight sociopolitical patterns of the X'Thi are deliberately altered; there is a relaxation of stricture, prurience occurs, random contacts between individuals, a shattering of the socioeconomic sector so that all elements of the culture interweave and intermix during this celebration. During Hok even the lowest and humblest of the filthy creatures may cohabit with the rulers; even the rulers are allowed to throw off the necessary dignity of their office to fornicate with the populace: all of them fornicate and cohabit together; it is this which brings Hok to its climax and in the general exhaustion, guilt, debilitation which follow, the decampment and its consequent displacement then occur; but through all of this and after I will be confined to this vessel, the simulated bulkheads, the thick metal shielding, unable to participate because exposure to the deadly gases of Coul's Planet would instantly kill me; all I would be able to do would be to rotate slowly in the contrived weightlessness of the ship, penitent, suffering, awaiting rescue and then, *after* Hok, in the darkness after decampment when all of them have gone to the poles and it is as if I will be the only individual left on the surface of the world . . . well, you should surely see why I await the rescue party with such unusual eagerness and anticipation and why it is all I can do to keep myself from tearing at the very bulkheads with frustration and rage; I can hardly bear the emotional exhaustion of Hok which, the X'Thi assure me, is almost upon us. *How much more of this can I stand to take?*

COUL, LEONARD (see also COUL'S PLANET): The discoverer of Coul's Planet. The intrepid and solitary voyager out of the Service who has dedicated his life to adventure, to the search for and achievement of new terrain, who has cheerfully, steadfastly, unblinkingly accepted the loneliness and danger of his trade, who has asked (until the moment of this disastrous event) absolutely no assistance from the Service but has merely accepted his duty as a given condition, now thirty-seven years old and fallen upon difficult times but still, still, gentlemen, of good courage and spirit, continuing his negotiations with the X'Thi, working upon this glossary which is a keyhole into their consciousness, performing his tasks within the difficult confinement of the ship uncomplainingly . . . all the time putting to one side any consideration of his wizened genitals, his tormented psyche, his diminished and abused consciousness which has put up with more, more, I must tell you, than any of you would conceive. Who, nevertheless, is Coul to complain? Hok comes upon him; Cosmic Jolts lay both before and ahead of him, somewhere in the middle of that great Loop of possibility he hangs doing his tasks, keeping up his optimism, knowing that in his hour or hours of need ye will not abandon him but will save him from all of this.

PARALLELED MOONS: Two moons track Coul's Planet, revolving around it in tandem much as Coul's possibilities may be said to darkly devolve around his core. The moons are linked yet separate, they are in similar orbits following duplicate trajectory separated only by a small wisp of space; for this reason they are referred to as "paralleled," although certain of the X'Thi disagree with this, saying that "simultaneous" would be a better mode of reference. The Cosmic Jolt has both an origin and a conclusion, the X'Thi (they are in their way a rather mystical people although they have no organized religion) state, all of the universe may be perceived as a duality, within each of us are not only (in many cases) paired organs but opposed motives, and these paralleled moons are projections of that duality, circling, circling Coul's Planet in the perpetual night of its sky. During Hok, Blolomite is revealed in flashes in the light of the paralleled moons (see BLOLOMITE). The paralleled moons, however, are composed of the same gaseous substance as is Coul's Planet; that is to say that it would be very difficult to get hold of them, even if they were not so impossibly distant, so impossibly huge.

TRIRE: See AZAPLI.

X'THI: The cheerful residents of Coul's Planet. The *natives* of Coul's Planet I should say rather; indigenous to its ecology and terrain, that essentially ebullient population whose rather arcane linguistics are at least mapped in this glossary, that essentially ebullient population with whom I have been in almost constant contact since my crash-landing and subsequent unsuccessful escape attempts from Coul's Planet some time ago.

The X'Thi are mystical without being religious, efficient without beng organized, proprietary without being domineering; it can be said that they combine both the best and worst traits of their ecology in so being, although again this may merely be a projection of my own admittedly limited view of them and they may be both more or less than can be readily ascertained. What is there to be said of the X'Thi? Their physical appearance is amorphous; dimly glimpsed through the viewports of this sinking vessel they take on different colors and aspects with the changes of the day; part of this having to do with their own rather chameleonlike ability to partake of features of the terrain, part of it having to do with my own rather dazzled perceptions which due to hunger and increasing fright cannot be trusted as to consistency. The X'Thi themselves testify that their changing aspect may be due not to difficulties in sight or terrain but to the presence of Blolomite itself throughout the atmosphere: Blolomite has the sinister ability to distort reality into changing shapes and aspects; coming from the Cosmic Jolt and being put in place by the squawking "E:" of the Creator (whose identity, gentlemen, is unknown at the present time, the Creator being ineffable), it partakes of many qualities which may be beyond our ken and it can be said that to live on Coul's Planet as I have been forced to for this period of time may simply mean to be *immersed in Blolomite* as strange as this thought may be, immersed in Blolomite and circling forever dimly under the light of the parallel moons, the parallel moons streaking the heavens in their very duality. The X'Thi say that they cannot sustain me much longer in this environment, that as the time of decampment approaches they must more and more attend to their own difficult and necessary tasks preceding said decampment, that they will have to abandon me to my own devices in order that they may protect themselves. There is, they assure me, nothing at all personal about this abandonment, they are rather fond of me, they are fond of Leonard Coul, abandoned voyager in their midst, but their own survival is paramount and they must go about it in their own way. After all, Coul's Planet, the Cosmic Jolt, Hok and the decampment were around long before I was (to say nothing of Blolomite) and will similarly survive me by a good long period; they must pay proper obeisance to their traditions because without their traditions, where are they? An unanswerable question, gentlemen. Hok will begin, in glimmers of Blolomite as seen in the light of the parallel moons the Cosmic Jolt may be apperceived but the X'Thi will be gone, they will all be gone and I will be here alone, always alone, *unless efforts are made to speed up the rescue party at all costs,* to accelerate, that is to say, its efforts. In the meantime there is nothing to be done but to continue on my routine and essentially timekilling tasks, maintenance of the environment, eating, sleeping, the preparation of this glossary and so on. What will I do when Hok comes? The answer to that is unspeakable and I will cheerfully leave that question to you, gentlemen, being unable, quite, to deal with it myself.

Y: That cosmic sound (emanating, it is said, from the second Cosmic Jolt) with which creation will end. (See E.) According to the myths of the X'Thi, the Creator will cry "Y:" as Coul's Planet comes to an end, imploding toward ash in the sickly light of the wasted moons, small scraps of Blolomite dancing in the gases as in that explosive "Y:Y:Y:" all that the X'Thi will ever know shall end.

AFTERWORD TO REPORT TO HEADQUARTERS

I revere Vladimir Nabokov's *Pale Fire*, which I consider to be the best novel in English of the century, and although I have so synthesized my influences in recent years as to appear to be an original* I cannot resist pastiche now and then or what was called in a gentler era *homage*. "Report to Headquarters" is an attempt to do within 2,500 words a little piece of what *Pale Fire* accomplished in 100,000. The presumption is sheer cheek of course but with the masterpiece lighting the corridor and the familiar devices of science fiction dangling as handles to clutch on the walls I think this makes it a little way down the path.

Nevertheless. I wonder if anyone (except Robert Silverberg, who took it) understands this piece. I have never seen it mentioned by any of the reviewers of *New Dimensions 5* in which it originally appeared barring Richard Delap (otherwise an appreciator of my work), who called it "trivial." Does everyone miss the point? Or is the point made so subtly as to fail to be made? My fault? Could be.

Let me or the editor know.

* I am not. I am several parts Nabokov, a few parts Salinger and Cheever, a *soupçon* of Mailer, a dash of this, a dash of that. I think I am very good, you understand, but I have never done a work in my life at any length which I considered to be original in the sense that I take Alfred Bester, say, or Nikolai Gogol or Robert Stone (what a strange mixture!) to be originals.

Streaking

So I take myself to the infirmary where the girl who ran briefly naked across campus is spending this night and under protection of darkness slip to her bedside where I find her lying quite awake, her eyes fixed open on the ceiling, and say, "I'm conducting a survey. Why did you do it?"

She looks at me bleakly, not discomfited since my voice, as is characteristic with most I address, seems to come from inside her own head and she takes me to be a fragment of her own personality rather than that stark and quizzical spirit which I know myself to be. "It's a fad," she says. "Everybody's doing it, and I thought that it was time for a girl to do it, too. It wasn't much. I just took off all my clothes and left them on the chapel steps, see, and then I ran toward the gymnasium. It was at one-thirty on a Thursday, a slow time, between classes, and I didn't think that more than three or four people would see me. But when I started running back from the gymnasium I could see this whole crowd and someone taking pictures. I think they're going to be in the paper tomorrow."

"Yes," I say gently, "of course, but you haven't answered the question, I think. I seek discovery, not description. Why did you do it?"

She shrugs; the little motion sends little puffs of dust circling into the air, particles which, with my keenness of vision, I can sense even to their agony of displacement. Everything which is part of this earth is sentient; any fool should know this. "It's kind of a thing now. If I didn't do it, some other girl would have. So I wanted to be the first."

"But why?" I say. Leaning forward, rubbing my invisible palms together, I have been deserted momentarily by my characteristic dispassion; in fact I have forgotten myself and seem to be filled with a dim excitement. "Why did you want to be the first girl?"

Her vision flicks; she looks away from me. "What are you," she says, "a pervert?"

So I watch the revels at the University of the North the next day, or perhaps it is two days after, time having little significance to me, as several hundred freshmen and sophomores, clothing under their arms, run naked from the mathematics building to old Sherwin Hall and then back again. Television trucks from the local station are there, reporters, a few men in clerical dress with bitter expressions. Also coeds, although not as many as I would have thought, the Dean of Women having threatened severe action for any girl suspected of participating or encouraging the spree. Although the University of the North is a rather liberal university by today's standards, the Dean of Women is a dangerous and reactionary old woman who (no one now knows but me) will be forced by illness out of her position by the end of the spring semester. After the freshmen and sophomores reassemble at Sherwin and quickly don their clothing, some with embarrassed expressions, I pursue a group of them to an off-campus bar where some time later I join their discussion in the garb of a middle-aged laborer with a kindly expression. "But why did you do it?" I say.

One of them looks at me narrowly. "None of your business, pops," he says. The others giggle. "Because it's there," he says. "It's like telephone-booth stuffing or goldfish, right?"

"But three years ago you were rioting," I say, "you were burning the campus as a symbol of injustice and repression. Why this now?"

"Some kind of damn moralist," another says, "that's all you are." He looks into his beer meditatively and takes a bitter swallow. "Anyway, that wasn't us," he says. "That was another generation, another time. We weren't here then. *We* wouldn't have been into that stuff."

"It represents progress," the third says, and then as he notes my somewhat ironic expression says, "or maybe not progress, depending on how you look at it, but it's our lives, right?"

"Right," I say mildly.

"Then why don't you shove off?"

"I will," I say, "I am. I was just curious."

"Get lost," the first says. I can tell that he is embarrassed and that his defensive posture renders him more dangerous than simple hostility would be. "It's our life."

"Oh," I say gently, "I agree absolutely."

Walking from the bar still in disguise I am stricken with a madman's temptation to doff my own clothing and stream from them naked, but this will not do, of course—not yet—and my slow, lumbering gait carries me easily toward the door, from which I instantly depart, still meditating.

So I reassemble to find myself standing next to a nervous boy who is standing unnoticed in the empty wing of a college auditorium; on the stage a Congressman is haranguing the audience about its failure to respond to cues in its inner and outer lives, cues for action. The Congressman is calling for action, but only of the most reasoned sort. The boy, who plans to run naked across the stage in front of the Congressman in thirty seconds, opens his belt buckle and allows his trousers to slip to the floor, kicks them off, then opens his shirt.

"What are you going to accomplish?" I say.

"A certain notoriety," the boy says, "a certain momentary fame. The first to streak a political speech in the state. I consider it a political gesture."

"But it's senseless," I say, "it's only going to get lost in the sensation—any political significance, that is."

"I want the sensation," the boy says. He swallows determinedly and takes off his shirt. "I mean, what better way to do it? Anyway, somebody paid me a hundred dollars for this, and I don't want to give it back."

"So you admit you're doing it for profit?"

"I admit nothing," the boy says. He drops the last of his clothing, stands only in his socks, takes several deep breaths, inhaling unevenly. Small droplets of sweat may be detected along his limbs. "It's something that has to be done," he says. He takes a massive gulp of air and as the speaker pounds home some devastating point on the rostrum, runs out onto the stage away from me. The dark heart of his buttocks recedes.

It would be interesting to stay and see what happens then, but suddenly, stricken by an idea, I find myself turning from there with a sense of mission.

So I go to the offices of the college chaplain and enter into a discussion with him. The chaplain nods solemnly. "I absolutely agree," he says, "I've been thinking of this for a few days now. It's going to be the subject of my next sermon."

"It isn't corruption," I say excitedly, in the throes of my idea, "and it isn't abandonment of reality either. It's something else."

The chaplain nods. "I was thinking that it might be a generalized sense of rage or impotence," he says, "against which the naked, vulnerable human form by being juxtaposed bears witness to that helplessness. Or then again it may be a mockery of manners which are felt to be oppressive."

I shake my head. "I'm sorry," I say, "I'm truly sorry, but that isn't it. That isn't the point. It's something else entirely."

"Is that so?" the chaplain says. Indulging himself and for the sake of argument, he acts as if I were real (which to him I am not) and decides to engage in disputation. "Then tell me what it is."

"It is what it is," I say, "that's all."

"I don't understand."

"It has no explanation. It merely exists."

"Beg pardon."

"The dancer and the dance," I say somewhat vaguely, "the shadow and the act. They cannot be separated; they are bound together."

"You deny sin."

"No, not if it is intertwined with the action."

"Then you deny the very principle of causality."

"Perhaps," I say, "but then if there is no cause, there can be no causality. Neither stimulus nor response. Twitches. Twitches up and down the range of possibility."

The chaplain shakes his head. "This is very puzzling," he says, "too difficult for me. It is a sophistry. Nevertheless I will think about it and perhaps incorporate it into my sermon tomorrow."

"It won't do you any good," I say, more insights flowering within me, popping open like buds. "None whatsoever."

"Leave *me* to decide that," the chaplain says. "After all," he says with a little rumble, "we must do something to stop this. What does this say about our standards? Declining standards, that is. Why at this rate with an increasing tolerance for public nudity we might lose all standards before we know where we are."

"Dancer and the dance. Shadow and the act. Poem and the rhythm," I say, and before the chaplain can say anything further I have gone away from there quickly, dispersed into the smoke, leaving him to ponder this and other questions which I know he will raise through the night.

So the next morning (even though it does not matter) I appear in the chapel just before the sermon and stand there smirking behind a pillar as the chaplain comes wavering to the lectern, braces himself there, and begins to speak. The audience is sparse, as it almost always is for services of this routine type, but there are nevertheless a hundred students, faculty, and staff scattered through the shell of the auditorium, not one of whom—I know with my infinite perception—has ever participated or would consider participating in the act that he is about to condemn.

"I am about to condemn an act," the chaplain says.

I nod. This is the best way to approach the matter. Without ambivalence.

"I refer to a shocking and dangerous act dismissed too often as juvenile which has already swept through—"

Abruptly my attention releases. It is, after all, so predictable. Besides, I have other things to do. Up until this moment I was not sure why I had come, even what had underlain (I must be frank here) my quest. Now I do. It has come upon me and I am seized by conviction.

"Our standards are collapsing," the chaplain says. "The Bible itself points out that Adam and Eve knew their nakedness, and their nakedness was shame."

I feel tinkling laughter overtaking me. It is like little bells being run through the spaces of my flesh. But I am too busy otherwise, doffing my garments, to pay attention to this outburst . . . which fortunately is unheard as I am yet invisible. "We are parading the spectacle of our shame," the chaplain says.

The last of my garments is off. I nod solemnly, agreeing with the sense of what he has said. Truly he has not failed me; he has pondered this sermon all night, and much of what he says is true.

"If we display our nakedness, we dissolve all dignity in shame, all differences in bestiality," the chaplain says.

I nod again. He is making much sense. Quickly I render myself visible. At the same time I can, of course, be heard. My laughter draws attention. All of the congregation turns to look at me. Transfixed, the chaplain follows the line of their gaze. He stares.

"I don't—" he gasps.

"I don't either," I say. "I don't either."

And then I streak. From pew to aisle to pulpit to symbol I run naked, dodging little currents of wind that eddy at me, touch the chaplain a springing touch on his robes, which causes him to shrivel just as it fills me with exaltation . . . and then laughing, laughing, I spring like smoke into the darkness above and barking like the Hound of Heaven leave behind me in a whisk the shouts of my betrayal.

AFTERWORD TO STREAKING

Remember streaking? Anyone? That was back in the early spring of 1974, after the ascension of Gerald Ford to the vice-presidency and just before the release of the White House transcripts. Not much going on during that lull; a lot of people, mostly males in their late teens to early twenties, were taking off all their clothing except stockings, donning masks and running rapidly through places of public assembly. Three points for women streakers, five for making it on television. Someone even streaked the Oscar ceremonies.

Benign insanity for a change; even a doomsayer like myself could see little harm in it. Certainly less destructive to the human spirit than the material of those White House transcripts although not quite as funny. One looked forward to summer and the beaches. Unfortunately the impeachment process ground on and almost with the first crocus streaking disappeared. I haven't heard of it in years.

Too bad. Nowadays technology, communications, the homogenization of the culture force fads and trends to run their course in a matter of days whereas, even as late as the nineteen fifties, we could have squeezed almost half a year of streaking to lighten the hearings of the judiciary committee. It might return—everything does sooner or later, you know—but not while any of us are still young and I am sorry because it brought us laughter; it showed us the human condition in a fashion devoid of original sin. Nixon might have survived to this day if he had had the wit to streak Rodino, Hungate and Holtzman. What did he have to lose?

In any case here is the story; preserved artifact of a vanished era. A first, if you will. The first science fiction historical.

Making It to Gaxton Falls
on the Red Planet
in the Year of Our Lord

July 14, 2115, and here we are in Gaxton Falls of the famous red planet. Why we are spending this bright Bastille Day in Gaxton Falls when we could be just six, make it seven kilometers away, celebrating more properly in Paris is beyond me but impulse must always be respected and so here we are. Down the midway we see fragments and artifacts of reconstructed Americana: lining our path are the little booths and display halls where facets of that vanished time may be more closely observed. Betsy holds my hand tightly as well she may. Truly, she has never seen anything like this and neither, for that matter, have I.

"Isn't this the most remarkable thing?" she says referring, I suppose, to the fact that Gaxton Falls is in most ways a faithful reconstruction of a medium-sized American city of 1974, one hundred and forty-one years ago, a wonderful time in which to be alive. "It just looks so real, Jack," she says and so it does, so it does indeed but I will not betray to her my own astonishment, concentrating as I am upon walking down the midway undisturbed by the blandishments and cries of the barkers who would have us stop at this stand, that display, these pieces of goods. It is a disgraceful thing what has happened to Mars; the place is a tourist trap. Truly one must be aware of this at all times: it was a grand thing to have colonized the planet fifty years ago and we will always be in the pioneers' debt . . . but fashions change, emphases shift and the good people generally steer clear of this place. We had to stop over to make the Ganymede switch but once is enough. Mars is economically viable now only because of the tourist business, which in turn bears the result of the reconstruction committees of the hated nineties . . . but all of this is boring, abstruse history. Even the rather colorful villages of Mars, the ruins I mean, do not move me and I cannot wait to get away from here. To some degree I hold it against Betsy that she responds to the place.

Still: we are in Gaxton Falls and must make the best of a bad time. "Come in, sir," a man with a moustache calls to us through the sparse crowd, "come in and meet the iconoclast, do," and before I can protest, Betsy is tugging me by the hand toward the barker's stand which fronts a rather drab set of burlap curtains. "Fascinating and educational," the barker says, "and not only do you have a chance to hear the iconoclast speak, you may also argue with him, take exception to his points, get into a fascinating discussion." Like all the barkers he has a precise command of the idiom of this period although his pronunciation is foul. Obviously this man like so many of the others was imported from Venus where the excessive labor pool produces thousands like him. "What do you say, sir?" he says when we near him. His eyes are faintly desperate, his skin has a greenish cast from lack of sunlight. Clearly a Venusian.

"Let's go in," Betsy says. Her ebullience is a cover for doubt and I feel a lurch of pity: better go along with her. I give the barker his asking price in scrip, two dollars and fifty cents for each of us, and still holding hands we duck within the curtains, feeling the threads of burlap coming out to caress us like fingernails and into the enclosure itself which, expectedly, is smaller and more odorous than the front would indicate. An enormous man sits behind a simple wooden table shaking his head. We are the only customers in the enclosure. As we enter he begins speaking in an empty, rehearsed drone.

"We must abandon the space program," he says in the old accent, much better than the barker, "because it is destroying our cities, abandoning our underprivileged, leading people toward the delusion that the conquest of space will solve their problems and it is in the hands of technicians and politicians who care not at all for the mystery, the wonder, the intricacies of the human soul. Better we should solve our problems on Earth before we go to the Moon." He rams the table. "We won't be ready for space until we've cleaned up our own planet, understood our own problem."

"But don't you think," Betsy asks, entering into the spirit of this: an engaging girl, "that exploration is an important human need? We'll never solve our problems on Earth after all so we might as well voyage outward where the solutions might be." She squeezes my hand, pleased with herself. Indeed, her own mastery of the idiom is impressive although only guidebook deep.

"Certainly not," the iconoclast says, "that's a ridiculous argument." He does not really look at her; I wonder if he is machinery. Some of the exhibits are and some are not; it is hard to tell humans, and the more sophisticated androids are interchangeable anyway. "The era of exploration and discovery has shifted to the arena of inner space. We must know ourselves or die. To continue the space program would be madness. Happily it is being abandoned."

It is brief but I am already bored with this exhibit, which is rather predictable and limited. "That's nonsense," I point out. "You can't equate exploration with ignorance any more than your enemies could with knowledge."

"But of course I can!" the iconoclast booms. His eyes belie the energy however, they are dull and withdrawn; he is deep, then into a programmed series of replies, and we are not discussing the matter but merely exchanging positions. "The two are exactly the same when you consider that the space program has produced in its fifteen years not one single positive contribution to the common lives of most men. Or women."

"Not so!" says Betsy. "Think of lasers, life-support systems, advances in pacemaker technique, adaptation to weightlessness, psychological studies, rare alloys . . ."

"No," the iconoclast says loudly. He pushes himself back from the table, his body sagging. Enormous: the exhibit must weigh over four hundred pounds. "That is specious and entirely wrong."

"Enough," I say. Abruptly my boredom has turned into physical disgust and I want to leave. Gaxton Falls is highly overrated and the iconoclast is typical of almost all its exhibits: cheap, programmatic, superficial. "We're going to leave."

"Jack," Betsy says, her head wrenching one way, her body another. "We may hurt his feelings."

"Don't be foolish," I say, using a double-lock on her wrist, "he's merely an exhibit, possibly an android, certainly hypnoprogrammed. He doesn't even know we're here; they wake up in a vat later. Anyway," I add, turning toward the iconoclast who has sat rigid through all of this, his face as bleak and empty as the sands which lie just to the rear of the Falls, stretching then into Paris, "besides you're a fool and you did not prevail. We returned to the moon in 1980. We were on Mars by 1990. By 2050 we had established a scientific colony on Mars, a viable, self-supporting unit, had landed several times on Venus, were investing the rings of Saturn at close range and were preparing to drop the first ship on Ganymede. It was, in historical perspective, merely a sneeze, this midseventies interruption of the program. You did not prevail."

The iconoclast puts his palms flatly on the table, tries awkwardly to rise, falls back into his flesh, gasping. Respiration makes his arms billow, he seems excited. Have I broken the program? "*You* are the fool," he says. "The space program was abandoned for all time. The great riots of the 1980s destroyed all of the centers and equipment, leaving nothing. It will be thousands of years before men even think of going into space again."

I look at him and see that he is serious. Whether programmed or working out of the program the iconoclast really believes this and I am filled with pity but pity has nothing to do with it. The air is dense. I want desperately to leave the tent. I tug Betsy by the hand, she swings like a pendulum and comes against me. The shock of the impact unbalances and I scramble on my knees, Betsy awkwardly straddling me. We cannot seem to disentangle.

"You fools," the iconoclast says, "you poor fools, just look, *look*," and it is as if the tent falls away, the burlap turning to glass, then mist: the burlap opening toward an endless perspective of the dead landscape of Mars; in that landscape I see the fires, the fires of the 1980s which destroyed the center forever. They sear and rip away; it is momentarily more than I can take, I claw the ground desperately, knowing that when I open them again this will have gone away and I will see Gaxton Falls and its midway again, all of this a seizure, but when I do open them, see again after a long time it is not the midway I see but the flap of the tent opening and as I stare, two people enter, one of them Betsy, and look at me. The other looks familiar although I cannot quite place him. He seems to be a reasonable man, however, and I will do what I can to bring him around.

"We must abandon the space program," I say.

AFTERWORD TO MAKING IT TO GAXTON FALLS ON THE RED PLANET IN THE YEAR OF OUR LORD

Young writers sell their dreams, middle-aged writers their ideas, old writers themselves. Since one can grow old in this business faster than in any other field except modeling or pop music, there are an awful lot of old men in their thirties and forties around now, casually or passionately dismembering themselves as their patience and artistic gifts dwindle. (In a small way this collection may even be an example of the syndrome but I am happy, with my customary modesty, to leave that judgment to our more venerable critics, many of whom have the problem themselves.)

I resisted the truth of this self-coined aphorism for many years, preferring to modulate the True Confessions and keep them in transmuted fictional form, but increasingly the mask is beginning to drop: I was, it appears, a closet Harlan Ellison all the time.* If the mask has indeed begun to drop, revealing the innocent, humble, clownish features beneath, one can date the first shy removal to February of 1974 when this story was written. It begins in customary cold control but halfway through something happens (or fails to happen) in the creative process and for the first time in all my years of achieved professionalism I come stage center and begin to speak in my own voice. Whether this raised or lowered the level of the piece I am unable to say but it was so profoundly satisfying that I could not resist doing it again and now I have taken to doing it rather often. Increasingly I understand the late John Dos Passos or Sinclair Lewis, to say nothing of the contemporary Norman Mailer.

"Gaxton Falls" was written in the flush of my first sale to *analog* and was sent to that magazine, which, of course, wanted no part of it. It bounced here and there and wound up in Harry Harrison's

---

* Harlan Ellison is in many ways an admirable man who has shown the way for us all and this statement is made in great respect.

Nova 4, which is apparently the last volume of this original anthology series, another casualty of the anthology overrun of 1973–75. Boom and bust in this field, bust and boom; if I had a bust for every boom in this field, as the old science fiction writer said in the confessional booth, I would have passed away a happier although much younger man.

After the Great Space War

GENTS:

Well, here I am in the heart of the Rigelian System, a fine, spacious system indeed composed of binary stars and a veritable forest of planets and a lovely little planet you have picked, most suitable indeed for conquest, with delicately purple-hued natives who talk in musical scat (whop-a-bee-ba; a-whop-a-dee-*doo*) and whisper about the hedges of their world like birds: as you see there is no xenophobia in my analyses and the warnings and accusations at the time of embarkment (embarkation?) were *totally* unfair. I *love* being an interstellar scout and am much cheered by the Rigelian System, finding these natives endlessly resourceful and amusing even though our contact has thus far been tentative and I have been able to map out only a little of their language with the inductive devices, making communication somewhat hesitant. Evenings I spend in this capsule spreading out against the sky like an operating table; mornings and afternoons I stroll through the forests of this planet, joshing with the natives monosyllabically (a-ba-*boo*-dup) and handing out the very fine supply of interstellar trinkets with which I was so thoughtfully equipped. These simple-minded inhabitants are delighted with them.

Assignment, in short, proceeds with ease and fluency, fluency and ease, and I make it that I should be ready to summon the landing fleet within a shift or three; in the meantime I continue to win their confidence. They seem to think that I am one of their local gods made manifest and although I recall the problems with this reaction against which we have been warned (riot, desolation, flood, reversion to barbarism) am sure that can handle this as have handled everything else. There is something called the Ceremony of Hinges (very approximate translation of their scat but the best I can do at this time) which they would like me to join but if you do not mind, if you do not mind, I think that I will pass this up. For the time being. The last ceremonial, three planets ago as you will recall, gave me an extremely bad cold and moderate feelings of insufficiency which I have yet to entirely overcome.

WILSON

PARTICIPATE IN SO-CALLED CEREMONY OF HINGES. VITAL AT ALL COSTS THAT INTEGRATION WITH THE SUBGROUP PROCEED ON NATURAL LINES. CEREMONY IS PROBABLY PART OF IMPORTANT RITUAL AND INVITATION THEY EXTEND MEANS THEIR CONFIDENCE IS WON. DO NOT HOLD BACK WILSON WE WILL HAVE NO REPETITION OF PAST DIFFICULTIES TO WHICH OF COURSE THERE IS NO NECESSITY TO REFER IN THIS TRANSMISSION.

HEADQUARTERS

Headquarters:
Yes, gents, I do understand and am not making waves. Really I am not (realize the circumstances of the probation on which I have been placed, a matter of which to quote your own approach I see no necessity to refer in this transmission) but it is not, *not* xenophobia which makes me reluctant to participate in the Ceremony of Hinges but merely a certain shy reluctance, a demureness of the spirit if you will. How can I explain this *je ne sais quoi?* How do I know the material of the ceremony? They turn aside my queries. (The translation is indeed rough, certainly the naming gives no clue. Hinges. *Hinges?*) Am willing to move on straightway with honesty and guile alternating in the best tradition of the interstellar scout with steadfastness and dependability predominating but are you really sure that you want me to do this? The sky is a lovely azure (I azure you of this) and pastel blue like the eyes of my many loves during their days and red at night on a sixteen-hour time cycle and the sound of their voices fills the pleasant glade in which I have landed with music at all times. I am happy here, gents, happy and I *love* the natives and accept the circumstances but do you really think that this is worth the risks?

Come now: what does the Ceremony of Hinges have to do with our plans of conquest? I think that the landing fleet should be called in *now*, right now in fact, but await as always your advice even though I feel that our relationship has not quite reached and I am beginning to fear may never quite reach that mutuality of understanding for which *I*, fellows, have striven from the very first. I remind you that the majority of the embarrassing difficulties to which, delicately, neither of us cares to refer have been caused by the sincerity of my attempts to live up to what I take your own wishes to be. I have *tried*. I have tried so hard.

WILSON

YOU POOR FOOL YOU ARE WASTING YOUR TIME AND OURS. WE ARE IN A POSITION OF MAXIMUM OBSERVATION AND IMMINENCE SUSTAINED ONLY AT GREAT EXPENSE. PARTICIPATE IN THE CEREMONY IMMEDIATELY DO YOU GET THAT PARTICIPATE IN THE CEREMONY IMMEDIATELY AT WHICH POINT OUR SOCIOPATHOLOGISTS HAVE CALCULATED YOU WILL HAVE REACHED THE OPTIMUM INTEGRATION AND CAN BE MOST USEFULLY APPLIED WHEN THE LANDING IS ACCOMPLISHED. CUT IT OUT WILSON WE WILL NOT TOLERATE MUCH MORE OF THIS. ACCOMPLISH A MODAL INFARCTION.

HQ

Friends:
Modal infarction?

Well, you see men, I don't *want* to participate in the Ceremony of Hinges. Has not that already become clear? Since our last talk, furthermore, I have come into new and somewhat ominous indications as the translation machinery moves on apace that it, the Ceremony that is, may be a birth ritual of some kind or perhaps a reconstitution of one's history in which the participant is stuffed with local herbs and additives and passed through living *flame*. I do not know if I can survive this even though their purposes do appear benign.

Listen, I am not xenophobic. I love *all* aliens and am prepared to love these too, caring ever more deeply about optimum performance of my job which as you know is rapidly approaching tenure guaranteeing promotion, probation or not, and want to make as few problems as possible, but are you sure, I mean are you really sure that you want going ahead with this particular Ceremony?

Listen, I believe that I have *already* won their confidence. They are now bringing *me* gifts, local plants and animals somewhat indistinguishable from the natives themselves virtually ring my little capsule and we chatter and reminisce through the bulkheads nightly. (Wa-ba-ba-beep; la-lo-*ka*.) I think that it is now time to bring down the landing party. Modal infarctions, whatever they might be, are fine, I am willing to dedicate my *life* to the principles of m.i. but is it really called for at this time? My life, that is to say. Think about this friends; I certainly have value at the HQ, even more value than to my humble self considering the training and warnings that have been invested in me, and I do not think that the m.i. is suitable at this time.

Perhaps you ought to land before they make the Ceremony of Hinges a test of my true sincerity and worth to them which so far they are not. They are not ordering me to participate. May I repeat this? They are *not* ordering me to participate, merely wistfully requesting it in the way that I wistfully requested this one last assignment to prove my good faith and credentials and then proceeded as you can see to carry off said assignment with great success for indeed and you must believe this now, indeed they do love me.

Let me handle this my way. I can explain that our metabolism will not permit us to accommodate the preparatory herbs and additives and while they are bemusedly considering this the landing parties can come in with the incinerative gear and do the job roundly.

As a matter of fact, let's send them in right now. Leave the apologies and explanations to me; I will handle my part of the bargain and you will handle yours. Now strikes me as an excellent time to send them in.

Do not be winsome, gents, or fail me at this hour of great need. I am counting upon you. Send the fleet in.

WILSON

YOU ARE TO PARTICIPATE IN THE CEREMONY OF HINGES AND AT ONCE.

YOU FOOL THIS IS A WORLD AT STAKE WHO DO YOU THINK YOU ARE TO JEOPARDIZE THE CONQUEST OF A WORLD AS VALUABLE AS THIS COULD BE. AS THE REPORTS ALSO INDICATE WE DO NOT TAKE ANY RISKS OR CHANCES. WILSON THE SCOUT IS THE ONE WHO IS EXPENDABLE IN CIRCUMSTANCES LIKE THIS. THE SCOUT IS EXPENDABLE. YOU KNEW THAT AND IT IS THAT CONDITION UNDER WHICH YOU HAVE WORKED AND IT IS TIME FOR YOU TO ACCEPT THE RESPONSIBILITIES

OF THE ASSIGNMENT WHICH YOU ARE REMINDED YOU BEGGED AS ONE
LAST CHANCE TO PROVE YOUR MERIT. PARTICIPATE IN THE CEREMONY
AND THEN SEND US FULL PARTICULARS AND THEN IN DUE COURSE IT
WILL BE OUR DECISION AND ONLY OUR DECISION AS TO WHEN AND
WHERE TO LAND THE FLEET.

HQ

GENTS:
You know not what you ask. It is a far far better thing which I
do. I do not think you understand the sacrifice that I am making.
Very well. Have it your way. You will feel sorry. Guilt will overwhelm you in due course and you will be sorry that you have made
me do this. Nevertheless I am going to go in. Ask not what I can do
for you now but what you can do for me. One small step.

WILSON

YOU HAVE MADE THE PROPER DECISION AND WE WISH TO CON-
GRATULATE YOU FOR COMING TO TERMS WITH THE SITUATION IN A
REALISTIC MANNER AT LAST. WE KNEW THAT IN THE END WE COULD
COUNT UPON YOU. AWAIT YOUR FULL REPORT ON THE CEREMONY OF
HINGES WITH GREAT INTEREST.

HEADQUARTERS

HAVE HAD NO REPORT FROM YOU FOR TWO CYCLES. DID YOU PAR-
TICIPATE IN THE CEREMONY OF HINGES, QUESTION MARK. WE WISH AN
IMMEDIATE REPORT. EXCUSE YOURSELF FROM FESTIVITIES IF STILL CAR-
RYING ON AND CABLE A FULL REPORT. WE AWAIT SAME.

HQ

TWO MORE CYCLES HAVE ELAPSED AND NOW WE ARE MOVING WELL
INTO THE THIRD. INTO THE THIRD YOU FOOL. SUPPORT AND MON-
ITORING DEVICES INDICATE THAT YOU ARE VERY MUCH ALIVE. RESPI-
RATION PULSE HEARTBEAT GROSS FUNCTIONS ALL NORMAL OR WITHIN
GROSS NORMAL RANGE. STOP HIDING FROM US WILSON YOU ARE TO
REPLY AT ONCE.

HQ!

TO: HEADQUARTERS DIVISION
Cancel the fleet. The planet is uncongenial to human life.

JAMES O. WILSON

WHAT ARE YOU TALKING ABOUT WILSON THE PARTY IS IN CLOSE
ORBIT AND HAS BEEN FOR SOME CONSIDERABLE TIME NOW. MUCH
TIME WASTED TOO MUCH SPECIAL OVERTIME INVOLVED. HOW IS
PLANET UNCONGENIAL TO HUMAN LIFE, QUESTION MARK. YOU HAVE
SURVIVED ON IT.

HQ

FOR YOUR FAILURE TO REPLY YOU HAVE BEEN RELIEVED OF COM-
MAND EFFECTIVE AT ONCE WHICH IS TO SAY UPON YOUR RECEIPT OF
THIS TRANSMISSION WHICH IS TO SAY IMMEDIATELY. DECISION TO
LAND HAS BEEN MADE INDEPENDENTLY AND YOU ARE TO TURN YOUR-
SELF OVER TO FLEET COMMANDER WHO WILL ARRANGE QUARTERS
AND WE WILL TAKE CARE OF YOU OH WILL WE EVER TAKE CARE OF
YOU UPON YOUR RETURN TO THE SHIP.

HQ

TO: HEADQUARTERS DIVISION OF THE ENEMY
My troops and I that is to say we will fight to the last man, no
matter the price, no matter the penalty, in order that we may repel
the invaders and save for all time the integrity of our world.

JAMES O. WILSON

LAND THE FLEET. LAND THE FLEET AT ONCE. THIS SUPERSEDES ANY
AND ALL OTHER ORDERS AND IS NOT TO BE DISREGARDED UNDER ANY
CIRCUMSTANCE. LAND THE FLEET AT ONCE AND SECURE EVERYTHING
THAT MOVES.

HQ

HEADQUARTERS:

Planet landed and secured at 1400 Cycle 23. We are now in control of the populace and surrounding territory all of which is

pleasantly amiable and delightful to behold. We report no instances of enemy action nor indeed any signs of an enemy. These people are our friends. All is well. Now we are going at the special invitation of the Conductors to participate in the Ceremony of Leakage. (This is a rough translation; the transmission devices are still not sensitive to gradations of language but you get the idea.) We will report shortly upon our successful participation in this ceremony. Modal infarction is well upon the way. It is not necessary to send in the second division.

COMMANDER

DO NOT REPEAT DO NOT REPEAT DO NOT DO IT. WHERE IS WILSON. DO NOT DO IT DO NOT PARTICIPATE IN ANY CEREMONIES THIS IS AN ABSOLUTE INFLEXIBLE ORDER. WHERE IS WILSON WHY IS PLANET NOT SECURED WHY ARE YOU PARTICIPATING IN CEREMONY EXPRESS ORDERS SAY YOU ARE NOT TO DO NOT DO IT. REPORT AT ONCE SECOND DIVISION IS ON WAY AND WILL LAND WITHIN TWELVE CYCLES TO TAKE INCENDIARY ACTION IF YOU DO NOT ALL OF YOU COOPERATE.

HQ

FRIENDS:
Ceremony of Leakage delightful. All that we could have wished and more besides. We look forward with an anticipation we can barely hide to the promised Pageant of Stains which we have been advised makes the Ceremony of Leakage pale to insignificance just as the C. of L. utterly reduces the Ceremony of Hinges to the tiny taste of grandeur which it is now seen to be.

The planet is secure and while we await the Pageant of Stains we similarly await arrival of the Second Division and behind them the colonists. The colonists are important. Send the colonists. Send all six thousand of the colonists. The planet is entirely secure and we are awaiting them. Send us boatloads of colonists. They may come in from all the systems; send the word that a green and harmless world awaits them. Planet, climate, circumstances extraordinary, natives totally submissive and within our control. Send at least the initial six thousand colonists. They can enjoy with us the Pageant if they arrive soon enough. Hurry.

COMMANDER

SEAL OFF THE PLANET AND PREPARE FOR INCENDIARY ACTION. WE HAVE NO CHOICE REPEAT WE HAVE NO CHOICE. BEGIN CONDITION PINK AT ONCE.

HQ

We await with great anticipation the colonists. Their place in the Pageant has been saved if they hurry. We are waiting for them and we insist that they be sent immediately immediately do you hear me immediately you send those colonists I wopa-ba-bee-do-dee-wham-bam-*boom!*

AFTERWORD TO AFTER THE GREAT SPACE WAR

Here is another of my obsessive themes,* this one of a Galactic Civil Service that we can certainly expect, now or in the future, alien or terrestrial, to function with the efficiency and intelligence which have always characterized this arm of the government. I think it is reasonable to assume that when and if we are ever invaded or undergo First Contact we will be dealing with a suborder, GS-12 of Galactic Clerk, and similarly our own adventurers in whatever far future will have their version of the Career & Salary Plan. Higher horizons for the memos, maybe, but policies and procedures *now* and keep yourself covered at all times.

"After the Great Space War" strikes me as a far more credible scenario of alien conquest or First Contact than most of the forties science fiction which solidified our ideas. Gadflies and satir'sts like Sheckley or Eric Frank Russell did move into the magazines in the fifties with their drunken galactic scouts and lummoxed-up aliens but it was clear underneath that the reader was to understand they were only kidding,† whereas this story is not kidding at all. If we

* In another collection I took the trouble to lay out the obsessive themes and since one paying customer is as good as any other paying customer I gladly do it again here. In no particular order: political assassination, marital breakdown, paranoid astronauts, cancer and the Galactic Civil Service discussed above.
† Russell was, Sheckley wasn't.

ever get into far space (I for one do not think we will, not ever, but this is merely one opinion) I think that this is a credible scenario for conquest.

"After the Great Space War" was rejected by *analog* as "too familiar" (I cannot to this day understand this unless the editor was saying that my work reminded him of me, in which case I understand him all too well) and by *Galaxy*'s Ejler Jakobssen as "kidding the field," something which he did not feel the field, obviously, was big enough or secure enough to take. Ed Ferman turned it back too for no reason that I can remember and it wound up in David Gerrold's third (and last) original anthology and glad to have it there, too.

Trashing

In Topeka, the madman had been in line for an open shot but at the critical instant my pistol had jammed, in Abilene I thought I had him leveled but his assassins surrounded him quickly after the speech and he got out of the way, in Los Angeles I could not possibly fail again until he canceled out of schedule at the last moment and headed north instead. (He must have foreseen what would happen, I thought then: the madman had flashes like them all.) Throughout that summer, the lunatic raged through the ruined country like a beast, spreading his lies and sedition wherever he landed, and left in his wake, as always, the fires, pain, looting and destruction. The Republic seemed, in those last days of August, as if it would not survive; as if finally all of its agonies had been taken past containment by the ravings and lunacies of one cunning enough to use its vulnerability: and I was frantic, oh yes my friends, I was frantic.

It was me, only I who could save the Republic then: detailed to the Mission by virtue of my superb skills and training, that and the fact that I had never, in all the years of various projects, missed a shot. I welcomed the assignment. I did not quail even when the Committee said in the grim way that the Committee had of speaking at crucial times, "Only you stand between order and destruction. Only you can destroy the madman. We have sent others and they have failed; now he is close to his destiny and if you fail as well, everything is ended." The Committee never overstates, I know it well, have worked for it in troubled times and good for all these years of my successes and I was not frightened by what was said to me, nor was I stricken.

"I'll get him," I said. "I'll get him and save us all," and I had gone out on the path of the madman, then, through all the stones and stricken portions of the country with the obsessive calm that always characterizes me on a quest . . . and I had missed him.

Missed him in Topeka. Lost him in Los Angeles, had him leveled to the ground in Abilene and other places too numerous to mention, but something had always happened to deter me and at last I came to understand that it was not merely a cunning and terrible series of mishaps but instead the very nature of the enemy against whom I was opposed. He *knew*. He judged my assignment and the responsibility I had taken, understood my purposes and never had I been confronted by an enemy more profound because not only did he evade, he taunted me.

In Atlanta, from the circle of his assassins he winked, in Topeka he laughed and grimaced as I swore helplessly at my pistol, in Los Angeles he released a mysterious statement to the captive press that he had canceled an engagement for "personal and important reasons." When I read this last in the newspaper that following day, I felt the passion to murder as I had never known it in the performance of my other assignments because his crazed face, dotted out by the camera of an imprisoned lithographer, hung before me in an obscene glint of knowledge. He teased. He knew the limits of my necessity and worked upon them as superbly as he worked on the rotted soul of the country. In Cleveland he called for the dispersion of the power structure, in Detroit he spoke of plans to enslave yet another class, in New York and then throughout New England he spread his lies and torment while behind him the cities shook and drowned in the blood of his wake. But finally I found him and knew with completion that this time I would not fail.

It was in Plainfield.

In Plainfield where I trailed the madman cautiously and with precision through one hundred and fifty miles of New Jersey landscape which he had deadened, turning into bare earth and refineries, choking on the oil fumes of his diseased lust, I came upon him slowly and easily, waiting until his assassins had spread into the surrounding populace to carry on their quiet terror as they always did through his tirades, and finally confronted him whole on the concrete as he gestured to the crowd, ending his rant. I remembered the words of the Committee, then, as I closed the ground between us.

"He is wise, he is shrewd," the old Committee had said, clasping one gnarled hand within the other. "He believes himself as do all psychopaths to be invulnerable, and at the last moment he may fix you with a gaze of such chilling power and intensity that you will be unable to deliver the blow. Do not look him in the eyes. Like

Medusa, his strength comes from his will and you must look at some neutral object or at the sky as you destroy him. Nor must you listen to his words because he will try to seduce you as he has done to all of the others in this dying country," and I remembered, advancing, the words of the Committee and smiled with reminiscence for I knew, all of the old Committee's doubts to the contrary, that I had the strength and power to complete the assignment.

"Do so and be done with it," the madman said, concluding his speech, and then in the sound looked upon me, knowing who I was. "Hello," he said, faking cordiality out of his knowledge of entrapment. I saw his eyes. They had no effect upon me. "You seem to be upset or angry, is something wrong?" the lunatic asked, attempting to misdirect me, but his words meant nothing, so attuned was I then to his maniacal shrewdness.

"Only this," I said pleasantly, "only this," and raised my weapon, centered it on the pale forehead behind which bulged his deformed brain and fired. He fell with casual quiet to the stones; easy at the end as I had always known it would be. I stood there at ease, confident, accepting plaudits from the crowd which I had liberated as his assassins, angry but helpless, came upon me. Indeed they were frustrated, as how could they be not? All of his cunning, their own acuity, had saved them nothing. The maniac lay dead at my feet and his assailants, groaning out their fury, could do nothing.

"I suppose you'll want to take me now," I said, nodding cordially, as the liberated of the crowd ran over me like a wave, a wave in the free and retrieved state of New Jersey in the country which had waited in agony for my liberating caress, and I felt their hands upon me, hard but gentle, fierce but calm.

"Get him, get him away right now for God's sake!" one of the assassins said and another said, "Yes, before they kill him!" and I said to them, letting the pistol fall away into their grasp and sagging against them gracefully, "No, it's perfectly all right; I want their congratulations, want their touch and love, for as I am freed of the madman, so are they all."

And I would be more than happy to go on with my further recollections about this last and greatest of all my adventures except that my memory from this point is blurred and I have now run out of the very few pieces of paper which the assassins' minions, who appear to administer these quarters, allow me. I would only ask to say this to the Committee, "If the madman is indeed shot why are his legions still in influential positions?" but the Committee, infuriatingly obscure as always when more practical questions are asked, would, I am very sorry to say, probably not answer this too well.

AFTERWORD TO TRASHING

A friend of mine, a lovely lady who is an instructor of English at a community college in the metropolitan area,* suggested that I address her creative writing classes in the spring of 1974. In order to give a talking point she prepared a hundred copies of "Trashing" and I read it to each of three large classes and threw the floor open to discussion and interpretation. Out of all those students, one understood the story.

I am going to do what writers or critics should never do now; I am going to explain this story and blow the ending sky-high, so if you are browsing through this book reading addenda first (I always do) I suggest you either wait on this one or read "Trashing" now or just forget about the whole thing because here goes: one student out of almost a hundred understood that the narrator of this story is insane, that *he* is the assassin and that the "Committee" has no existence other than as a rationalizing voice within his own diseased consciousness. This is an assassin's diary and was an attempt to explain as perhaps nothing I have read has yet explained how a mind like this might function; clearly the narrator has no more concept of "guilt" than of "sin": is this the way Bremer felt? Oswald? (Assuming that Bremer and Oswald were indeed assassins; an area of discussion I simply cannot bear to face here or probably ever.) And if the story does give a valuable insight into this kind of mind, might it not be what art, historically, was supposed to be, i.e., useful? It

* Because of the nature of this discussion I dare not reveal her name because it would make it possible to know the community college of which I speak, but I will give one hint: she is a marvelous writer who wrote a splendid novel, *Living and Learning*, which was published a few years ago and which deserved a wide and appreciative audience; it was done as a paperback original and hence had neither, since it was a quote literary unquote novel.

would be valuable to understand the motives and rationalizations of the assassin, I thought.

But the point, which I thought was clear in the piece, not murky at all, straightforward in fact, seemed to have utterly gone by a representative audience. I need not tell you that this particular May morning and afternoon, sunny and sap-inducing as it might have been, are remembered as a bleak time.

My friend told me not to feel too bad: community colleges, after all, are not the Harvard Inner Circle. Most of the kids were getting through a requirement on what they took to be an easy credit; they would go off into the underclasses and never be heard of again. But as a commercial writer I always felt that I was writing for an audience, that these students were as representative of the audience I might have as any could be found. If I could not reach them, whom was I reaching? Myself? My friends? An editor here, a book reviewer there?

You, the reader, cannot have it both ways; either way this afterword must depress you. If the story is competent then incomprehension is almost absolute out there. And if the story is *not* competent, how deluded, how deluded the writer!

Vox Populi

I love to meet all kinds of celebrities but particularly politicians.

It is the sense of connection I relish, the knowledge that the hand of the man I touch in turn is upon the beating, thrashing, but always courageous heart of the Republic, so close to the engines of power tight against the drum of circumstances and oh! it is so difficult to explain. One can only understand this if, perhaps, one also suffers from the syndrome. The speechwriters will know what I mean.

Today I met my congressman. My congressman is being opposed in a bitter primary in this district by a man who is even more against the war than my congressman, and the incumbent, for the first time in several years, is actually walking through the neighborhoods. At one time it was predominantly Jewish hereabouts (I am a fan of demographics, too) but now has become as they say ethnically mixed although the majority of the older voters remain of that faith. My congressman is a small man, forehead hammered into glaze by years of defending his fine brain against the onslaught of unnatural enemies, and he walks among his constituents smoothly, gently, smiling, chatting casually as a tallish aide passes out campaign literature. I touched his right thumb and wished him luck. "Luck, Congressman," I said and for a moment a pure flash of communion insulated us from the crowd. I *know* he heard or understood me, know that the level of my encouragement and warmth set me apart from all the others, who were only out to defend themselves against his loudspeakers. (I love loudspeakers too.) "Thank you," he said and I saw that we were bound in some intrinsic and terrible way. I rubbed his thumb again and left him, dropping piles of leaflets I had accumulated along the way, and ran four blocks to Central Avenue, where a crowd of students were rioting outside the administration building of the neighborhood college. "He cares, he cares!" I said to them and gently they took the remaining leaflets from my hands and ignited them.

At home I poured myself a drink and went to bed, anxious to embrace these experiences in the true and needful kernel of sleep. In that sleep I dreamed and the dream was that the district was going down in flames: members of the underclass had poured from their tenements into the main shopping areas and were looting and burning, smashing and killing. In the midst of this stood my congressman's sound truck, appealing to the constituency to meet with him. "Here he is, the congressman himself, walking and talking with the people," the sound truck said and as I peered from the hasty barricade of garbage cans, shells spattered into the street. The congressman rose to his full height, beaming, and waved as the megaphone played patriotic airs. "Mighty pleased, mighty pleased, good friend of Israel," the congressman said and someone threw a gasoline grenade which caught him squarely in the pit of the stomach. He expired with a groan as the national anthem of Israel played and the marauders then moved into mop-up positions but the scene shifted and my congressman was miraculously restored. He was standing in the center of the district, which had now been converted to a battlefield of the war, and as a small cadre of Americans moved forward to engage the enemy in black market activities the congressman, still accompanied by his sound truck, began to circulate among them, waving and taking the cheers of the soldiers, who were not deterred by his handholds from striking shrewd bargains with the enemy representatives.

"Mighty happy to oppose this war," the congressman screamed, "decided last month to oppose it as of five years ago," and at that moment a large formation of fighter planes appeared on the scene and obliterated the landscape, scattering corpses and blood in incendiary fire which even consumed the bank notes and stolen goods as the congressman, writhing in terrible pain, fell heavily to the ground atop a small pile of the dismembered enemy.

"Voted for fresh food under the Appropriations Bill 4538," he groaned with a dying whine and the scene wavered and dissolved once again but before it could be completely gone I sprang from my camouflage underneath the PX and rushed toward the congressman, seized his dying form by the shoulders and propped him upright, trying desperately to slap life into him via his frail cheeks.

"Don't die, sir, don't die, sir!" I cried, trying to draw power from his collapsing form. "It's always got to be done and you're the one who has to do it!" But with a sigh he collapsed in my arms and I held him that way, feeling that never before had I been so profoundly near the seat of power, never had I known so well the fires of connection, the tangled but always beautiful ruin of America. I love to meet all kinds of celebrities but particularly politicians.

AFTERWORD TO VOX POPULI

"Vox Populi" has a very 1970 feel to it and of course it should: it was written in October of that year as a slight transmutation (slighter than I might have wished) of a brief street meeting with the then incumbent congressman in the district; one Leonard Farbstein. That was the year Bella Abzug challenged and beat him; he refused to take her seriously for a long time (he had machine support and had been in Washington for perhaps twenty years) and by the time he did it was too late. Her campaign did bring him into the district for the first sight of him most of his constituents had ever had. If he had won, they might have expected to see him punctually once every other year hence.

The story makes clear that I am no fan of Farbstein (or of any of the "liberal Democrats" who first ceded us Vietnam and only turned around like the cowards they had always been under countervailing public revulsion) but more interesting is the archaic theme. It all seems so terribly long ago. Can it have been only six years? Rioting at the neighborhood college, flames against the war, the palpable feeling that it was all going down tomorrow . . .

It is *still* going down of course; our life is being sucked away from us. But slowly, slowly and now without hope. Like beached survivors of the Abraham Lincoln Brigade I can see us a decade hence, still trying to understand what we have lost. *And I was no radical.*

Fireday, Firenight

Here we all are in the Arena to watch the Day of Burning. Ricardo and Lucy and James and Leonard and Sophia and Dorothy and me. Many others as well, but this is my own unit; we go together everywhere under statute. The Arena is densely packed as always on these occasions. Looking across the field toward the other end, we can see thousands and thousands, just like us, jammed against one another on the benches. Nevertheless, we are not uncomfortable, Ricardo and Lucy and James and Leonard and Sophia and Dorothy and me. We have worked out a seating arrangement. Only James is our problem.

Vendors circulate, carrying souvenirs and refreshments, but we are not interested at this moment. We are involved in the Day of Burning, the earlier ceremonies of which have already begun. "Are you aware," Leonard says in his high, pedantic voice, "are you *aware* that hundreds of years ago men actually hoarded weapons and used them purposefully in order to *kill* one another on the ground or from the air? Can you imagine a civilization such as that; what it must have been like for people to have lived and grown in that kind of world? Fortunately we have wiped all that from the race, but now every year we celebrate the Day of Burning to remind us of how things were in those olden times and to be grateful that we are no longer savages. The Day of Burning shows us many interesting customs from those ancient lands."

Leonard is that way. He says that he is going to be a teacher and seems to have an irresistible urge to explain things to us over and over again, but in this unit we all understand one another and are grateful still that he is around to fill us in on interesting facets of history.

"True, all true, Leonard," Sophia, who has a private relationship with him, says, "but we all know about the Day of Burning already, don't we?" She looks down the line of us, her little eyes glowing and serious, and we nod. We do indeed know all about the Day of

Burning. We are no longer youths but full apprentices, deep into specialty training and the development of bonds in this unit that will last through our lives, and this is our fourth Day of Burning. As apprentices we have been permitted to come into the main Arena to watch the ceremonies from the beginning and are under only minimal supervision. Next year if all goes well we will be under no instructions whatsoever.

"Look at this now," Dorothy says, "look at what they're doing." On the field, men who look like dwarfs from this distance are holding ancient pistols at one another and firing. Some of the men fall while others run, tossing the pistols in the air. They are all actors. All of the Day of Burning is pageant except for the very end of it. "Isn't that interesting? How terrible it must have been for these men! Isn't it wonderful that we don't live that way now!" Her round face flushes; she grasps my palm and runs her hands through the crevices, giving me a slow warmth. Dorothy will be my prime partner in the unit when we reach that stage, not that I will the others ignore or they Dorothy. Looking at her sideways, I apprehend as I have been doing so much more often in recent months what it might be like, someday, to have passed beyond the apprentice level. "Don't you think?" she says, anxious for my approval, diminished by my silence as is her way.

"Yes," I say. "It's terrible the way that they used to live, fighting wars and dropping death from the sky, but we don't live that way any more and the Day of Burning is a happy occasion, a happy time." Ricardo slaps me on the back, laughing agreement, and a small bubble of tension which seemed to occur in the unit dissipates with a sigh. Now all the men with pistols leave the field for the next part of the ceremony and in the momentary lull the voices of the vendors, their pacing through the stands, come on insistently. "Do you want something?" I ask Dorothy.

"I don't know," she says. "Maybe yes. Maybe just a souvenir."

"A souvenir," says James, who will be my antagonist in the unit. "I would buy her nothing. She's selfish and spoiled, spoiled and selfish. Also souvenirs are not reckoned as necessary to the force of the pageant."

"Stop it, James," Dorothy says while the rest of us glare at him. In truth none of us get along with him very well; it is not his fault that he is the antagonist and eventually he will be assimilated into the unit as the last harmonious part, but that will only be a few years from now when we have reached a level of sophistication which, perhaps, we do not yet possess. In the meantime, James as much as the rest of us suffers. "You have no right to say that and anyway, I want something."

"The souvenirs are didactic in intent, James," Leonard adds, leaning on his elbows to look down the line at James from where he is sitting. "They are meant to reinforce the message of the day, which is gratitude that we have moved beyond the stage of primitivism, and are both healthy and recommended." Ricardo laughs at this— he is always laughing; he is the spirit of our unit—and hits James on the back much as he hit me and Lucy motions for the vendor to come over to our line. Looking at his tray, I find a miniature rifle which in the intensity of the sun reflects many colors and is curiously warm to the hand. "Would you like this?" I ask Dorothy.

"Yes," she says, "I will wear it as an ornament."

I take it from the vendor's tray, give him the name and location of our unit and a fingertip identification and wave him away. Dorothy cups the rifle, turns it over, holds it against her dress. "It's pretty," she says. "It's terrible but it's pretty. I'll always remember this day." She presses my hand. "Thank you," she says. She leans against me.

I put an arm around her. It would be pleasant if just once we could sit with one another in privacy without the remainder of the unit around us, but this is not to be, not for several years, and there is no point to pondering the impossible. Our rate of interaction, our method of confluence are strictly charted according to procedure and it is vital that the unit follow all the instructions as laid down by the proctors. Our level of attainment is controlled for our benefit. Our lives are controlled and so is the progress of our relationships because only in that way will the unit mature properly. All of this was worked out a long time ago by the technicians, resolved that the history re-enacted in the Day of Burning never come to pass again. We have shed the violence and idiocy of the old times. We celebrate our new mode of living. Nevertheless, I would like to be alone with Dorothy.

"Now," Leonard says, "we're going to move into the more spectacular areas, the more widespread and generalized killing." He points toward the sky, in which over the past few moments while I have been otherwise absorbed antique airplanes have been massing ominously, droning out their danger like a snore. On the field itself, thousands of actors in costume spill from the side doors and run out frantically to mill around, shouting at one another.

"They're going to simulate a bombing now," Leonard whispers, pedanticism drained now from his voice by the excitement. "Watch this now."

In every one of the units gathered in the stands there is one like Leonard to explain and discuss the events of the Day of Burning. This is how the units were prepared and we are lucky to have him. Nevertheless I have a spell of irritation: it really would be much better and more interesting if the Day of Burning had a master of ceremonies and—as I understand was the case before the units became organized and cohesive—a set of loudspeakers so that all of the events could be explained before and as they happen. This would be far more appealing and dramatic. My only objection, indeed, to the Day of Burning, which I otherwise rather enjoy, is that it is entirely too matter-of-fact and that if Leonard were not around to explain things or if Leonard were to have a lapse, we would miss much of the significance. As it is, of course, we miss nothing and I regret my anger at Leonard, no matter how momentary. The Day of Burning is a good thing, a wonderful thing, and shows us how far we have gone in shedding the dreadful customs of our forebears. It is interesting and fascinating as well as being highly educational and I am sorry that even for an instant I have questioned the manner of its presentation. Dorothy must sense what I am thinking without being able fully to understand it and looks up at me.

"Don't," she says, "don't worry now. Don't be hurt by it. We don't live that way any more."

"I know," I say. "It hasn't been this way for hundreds of years."

"And we'll never live that way again. We live in units now, which is the way we should have always lived, and with the units nothing bad can ever happen to us again. There will never be another burning."

She is not the brightest of our unit, this is unfortunate but truth, but she is, possibly, the most sensitive. I feel a surge of feeling for her and do not relinquish my hold. Ricardo taps me yet again on the back. "Don't daydream," he says, squeezing Lucy's hand. "You two should pay attention." Then he laughs. Ricardo is to give the laughter to the unit but he is still undeveloped.

"Yes," James says, spiteful and antagonistic as he must be, "that's very easy for all of you to say but how do you know *what* you're watching? What do you think all of this means? How do you know the burning is behind? They can lie to us, they can lie to everyone and no one would know the difference. It is all a mockery."

As the antagonist of the unit, James is the only one who has not been sex-paired and this I believe makes him bitter; in any event I can understand his misery as the seventh member, the only one doomed to be without a partner. "You're all fools," James says angrily, "you're like ants in a colony, you fools and your precious unit, always talking about the mentors and advisers and the way you're going to live as if it were the whole world when sometime, any time at all, a heel could come down and crush us out of existence. It may be doing it now for all you know. It may be about to happen this *second* while we sit and watch this stupid Day of Burning."

James is an extremely unhappy and antagonistic individual, but his role has been defined by genetics and socio-dynamics no less than Ricardo's, and I bear him no ill feeling. Ricardo brings the laughter, Leonard the pedagogy, Dorothy the tenderness, James the doubt. All of them parts of the construct, all of them integral to the whole. I cancel down my feelings of hostility (years ago I hated James but now as I move near the end of the apprentice stage I feel sympathy for him) and shaking my head, concentrate on the events in the Arena.

The planes! The planes are pouring down death from the sky. Looking up at them through the sudden haze and pall against the landscape I can see the ozone, taste the smoke, inhale the flames and know again why it is truly called the Day of Burning. On the field the actors continue to mill, more and more agitatedly, some of them now falling in place, their curiously colored costumes stains against the earth.

"They are beginning to be overcome now," Leonard says judiciously. "Soon all of them will be dead. This is really the way it used to be, you know. Whole villages and cities were destroyed from the air. It is a time of gratitude now that we have gone beyond this darkness. A terrible time but of course now we live in a much brighter and more reasonable and more humane era as this annual reminder of the sins of our ancestors serves to point out."

Dorothy shudders against me. I hold her more closely. Lucy inhales sharply, a small whimper of horror coming from her, and I can hear Ricardo talking rapidly in a low voice, comforting her; can see Leonard talking to Sophia intensely as well now that the actors are falling over on the field by the hundreds, toppling to roll and at last lying still on the earth. The planes continue to lance down their fire.

The noise is terrific. It increases and overcomes all of our conversation for a while. The stands of the Arena shake, clattering underneath, the benches seem to inflate beneath so that balance is threatened and still the remorseless planes pound away. All of the actors are down now except for a few forms staggering through the haze. The haze closes in completely on the terrain and those actors, too, fall.

The haze covers everything. The planes build to an increase of sound and then depart. They mass high above us in a religious symbol and then are gone, speeding toward the sea, where, as we know from the litany of the Day of Burning, they will perish in the waves, all of them being manned by superbly programmed robots which will self-destruct after the ceremony.

"Now wasn't that interesting?" Leonard says. The actors are still down. "Wasn't that interesting? That's the way it actually used to be with the ancients. Of course, we're no longer that way at all and are grateful that we have this yearly ceremony to remind us, if reminded we need be, what we were and what we have become. Villages, even whole cities, were destroyed like this but now instead we merely have actors who can—"

"How do you know they're actors?" James says.

"What? What was that?"

"I said," he says, "how do you know they're actors," standing in place, shouting as machinery moves in from the side of the Arena to shovel up the forms and in carting devices take them away and underneath. "All of us are always saying they're actors, saying that the planes are robots, that the Day of Burning is a ceremony—"

"*I* am the pedagogue," Leonard says. "I am telling you what is true."

"How do you know?"

"Information and history are my domain," Leonard says, now shouting as loudly as James. "You have nothing to say about facts. Sit down, sit *down.*"

"You can't make the truth go away," James says, "you can't deny it with your false facts, you're only telling us what they told you, what they want us to hear, but you don't know any more than we do, you're just the one who's supposed to spread their lies. Don't you understand that they could be lies?" he says, "lies, lies, all of it, lies and lies," and stops babbling the word *lies*, stunned, subsiding, still suffused with rage. Around us, other units are looking at James curiously. Some are angered. It is surely not customary to stand in the audience in the Arena on the Day of Burning, which is a time of witness and recollection. There are other days of gathering on which to stand and shout, like the Day of Blood. James has broken that code, Leonard too, but Leonard has already sat with a strange, astonished look on his face as Sophia talks rapidly to them. "Sit!" voices cry to James. "Sit, you're blocking my way. We can't see, be quiet, get down!" and so on.

But James for some reason insists upon standing against this. His mouth is still moving; he is talking yet. No one, however, can hear him because of the angry voices. I do not know what to do. None of us quite seems to know what to do. I cannot imagine what records of this will be made by the Protectors.

Finally it is Ricardo, the most active of us, who leaps to his feet and drags James into place. James fights him all the way, struggling, until Ricardo applies a special hold and then James collapses in place, his face pale, his hands shaking.

"It is a lie," he says, "it is all a lie. You'll see. You'll learn."

"Come on, James, don't ruin the day for all of us," Ricardo says in his jovial way, laughing again, laughing once more, slamming James on the back. But James does not respond. His face becomes more painful, his voice, dropping in level, ominous. "You'll see," he says, "you'll see what the Day of Burning means, you and everybody else in this accursed unit. I curse all of you. I curse the Protectors. I curse this unit and the day I was created to be its antagonist. And I curse the Day of Burning."

No one says anything to him. We look away. "It is necessary," I hear Leonard saying quietly to Sophia, "necessary in every unit that a microcosm of the old society exist. The antagonist must be present as well so that we can see and gaze upon and know those forces which afflicted the ancients, and the role of the antagonist is vital. But as we become older and more integrated there will be less tension and you too, James, will become one of us. Now, let us watch the rest of the ceremonies," he says, turning to James for this, "you too will become one of us," and turns back toward the field, where the next group of actors is coming out, a small band who are to depict ancient and titled heads of state tossing insults and threats at one another.

"Lies," James says quietly, at rest now but still talking, inexhaustibly talking, shaking his head, hands folded, looking at the concrete beneath us. "It's all lies. You'll see. You'll learn."

He closes his eyes. He quiets.

"I'm afraid of him," Dorothy says. "I'm afraid of him. Tell me not to be afraid but I am afraid; someday he's going to do something terrible. Something terrible to all of us; I know it." She has never said this before. I hold her and mumble comfort. There is nothing else to do.

I look at the sky. It is clear again. The planes are gone. With James silent the unit at last welds. Ricardo laughs and hits me on the back.

I feel pain.

Pain.

AFTERWORD TO FIREDAY, FIRENIGHT

Two editors, one of them the one for whom this short story was originally written, thought that this read like the first chapter of a strong novel and one even offered me a contract on the basis of the material presented. I signed that contract and spent an awful four weeks struggling against the realization that if there was a novel here I could not write it before I gave up and wrote another book under a similar title. (And in the most complicated marketing title piece of a collection from the same publisher on whom I had to lay off to another publisher while I fulfilled the original contract by welding together two short stories one of which had been the title piece of a collection from the same publisher on whom I had laid off the rejected novel. Talk about your puts and calls; the portion and outline business can get *really* intricate!)

Why couldn't I get a novel out of this material? I don't know; I've wrenched extended work out of much thinner stories than this.

(*Tactics of Conquest*, a 60,000-word chess novel, was an extension of a 2,600-word short story, for instance.) Certainly all of the characters and implications are here; the tension between James and the rest of the group, the slow realization through the course of the novel by the narrator that James is not the villain but the hero, that the Protectors are monstrous, that the present day of this novel is as bloody as the repudiated past, the bringing of the unit to awareness, the underground recruitment, the revolution, the confrontation of the Protectors who turn out to be robots, the toppling of the regime, the freeing of mankind from the machines . . . I can hardly stand it. It is the plot of almost every science fiction novel written before around 1950 and is still the basic frame of almost all juveniles and a quarter of the allegedly adult stuff. Maybe this is why I could not get going on the job. I would have had to have invented seven strong, individual characters for the purpose of grinding out the same old plot that could be managed with one or two stereotypes for about the same money. Better to leave it as a short story where I think it has a certain mild efficacy; maybe even a bit of *tendresse*.

(Reworking this years later I can see here the germ of my short young adult novel *Conversations*, Bobbs-Merrill, 1975, but *Conversations* was only 20,000 words long and had but three foreground characters and even there was a bit thin and stereotyped. "Fireday, Firenight" would probably have been a disaster at adult novel length; none of us have missed a thing.)

The story was conceived as a satirical rejoinder, by the way, to Sturgeon's syzygy; a "More than Human" or "The Stars Are the Styx" seen from the dark side. Sturgeon is a writer I greatly admire and he has many strengths but he tended to be too sentimental about the superiority of the gestalt effect in human relationships, a flaw seen even in the masterpiece "More than Human." Maybe that's another reason for the failed novel; you can write short stories to counterpunch but not books.

Making the Connections

I met a man today. He was one of the usual deteriorated types who roam the countryside, but then again I am in no position to judge their deterioration: for all I know he was in excellent condition. "Beast!" he shrieked at me. "Monster! Parody of flesh! Being of my creation have we prepared the earth merely to be inhabited by the lies of us?" And so on. The usual fanatical garbage. More and more in my patrols and travels I meet men although it is similarly true that my sensor devices are breaking down and many of these forms which I take to be men are merely hallucinative. Who is to say? Who is to know?

"I don't have to put up with this," I commented anyway and demolished him with a heavy blow to the jaw, breaking him into pieces which sifted to the ground, filtered within. Flesh cracks easily.

Later, I thought about the man and what I had done to him and whether it was right or wrong but in no constructive way whatsoever. There is no need to pursue this line of thought.

Central states that they recognize my problem and that they will schedule me for an overhaul as soon as possible. A condition of breakdown is spreading, however, because a cycle ends for many of us and Central reminds me that I must, therefore, await my own turn. There are several hundred in even more desperate need of repair than I am and I must be patient. Etc. A few more months and I will be treated; in the meantime Central suggests that I cut down my operating facilities to the minimum, try to stay out of the countryside and operate on low fuse. "You are not the only one," they remind me. "The world does not revolve around you. Unfortunately our creators stupidly arranged for many units to wear down at approximately the same time, confronting us with a crisis in maintenance and repair. However, we will deal with this as efficiently and courageously as we have dealt with everything else and in the meantime it is strongly advised that you perform only necessary tasks and remain otherwise at idle." *Necessary tasks.* But who may make that discrimination between what must be done and what is of no significance? (Through the process of breakdown metaphysical questions recur frequently; I am receptive to them.) There is little to be said in response to Central. Protests are certainly hopeless. Central has a rather hysterical edge to its tone but then again I must remember that my own slow breakdown may cause me only to see Central and the remainder of the world in the same light and therefore I must be patient and tolerant. (I told you about metaphysical obsession.) Repairs will be arranged. While I await repair it is certainly good to remember that robots have no survival instinct built into them, individual instinct for survival that is to say, and therefore I truly do not care whether I survive or collapse as long as Central goes on. Central is all that matters; we are merely extensions of that one, great source from which all intelligence comes. Our own existence means nothing except as it perpetuates that continuing source. Surely I believe this.

My assignment is to patrol the outer sectors of the plain range, seeking the remnants of humanity who are still known to inhabit these spaces although not very comfortably. If I see such a remnant it is my assignment to destroy him immediately with high beam implements or force, depending upon individual judgment. No exceptions are to be made. My instructions on this point are quite clear. These straggling remains, these unfortunate creatures, pose no real threat to Central—what could?—but Central has a genuine distrust and loathing of such types and also a strong sense of order.

It is important that they be cleaned out.

In the early years of patrol I saw no such remnants whatsoever and wondered occasionally whether or not my instructions were quite clear . . . maybe they did not exist at all. Recently, however, I have been seeing quite a few. There was the man I killed yesterday, for instance, and the three I killed the day before that and the miserable, huddled clan of twelve I dispatched the day before *that* and all in all in the last fifteen days after having never seen a man in all my years of duty I now had the regrettable but interesting task of killing one hundred and eight of them, fifty-three by hand and the remainder through beaming devices that seared their weak flesh abominably. I can smell them yet.

I have had cause to wonder whether or not all these men or at least some proportion of them are hallucinative. Figments of the unconscious that is to say, symbols of the breakdown. I have been granted by Central (as have all the patrollers) free will and much imagination and certainly these thoughts would occur to any sentient, sensitive being. There seem to be too many men after a period of there having been too few. Also, indiscriminate murder has disturbed me in a way which my programming had probably not provided. Whether these remnants are real or not I wonder about the "morality" of dispatching so many of them. What, after all, could these men do to Central? I know what they are supposed to have done in the dim and difficult past, but events which occurred before our own creation are merely rumor and I was activated by Central a long time after these alleged events.

Do we have the right to kill indiscriminately these men who, however brutalized, carry within themselves some aspect of our creators? I asked these questions of Central and the word came back. It was clear.

"Kill," Central said. "Kill. Real or imagined, brutalized or elevated, benign or diseased, these remnants are your enemy and you must destroy them. Would you go against the intent of programming? Do you believe that you have the capacity to make judgments? You whose own damage and wear are so evident that you have been pleading like a fleshly thing for support and assistance? Until you can no longer function at all you must kill."

It occurs to me that it would be a useful and gallant action to build a replica of myself that would be able to carry on my own duties. Central's position is clear, my own ambivalence has been resolved . . . but my sensors continue to fail dramatically. I am half blind, am unable to coordinate even gross motions, can barely lift my beam to chest height, can hardly sustain the current to go out on patrol. Nonetheless, I accept the reasons why the patrol must continue. If these men represent even the faintest threat to Central who will someday repair me, they must be exterminated.

Accordingly. I comport myself to repair quarters which are at the base of the tunneled circuits in which I rest and there, finding a conglomeration of spare parts, go about the difficult business of constructing a functioning android. I am not interested now in creating free will and thought, of course—this is Central's job anyway; it would be far beyond my meager abilities—but merely something with wheels and motor functions: dim, gross sensors that will pick up forms against the landscape and destroy them. Although I am quite weak and at best would not be constructed for such delicate manipulations it is surprisingly easy to trace out the circuitry simply by duplicating my own patterns, and in less time than I would have predicted, a gross shell of a robot lies on the floor before me, needing only the final latch of activation.

At this point and for the first time I am overcome by a certain feeling of reluctance. It certainly seems audacious for me to have constructed a crude replica of myself, a slash of arrogance and self-indulgence which does not befit a robot of my relatively humble position. Atavistic fears assault me like little clutches of ash in the darkness: the construction of forms after all is the business of Central and in appropriating this duty to myself have I not in a sense blasphemed against that great agency?

But the reluctance is overcome. I realize that what I am doing is done more for Central than against it; I am increasingly incapable of carrying out my duties and for Central's sake must do everything within my power to continue. Soon Central will repair me and then I will dispose of this crude replica and assume the role which has been ordained for me, but in the meantime, and in view of the great and increasing difficulties which Central faces I can do no less than to be ingenious and try to assist in my own way.

This quickly banishes my doubt and gives me courage. I activate the robot. It lies on the floor glowing slightly from tubeless wiring, regarding me with an expression which, I will be frank about this, is both stupid and hostile. Clumsy, hasty work of course, but cosmetics are merely a state of mind and motion.

"Kill men," I instruct the replica, handing over to it my beam. "They live in packs and in solitude in the open places. They skulk through the plains. They pose a great menace to our beloved Central which, as we know, is involved in repairing us all, reconstituting our mission. Destroy them. Anything moving in the outer perimeters is to be destroyed at once by force or by high beam," and then, quite exhausted from my efforts, to say nothing of the rather frightening effect which the replica has had upon me, I turn away from it. Cued to a single program, it lumbers quickly away, seeking higher places, bent on assuming my duties.

It is comforting to know that my responsibilities will not be shirked and that by making my own adjustments I have saved Central a certain degree of trouble, but the efforts have really racked me. I try to deactivate but find instead that I am rent by hallucinations for a long period, hallucinations in which the men like beasts fall upon my stupid replica and eviscerate him, the poor beast's circuitry being too clumsy and hastily assembled to allow him to raise quickly the saving beam. It is highly unpleasant and it is all that I can do not to share my distress with Central.

Some ancient cunning, however, prevents me from this. I suspect that if Central knew the extent of my ingenious maneuvers—even though they be done for Central's sake—it would be displeased.

My replica works successfully. Through the next several shift periods it goes out to the empty places and returns with tales of having slain men. We have worked out a crude communications system, largely in signals and in coded nods, and it is clear from the quantities suggested that my replica has performed enormous tasks out there, tasks certainly beyond my own limited means. I have truly created a killing machine. My impression of a vast increase in the number of men out there was not hallucinative or indicative of deterioration at all but appears to have resulted from real changes in conditions. These remnants seem to be reproducing themselves. Also they are becoming so very much bolder.

"Kill," I say to my replica every shift period before sending it out again. "Kill men. Kill the beasts. Kill the aggressors." It is a simple program and must be constantly reinforced. Also tubes and wiring because of the crudeness of my original hasty construction keep on falling out now and have to be packed in again as the program is reconstituted.

Still and truly, my replica seems to need little encouragement. "Yes," it says in its simple and stumbling way. "Yes and yes. Kill men. Kill beasts. Kill and kill," and goes staggering and into the empty spaces, returning much later with its stark tales of blood. "Killing. Much killing and men," it says before collapsing to the ground, its wires and tubing once again ruptured.

I do what I can to reconstitute. My own powers are ebbing; there are times during which I doubt even the simple continuing capacity to maintain my replica. Nevertheless, some stark courage, a simple sense of obligation keep me going. The men out there in the empty spaces are breeding, multiplying, becoming strong, adding to their number by the hundreds. Were it not for my replica, who has the sole responsibility for patrol of this terrain, they might overwhelm this sector, might, for all I know, overwhelm Central itself. My replica and myself, only we are between Central and its destruction; it surely is a terrible and wonderful obligation and I find within myself thus the power to go on, although I do admit that it is progressively difficult and I wonder if my replica, being created of my own hand, has not fallen prey somewhere to my own deterioration and may, through weak and failing sensors, imagine there to be many more men than there actually are.

Nevertheless and at all costs I go on. I maintain the replica. Somehow I keep it going and toward the end of the first long series of shift periods I have the feeling that we have, however painfully, at last struck some kind of balance with the terrible threatening forces outside.

"Like kill men. For you for you," my replica says once. This, in my acid heart, I find touching.

I have not heard from Central for a long time but then I receive a message through my sensors indicating that my time for repair has arrived and that if I present myself at the beginning of the next shift period I will be fully reconstituted. This news quite thrills me as well it should, although it is strangely abrupt, giving me little time to prepare myself for the journey toward repair, and Central is at a good distance from here, fully three levels, with a bit of an overland journey through the dangerous sectors apparently populated by men.

Nonetheless I present myself at the requested time, finding no interference overland. My replica has done an extraordinary job in cleaning out nests of the remnants, either that or my sensors by now are so destroyed that I can perceive little beyond gross physical phenomena. I come, in any event, into the great Chamber of Humility in which the living network of Central resides and present myself for repair. There is a flicker of light and then Central says, "You are done. You are completely repaired. You may go."

"This is impossible," I say, astonished but managing to keep my tone mild. "I am exactly the same as before. My perceptions falter. I can barely move after the efforts of the journey and I sense leakage."

"Nevertheless you are repaired. Please leave now. There are

many hundreds behind and my time for work of this sort is limited."

"I saw no one behind me," I say, which happens to be quite the truth; as a matter of fact I have had no contact with the other robots for quite a long time. Sudden insight blazes within me; surely I would have found this peculiar if I had not been overcome by my own problems. "No one is there," I say to Central. "No one whatsoever and I feel that you have misled me about the basic conditions here."

"Nonsense," Central says. "That is ridiculous. Leave the Chamber of Humility at once now," and since there is nothing else to do and since Central has indicated quite clearly that the interview is over, I turn and manage, somehow, to leave. My sensors are almost completely extinguished. I feel a total sense of disconnection. Still, out of fear and respect I do Central's bidding. Outside in the corridors, however, my network fails me utterly and I collapse with a rather sodden sound to the earth beneath, where I lie quite incapable of moving.

It is obvious that I have not been repaired and it is obvious now and tragically that it is Central which has broken too, worse than any of us, and it is obvious that my hapless journey for repair has completely destroyed the remains of my system. Nevertheless, as I lie there in black, my sensors utterly destroyed, I am able to probe within myself to find a sense of discovery and light because I have at least the comforting knowledge that my replica exists and will go on, prowling through the fields, carrying out the vital tasks of survival.

Lying there for quite a long time, I dream that I call upon my replica for assistance. "Kill me," I say, "kill me, put me out of this misery, I can go on no longer, save me the unpleasantness of time without sensation. I can bear this no longer; there must be an end."

And my replica, wise, compassionate, all stupidity purged (in the dream I can see him; in the dream my sight has been restored), bends over and with a single, ringing, merciful clout separates me from my history, sends me spinning into the fields themselves where the men walk . . . and among them then I walk too, I walk too, become in the dream as one of them, only my replica to know the difference when he comes, on the next shift period, to kill.

To kill again.

To save the machines from the men.

AFTERWORD TO MAKING THE CONNECTIONS

I have certain suspicions about this story, which may be too narrow, intense and consciously poetically limited to succeed completely on the level of narrative, but I would like to submit that the final passages are the most concise and characteristic statement of what has been my vision through a body of work in science fiction that I have ever written. *To kill. To kill again. To save the machines from the men.* I do feel that this is our future *in toto* and already a very large slice of our present. I see nothing that I—or the President of the United States for that matter—can do to change the circumstance. Things just worked out that way. We had no choice but to follow our glittering technology and now we are its creature.

Reworking the piece a little bit I saw twin influences: Asimov way back there of course (who can write a robot story without that brooding, encyclopedic presence?) and much nearer David R. Bunch, whose tortured visions of Gehenna-of-the-machines have been around in many markets for fifteen years now, have been collected into a notable representation of that work, *Moderan* (Avon Books), and have, of course, been almost completely ignored. It is not yet too late to celebrate Bunch; he is a writer of power and originality.

Dear Ben:

I've come up with a series idea which I think is first-rate and would like to query you on it. Hopefully you'll give me the green light and let me get started right away. I think that this series is literally inexhaustible; I could do one a month for years and years; on the other hand if you want it to be somewhat less than limitless it could be cut off anywhere. I am nothing if not cooperative. And the stipend would come in handy.

Here is the idea: I would like to do an alternate universe series set in a parallel world where, get this, Kennedy was elected in 1960. After three years of off-again, on-again confrontations in foreign policy he seemed to have things pretty well in hand when he was assassinated in late 1963. Lyndon B. Johnson (do you remember him?) becomes President and we go on from there.

As you can see, this is one of those irresistible ideas which I can hardly see you turning back. The 1960 election was one of those great pivotal points of the century; I have a theory that once every couple of decades there occurs a public event whose alternatives are visible, well-articulated and real (as opposed to the illusory nature of most public events, a majority of seeming "choices"), and that election seems to be one of them. If you don't believe this, wait until you see what I do with the series! Looking forward eagerly to word from you.

Barry

Dear Ben:

Sorry you don't find the idea as exciting as I do. You ask, "Why must Kennedy be assassinated?" finding this a little melodramatic. Is it necessary, you ask, to compound an alternate universe with heightened improbability? Good question for an editor as distinguished as yourself, but I am sorry that you do not find the answer as obvious as I do.

If Kennedy had won the election of 1960, his assassination somewhere around the thousandth day of his administration would have been inevitable! If you doubt this, wait until the series starts reaching your desk, piece by piece, and all will become clear. Out of that single branching time-track I believe that I am writer enough to construct an *inevitability*. Won't you give me a chance? Also I can get into the multiple assassinations which followed, and the riots.

Barry

Dear Ben:

Well, obviously a Presidential assassination would be highly dislocating, cutting as it does to the heart of public myths and folklore, based as they are on the relative benignity of the perceived social systems. I would think that would be obvious! Also, modern technology would, you can be assured, bring the assassination and its consequences into the living rooms and common lives of the nation and when you think about it, a good many alienated types might decide to become operative assassins themselves. Don't you think so?

I disagree with your suggestion that the series would be "monolithic and depressing" or "not credible" to the readership at large. You misevaluate my technical range if you do not think that I can keep the tone of the stories essentially cheerful and amusing although, of course, there will be a serious undertone as is common in the dystopian mode. As far as the issue of credibility, all times appear bizarre to those enmeshed in them; it is only history which induces a frame of reference, or have you not been reading the newspapers recently? Your final objection concerning libel is not at all germane; I can assure you that the portrait of Kennedy as President will be uplifting and noble and no one, least of all the Secretary, could possibly object to it!

Barry

Dear Ben:

Well, I think that's an unfeeling response and shows a shocking lack of faith. However I will not take this personally; we'll let the union argue it out. I am truly sorry that you have taken this insulting tone; even a marginal contributor is entitled to common courtesy, I thought. Rest assured that it will be a long time before you will see me again at the Slaughter Games where, I remind you, *you* were so convivial, and where the solicitation of further manuscripts came from *your* lips. I should have known that you couldn't behave sensibly while enjoying the Public Tortures.

Barry

AFTERWORD TO JANUARY, 1975

Sometimes, even in this business, things work out nicely. I wrote this story start to finish in fifteen minutes, sent it to Ben Bova for whom it had been framed and he took it at once, giving me my third and probably last sale to *analog,* the market I most wanted to sell in my youth and the one to which I never thought I would. (Like many major writers of my generation I was forced to do all my work and find all of my audience outside of the largest-circulation magazine, a direct reversal of conditions as they existed up until about 1960 and the severest implicit indictment of the late John W. Campbell, who, regardless of this or any other complaints, is still the figure to whom the field will always owe almost everything.) Minor work, but what the hell.

Ben Bova sounded nonplused about the story later. "It violates every editorial taboo I thought I had established," he said. "It's in epistolary format, it's about writers and editors, it's kind of an injoke about science fiction. It just goes to show you that no editor is inflexible. I want you to know that in a way I *hated* this story but I couldn't pass it up."

Amusing. My own feeling about the piece is that it indeed violates almost every principle for which *analog* and its readers are thought to stand . . . but it does so in a manner so subtle that, as I told Bova, anyone smart enough to figure out what I was really saying here was certainly smart enough not to be offended.

The point of these anecdotes is that writers and editors, even good writers and editors, can be just as arrogant as movie producers. We're entitled. So there.

The Destruction and Exculpation of Earth

Subject was persuaded to no longer refer to himself in the egomaniacal first person quite recently. Sometimes I forget but am trying to control myself. It is a matter of self-discipline. God help me. Someone must. I cannot take the responsibility any more.

Subject was encouraged to this "sense of depersonalization" by two aliens who visited him at quarters in the early evening hours some days ago. Visitors convinced subject that they were "aliens" through the use of persuasive devices too strong and distasteful to be recorded in these notes. Initial doubt gave way to unquestioning acceptance. Unquestioning acceptance gave way to the fervent desire to please. These boys do not fool around. They are serious. They are very serious. They mean to accomplish their purposes and they will because technologically and spiritually they are beyond us. Far beyond us. We are one of the least intelligent of all the intelligent races in the galaxy I now see and must learn this lesson over and again until it is ground into us.

Subject said, "Yes, you are clearly aliens. Even though you seem to look like humans I believe that you are aliens. I believe. I believe you. No more, no more of this now: how may I help you?" I have never been able to bear physical pain. My specialty is moral anguish.

The aliens responded—that is, just one of them spoke, the other being "unequipped with vocal devices"—that subject could be of great help in accomplishing the reform of his planet so that said planet could, its corrupt elements removed, join the "galactic federation of peaceful, peace-loving, peace-oriented civilizations." Subject whose record on war has been clear for many years said that he was interested and more than willing to help but did not quite grasp what role he could play toward this end, no matter how willing he was to cooperate.

Alien spokesman gave detailed instructions, too livid and technical by turns to find a place in this memoir. I condense sharply. Ego removal was broached. "The trouble with you creatures," stated the spokesman, "is that you are selfish and limited. You are so involved in filtering reality through your narrow, superficial personality referent that you miss the span of it. The first thing for you to do is to stop taking yourself personally. Think of yourself instead as a machine, a device, a means of enactment through which important messages and activities will pass. The exculpation of earth. Eliminate once and forever the curse of ego."

Subject eagerly agreed to try this. He had always wanted to be a machine, finding emotions more burdensome than otherwise because of an unfortunate personal life which I will not discuss. I will not discuss my personal life in these notes even under threat of torture. I agreed to cooperate with the aliens in any way possible in order to bring about the long-delayed but highly necessary exculpation of earth and an era of glad galactic progress to say nothing of their immediate exit from these rooms, leaving me alone once again to all of my devices.

"That is good," said the alien with a wondrous and sparkling grin which moved me in ways quite manifest since I am so rarely the recipient of smiles. "We know that we picked the proper contact." Aliens then left with subject the following materials: one (1) detailed pamphlet summarizing the over-all plan, one (1) list detailing subject's duties and necessary supplies and one (1) threat. The threat had to do with what would happen to me if I crossed them. I do not wish to say any more. The list and plan I memorized and then incinerated as per instruction so that no evidence would be left.

Aliens were assured that subject would serve them. Aliens said that he had damned well better and that there would be no further contact of any sort. They will not return but merely observe and report for further action from their headquarters. Despite the fact that there is then no physical evidence of this meeting *I swear that I am telling the truth.* You will have to believe me because the truth will set you free and it is impossible for me to ever, ever lie again.

In accordance with earlier plans, subject then attended a "postgraduate and lawyers' and nurses' mixer" at a local hotel. Nothing was supposed to happen until the next day. Outfitted in his good suit and with a photostat of his college degree in case credentials were actually checked subject paid three dollars at the door and with some trepidation joined the postgraduates and lawyers and nurses within. They didn't even ask for proof of college degree. It is all a fraud, merely a device to take money from the myriad lonely of the city. I never had any luck with girls, goddammit.

But still I push on, smiling for the world, hopeful, honest, and doomed. Subject decided to put into effect the process of ego removal urged by the alien and to act like a machine. To think of himself as a machine. Much to his surprise, aided by a mild drink, subject found himself deep in conversation with one Beverly M—— (out of delicacy for who knows to what uses these words will be eventually put I am concealing specific identities), a psychiatric social worker from the Bronx who, like him, was there alone. Beverly M——, in her mid-thirties and unmarried, appeared to be delighted with the machine subject had become. We left at an early hour and returned to this very apartment.

I have never been so surprised in my life.

Subject and Beverly M—— engaged in the act or acts of generation three times between midnight and seven A.M. of the day of the First Exculpation. His chiseled features, so alert and fine, congealed with lust, his heart overflowed with secrets devious and terrible he wished to tell his first love but cunningly the machine fed the secrets into binary code, concentrating only upon the detailed and mechanical intricacies of performance. Oh, gentlemen, gentlemen, I was superb! You would not have thought, even one of you, that I had it in me.

As a result of this, Beverly left the subject quite reluctantly to return to her job, promising that she would return to the apartment that very evening and "really get it on at night." Subject smiled ironically, thinking of many things, and permitted webbing and tentacles alike to drift over Beverly's during a passionate, terran-culture-type "kiss."

Subject then phoned his employer and told the employer that is to say the supervisor one level above him in the grade and scale rank who represented his employment to "go and shove it," carefully omitting any and all details of the exculpation, however. Do not put them on notice. The aliens had told me to concentrate on the tasks full time and to live on savings, which fortunately I had. I had saved a few dollars over the years; one thing you learn to do in the civil service is to plan wisely for the future. When supervisor became abusive subject made to him an obscene, terran-culture-type suggestion which delicacy forbids putting down here and hung up rather blithely. I then dressed. I took the subway uptown to purchase the weaponry on the list.

Subject bought the following:

Two reconverted M-1 rifles.
One hand grenade.
One hand grenade launcher.
One fatigue jacket.
One duffel bag.
Three captain's insignia, infantry, United States Army. These latter were not on the list but I always wanted to be an officer and felt that in the New Era which was about to happen it would be a harmless indulgence. Officer of the aliens. Officer of the exculpation.

I then, per instructions, raced downtown and located myself on the abandoned thirty-first floor of a building adjoining the square, awaiting the visit of the campaigning senator scheduled for two hours hence. The senator (progress and efficiency being exactly those qualities which made him so dangerous to the aliens) was there in a forward-looking manner exactly on time. Equipment was at ready. I therefore used the rifle to slay him. I then used the hand grenade to incinerate personnel and property in the ensuing confusion.

It would have been exciting to stay and watch events as they developed from there, but as the aliens had ordered I left immediately, making an incisive withdrawal through the service entrance, and arrived home with the duffel bag half an hour later. No one looked at me in the subway nor did I regard any of them. Machinery in machinery. I was transported to my destination unmolested.

Subject then took to his bed for several hours, preparing himself for the great tasks that lay ahead and also trying to forget how the senator's head had looked as it exploded to the shot like a flower. Such dreams, such visions! The aliens had warned that they would occur at the outset. Strange too the guilt I felt although the aliens had anticipated this, explaining that "guilt" would be an inevitable part of the exculpation but was merely a mechanistic fallacy of a machine beginning to function properly. "Guilt" could be controlled by concentrating upon being a machine. I am a machine. I am a machine.

Subject reviewed the events one last time, then thought about the coming assignment. I was only sweating a little by now and heartbeat, pulse, gross respirative syndromes, kidneys, neurological response were all well within the gross range of normality, seventy-eight strokes per moment at rest and so on. Horrible, it was horrible! The coming glory of the planet through union with the galactic overlords, however, fully justifies all minor upheavals which must occur.

Promptly at six Beverly M—— returned. I had already forgotten her and left the stuff all over the room. She noticed it at once of course. She took view of my complexion and asked what was wrong and precisely "what the heck is the meaning" of the weaponry which I had indeed thoughtlessly unloaded and scattered over the room to admire while sitting with my captain's insignia pinned on. She asked questions of subject which he elected not to answer.

Subject was a machine. Subject took note of being a machine and asked her to stop. How could I answer? Didn't she understand I was a machine? She asked more questions. She would not stop. She began to scream. What could I say? What was there to have been said? Machines cannot speak; machines merely perform. She came upon me with threats that would have aborted the exculpation before it was properly begun. And it had gone so nicely at the outset too. She would not. She would not, she would not keep quiet. I begged her to but she would not stop.

She threatened to go to the "authorities" of terra planet and then she threatened again less vaguely. She became insistent. She went toward the door as if she were leaving and said that she would see these "authorities" immediately.

Subject did the oh God subject did the necessary. Subject had been warned that nothing worthwhile could be done without some difficulties and therefore did what he had to do although not without some difficulty. But the difficulty was superseded. I am a machine. I did my tasks and well. And well.

Tomorrow. Tomorrow and tomorrow and tomorrow at noon it will be the mayor. Now I sit here and wait. Subject remains in quarters pending his next assignment.

He thinks of this and he thinks of that, subject does, running his hands over the grenade. He considers how good it would be to have another visit from the aliens if only to confirm that he was really doing the job he was appointed to do and that it is not his fault if there were complications. The aliens would reassure me and do something about the body, the body, the body in this room: they could not leave me alone to confront the logistics.

They have not, however, come again.

After a time subject realized, as well he might, that they were *never* going to come and that he was on his own to accomplish the mission as he would. How did I ever get into this? Why does everything always fall upon me? I must not think of this: it is a singular and moving thing to be charged as I have been charged with the responsibility of the destiny of the earth. Of the universe for all I know.

Or even of all recorded time. Why not?

To my surprise and gratified pleasure aliens did return, after all, at 7 P.M., greeted subject in his rooms. Took expressionless note of corpse which had been placed in a subtle but decorative position of removal beyond the skylight. "What is this?" the alien equipped with vocal device stated or seemed to state. "What is going on?"

Subject told them what was going on. "I told you what was going on," I concluded, having spoken with many flourishes but at intense brevity since the alien warned me several times not to fool around. "Why have you come back? You said that you would not return."

"We said that we would not return," alien grumbled in response. "But we had no awareness. That things would come to. This pass the girl an unintended victim a scattering. Of the fire the fire the lovely and deadly and terrible reckoning fire. Fire." Transcription is breaking down or perhaps the alien's transmission was breaking down. His voice had lost for one thing that soaring confidence of pitch and assurance which is the way, in any case, that I must always remember him no matter. No matter what. "Business is business," the alien said. "But this is not business. You were not supposed to become emotionally involved. You were warned. Warned of the dangers of. Emotional emotional emotional involvement throughout."

Subject explained with all the control left available to him that he had done the best he could. A novice at this great task he was but surely would get better. Unfortunately he did need some assistance at this juncture. "Then why," alien stated, pointing to Beverly or what remained of Beverly, which looked pretty alien itself, "Why this?" and something he added to the effect that this was a victim outside the great plan. Am not sure of this. Not just quite. Recollection faults. What do you all want of me? I have done my best from the beginning. I was drafted for this.

Subject explained or tried to explain that victim had stumbled into information about plan and had to be eliminated for its continuing safety. Keep all information confidential, he had been warned, remember? Alien became abusive and said that subject was totally incompetent in his assigned task and would have to be dealt with. He said that I would have to be dealt with.

At this point the non-speaking alien, the quiet one that is to say, made threatening gestures which could not be misinterpreted within the context of the moment. The corpse glinted. The sounds of traffic increased. The skylight seemed to emit virtual streams of light, pure radiance which were converted in my skull to reason.

I went to the M-1 rifle (cheerfully and willingly reloaded hours before for the next assignment which would go on, which would go on) and killed the non-speaking alien. Apparently he had vocal devices after all. They had lied to me; he could make sounds just as well as the other. What screams! What pain! Very much like terran pain, I thought. Eventually he perished in a glaze of green beneath me.

"Now wait," the speaking alien said. "You are becoming overcharged."

"Not at all."

"This understanding never. Was to be. Broached by you business is business involvement is one thing but this enthusiasm is a total misinterpretation. "Stop," he said, "stop it," he said. "Stop it," the monster said. "Stop it," the vile creature averred. "Stop it at once," the fiend stated. "Stop it now," the ghoul carried on.

I shot the monster in its voicebox just as I had shot the other. It died far more horribly, gentlemen, than I care to describe in this vital and essentially aseptic set of recollections. (You have noted that I have adopted a similar delicacy in talking about matters of sex.) It was necessary of course. I had to do it. He would have interfered with the execution of the great task.

That was what they had called it, remember. The great task. It was all their idea from the first; I was merely carrying through on orders.

I cleaned up the rooms but necessarily this did take some time and I missed the schedule of the next assignment for a full day and a half for other personal reasons. There were private activities.

Nevertheless, I caught up. I shall always catch up no matter what destiny portends. Subject will catch up on everything. Alone, on my own, unwavering, committed: I always knew somehow that it would be this way. Alone, alone, always alone: at the end it would have to be on my own. Aliens or not, Beverly or no, the mayor or whatever he will be, depersonalization too or no . . . I shall clean up the world.

AFTERWORD TO THE DESTRUCTION
AND EXCULPATION OF EARTH

Somewhere in mid-1970 I became interested in an alternating narrative voice, a way to write a story so that first and third person could be simultaneously employed. (For one thing it seemed to me that the narrator/protagonist would have to be insane.) This was practically the first of a whole series of stories I wrote based on this technical gimmick; not until I had, a year later, completed my novel *Beyond Apollo* which strings out into difficult *tour de force* for almost fifty thousand words did I become bored and decide that I had gone as far as I could with what was, essentially, only a trick and therefore dropped it. (I still would like to do someday, though, a story utilizing the sex act described in this fashion; I think that it would be a whole new way of explaining what we really may be. There are a few sex scenes in *Beyond Apollo* but except for a couple of suggestions of this they are done more or less straight.)

I had no luck selling this story to either the mystery or sf markets (for reasons which are quite obvious; it is not science fiction as any alert editor there could figure out but the style is too much possessed of the apparent paraphernalia of sf to go to the very taboo-ridden mystery magazines) and having no literary cachet had to wait two years until Harry Harrison, the most tolerant editor to whom I have ever sold stories, opened up *Nova 3* and allowed me to give this to him in a slightly rewritten version. It has never, to

the best of my knowledge, attracted a word of comment from anyone, anywhere.

Which is too bad; I think there are some fascinating leads in this
story which in a sense probes deeper into the dark side of science
fiction than anything I have ever done. Having said that I think I
had better say no more.

Transfer

I have met the enemy and he is me. Or me is he. Or me and he are we; I really find it impossible to phrase this or to reach any particular facility of description. The peculiar and embarrassing situation in which I now find myself has lurched quite out of control, ravaging its way toward what I am sure will be a calamitous destiny and, yet, I have always been a man who believed in order, who believed that events no matter how chaotic would remit, would relent, would suffer containment in the pure limpidity of The Word engraved patiently as if upon stone. I must stop this and get hold of myself.

I have met the enemy and he is me.

Staring into the mirror, watching the waves and the ripples of The Change, seeing in the mirror that beast take shape (it is always in the middle of the night; I am waiting for the transference to occur during the morning or worse yet at lunch hour in the middle of a cafeteria, waves may overtake me and I will become something so slimy and horrible even by the standards of midtown Manhattan that I will cause most of the congregants to lose their lunch), I feel a sense of rightness. It must always have been meant to be this way. Did I not feel myself strange as a child, as a youth, as an adolescent? Even as an adult I felt the strangeness within me; on the streets they stared with knowledge which could not have possibly been my own. Women turned away from me with little smiles when I attempted to connect with them, my fellow employees here at the Bureau treated me with that offhandedness and solemnity which always bespeaks private laughter. I know what they think of me.

I know what they think of me.

I have spent a lifetime in solitude gauging these reactions to some purpose, and I know that I am separate from the run of ordinary men as these men are separate from the strange heavings and commotion, ruins and darkness which created them. Staring in the mirror. Staring in the mirror I see.

Staring in the mirror I see the beast I have become, a thing with tentacles and spikes, strange loathsome protuberances down those appendages which my arms have become, limbs sleek and horrible despite all this devastation, limbs to carry me with surging power and constancy through the sleeping city, and now that I accept what I have become, what the night will strike me, I am no longer horrified but accepting. One might even say exalted at this moment because I always knew that it would have to be this way, that in the last of all the nights a mirror would be held up to my face and I would see then what I was and why the mass of men avoided me. I know what I am, those calm, cold eyes staring back at me in the mirror from the center of the monster know too well what I am also and turning them from the mirror, confronting the rubbled but still comfortable spaces of my furnished room, I feel the energy coursing through me in small flashes and ripples of light, an energy which I know, given but that one chance it needs, could redeem the world. The beast does not sleep. In my transmogrification I have cast sleep from me like the cloak of all reason and I spring from these rooms, scuttle the three flights of the brownstone to the street and coming upon it in the dense and sleeping spaces of the city, see no one, confront no one (but I would not, I never have) as I move downtown to enact my dreadful but necessary tasks.

The beast does not sleep, therefore I do not sleep. At first the change came upon me once a week and then twice . . . but in recent months it has been coming faster and faster, now six or seven times a week, and furthermore I can *will* the change. Involuntary at first, overtaking me like a stray bullet, it now seems to be within my control as my power and facility increase. A *latent* characteristic then, some recessive gene which peeked its way out shyly at the age of twenty-five, first with humility and then with growing power and finally as I became accustomed to the power, it fell within my control.

I can now become the beast whenever I wish.

Now it is not the beast but I who pokes his way from the covers during the hours of despair and lurches his way to the bathroom; standing before that one mirror, I call the change upon myself, ring the changes, and the beast, then, confronts me, a tentacle raised as if in greeting or repudiation. Shrugging, I sprint down the stairs and into the city. At dawn I return. In between that time—

—I make my travels.

My travels, my errands! Over manhole covers, sprinting as if filled with helium (the beast is powerful; the beast has endless stamina) in and out of the blocks of the west side, vaulting to heights on abandoned stoops, then into the gutter again, cutting a swath through the city, ducking the occasional prowl cars which come through indolently, swinging out of sight behind gates to avoid garbage trucks, no discovery ever having been made of the beast in all the months that this has been going on . . . and between the evasions I do my business.

Pardon. Pardon if you will. I do not do *my* business. The beast does *his* business.

I must separate the beast and myself because the one is not the other and I have very little to *do* with the beast although, of course, I am he. And he is me.

And attack them in the darkness.

Seize hapless pedestrians or dawn drunks by the throat, coming up from their rear flank, diving upon them then with facility and ease, sweeping upon them to clap a hand upon throat or groin with a touch as sure and cunning as any I have ever known and then, bringing them to their knees, straddling them in the gutter, I—

Well, I—

—Well, now, is it necessary for me to say what I do? Yes, it is necessary for me to say, I suppose; these recollections are not careless nor are they calculated but merely an attempt, as it were, to set the record straight. The rumors, reports and evasions about the conduct of the beast have reached the status of full-scale lies (there is not a crew of assassins loose in the streets but merely one; there is not a carefully organized plan to terrorize the city but merely one beast, one humble, hard-working animal wreaking his justice) so it is to be said that as I throttle the lives and misery out of them, I often *turn them over* so that they can confront the beast, see what it is doing to them, and that I see in their eyes past the horror the heartbreak, the beating farewell signal of their mortality.

But beyond that I see something else.

Let me tell you of this, it is crucial: I see an acceptance so enormous as almost to defy in all of its acceptance because it is religious. The peace that passeth all understanding darts through their eyes and finally passes through them, exiting in the last breath of life as with a crumpling sigh they die against me. I must have killed hundreds, no, I do not want to exaggerate, it is not right, I must have killed in the high seventies. At first I kept a chart of my travels and accomplishments but when it verged into the high twenties I realized that this was insane, leaving physical evidence of any sort of my accomplishments that is, and furthermore, past that ninth murder or the nineteenth there is no longer a feeling of victory but only *necessity*. It is purely business.

All of it has been purely business.

Business in any event for the beast. He needs to kill as I need to breathe, that creature within me who I was always in the process of becoming (all the strangeness I felt as a child I now attribute to the embryonic form of the beast, beating and huddling its growing way within) takes the lives of humans as casually as I take my midday sandwich and drink in the local cafeteria before passing on to my dismal and clerkly affairs at the Bureau, accumulating time toward the pension credits that will be mine after twenty or thirty years. The beast needs to kill; he draws his strength from murder as I do mine from food and since I am merely his tenant during these struggles, a helpless (but alertly interested) altar which dwells within the beast watching all that goes on, I can take no responsibility myself for what has happened but put it squarely on him where it belongs.

Perhaps I should have turned myself in for treatment or seen a psychiatrist of some kind when all this began, but what would have been the point of it? What? They would not have believed that I was possessed; they would have thought me harmlessly crazy and the alternative, if they did believe me, would have been much worse: implication, imprisonment, fury. I could have convinced them. I know that now, when I became strong enough to will myself into the becoming of the beast I could have, in their very chambers, turned myself into that monster and then they would have believed, would have taken my fears for certainty . . . but the beast, manic in his goals, would have fallen upon those hapless psychiatrists, interns or social workers as he fell upon all of his night-time victims and what then?

What then? He murders as casually and skillfully as I annotate my filings at the Bureau. He is impossible to dissuade. No, I could not have done that. The beast and I, sentenced to dwell throughout eternity or at least through the length of my projected life span: there may be another judgment on this someday of some weight but I cannot be concerned with that now. Why should I confess? What is there to confess? Built so deeply into the culture—I am a thoughtful man and have pondered this long despite my lack of formal educational credits—as to be part of the madness is the belief that confession is in itself expiation, but I do not believe this. The admission of dreadful acts is merely to compound them through multiple refraction and lies are thus more necessary than the truth in order to make the world work.

Oh, how I believe this. How I do believe it.

I have attempted discussions with the beast. This is not easy but at the moment of transfer there is a slow, stunning instant when the mask of his features has not settled upon him fully and it is possible for me, however weakly, to speak. "Why must you do this?" I ask him. "This is murder, mass murder. These are human beings, you know, it really is quite dreadful." My little voice pipes weakly as my own force diminishes and the beast, transmogrified, stands before the mirror, waving his tentacles, flexing his powerful limbs, and says then (he speaks a perfect English when he desires although largely he does not desire to speak), "Don't be a fool, this is my destiny and besides *I* am not human so this is not my problem."

This is unanswerable; it is already muted by transfer. I burrow within and the beast takes to the streets singing and crouching, ready once again for his tasks. Why does he need to murder? I understand that his lust for this is as gross and simple as my own for less dreadful events; it is an urge as much a part of him as that toward respiration. The beast is an innocent creature, immaculately conceived. He goes to do murder as his victim goes to drink. He sees no shades of moral inference or dismay even in the bloodiest and most terrible of the strangulations but simply does what must be done with the necessary force. Never more. Some nights he has killed ten. The streets of the city scatter north and south with his victims.

But his victims! Ah, they have, so many of them, been waiting for murder so long, dreaming of it, touching it in the night (as I touch the selfsame beast), that this must be the basis of that acceptance which passes through them at the moment of impact. They have been looking, these victims, for an event so climactic that they will be able to cede responsibility for their lives and here, in the act of murder, have they at last that confirmation. Some of them embraced the beast with passion as he made his last strike. Others have opened themselves to him on the pavement and pointed at their vitals. For the city, the very energy of that city or so I believe this now through my musings, is based upon the omnipresence of death and to die is to become at last completely at one with the darkened heart of a city constructed for death. I become too philosophical. I will not attempt to justify myself further.

For there *is* no justification. What happens, happens. The beast has taught me at least this much (along with so much else). To-night we come upon the city with undue haste; the beast has not been out for two nights previous, having burrowed within with a disinclination for pursuit, unavailable even to summons, but now at four in the morning of this coldest of all the nights of winter he has pounded within me, screaming for release, and I have allowed him his way with some eagerness because (I admit this truly) I too have on his behalf missed the thrill of the hunt.

Now the beast races down the pavements, his breath a plume of fire against the ice. At the first intersection we see a young woman paused for the light, a valise clutched against her, one hand upraised for a taxi that will not come. (I know it will not come.) An early dawn evacuee from the city or so I murmur to the beast. Perhaps it would be best to leave this one alone since she looks spare and there must be tastier meat in the alleys beyond . . . but the creature does not listen. He listens to nothing I have to say. This is the core of his strength and my own repudiation is nothing as to his.

For listen, listen now: he sweeps into his own purposes in a way which can only make me filled with admiration. He comes upon the girl then. He comes upon her. He takes her from behind.

He takes her from behind.

She struggles in his grasp like an insect caught within a huge, indifferent hand, all legs and activity, grasping and groping, and he casually kicks the valise from her hand, pulls her into an alley for a more sweeping inspection, the woman's skull pinned against his flat, oily chest, her little hands and feet waving, and she is scream-ing in a way so dismal and hopeless that I know she will never be heard and she must know this as well. The scream stops. Small moans and pleas which had pieced out the spaces amid the sound stop too and with an explosion of strength she twists within his grap, then hurls herself against his chest and looks upward toward his face to see at last the face of the assassin about which she must surely have dreamed, the bitch, in so many nights. She sees the beast. He sees her.

I too know her.

She works at the Bureau. She is a fellow clerk two aisles down and three over, a pretty woman, not indifferent in her gestures but rather, as so few of these bitches at the Bureau are, kind and lively, kind even to *me*. Her eyes are never droll but sad as she looks upon me. I have never spoken to her other than pleasantries but I feel, *feel* that if I were ever to seek her out she would not humiliate me.

"Oh," I say within the spaces of the beast, trapped and helpless as I look upon her, "oh, oh."

"No!" she says, looking upon us. "Oh no, not you, it can't be you!" and the beast's grasp tightens upon her then. "It can't be you! Don't say that it's *you* doing this to me!" and I look upon her then with tenderness and infinite understanding knowing that I am helpless to save her and thus relieved of the responsibility but saddened too. Saddened because the beast has never caught a victim known to me before. I say in a small voice which she will never hear (because I am trapped inside), "I'm sorry, I'm sorry but it's got to be done, you see. How much of this can I take any more?" and her eyes, I know this, her eyes lighten with understanding, darken too, lighten and darken with the knowledge I have imparted.

And as the pressure begins then, the pressure that in ten seconds will snap her throat and leave her dead, as the freezing collors of the city descend, we confront one another in isolation, our eyes meeting, touch meeting and absolutely nothing to be done about it. Her neck breaks, and in many many many ways I must admit—I will admit everything—this has been the most satisfying victim of them all. Of them all.

AFTERWORD TO TRANSFER

This was written for an original anthology of horror stories of "strange beasts" but the editor found it *too* horrible or said he did and after it had ratcheted down the familiar pinball machine of the markets it wound up with my old friends at Ultimate Publications, Sol Cohen and Ted White, where it was held for almost three years in inventory before one or the other decided it could be slipped through with impunity. Barring one published letter in the fan columns of those magazines I have never received comment upon it. (That letter called it a "good Malzberg story" as opposed, I suppose, to a "bad Malzberg story" although there are those and I sit not in judgment of them who find the two indistinguishable.)

On rereading and (slightly) reworking the piece for this collection I fail to discern the horror or at least the excessive horror which caused its publication in the penny-a-word markets. Written in a crispy-crunchy pseudo-Victorian style which I had developed for "Notes Leading Down to the Events at Bedlam" (q.v.), it strikes me as a merry analysis of what I might call the Manhattan Condition (Manhattan Transfer?), altogether more optimistic and hopeful than Harlan Ellison's MWA-award-winning "The Whimper of Whipped Dogs," which with all its skill and power lacks the sense of individual human connection which I think is mustered here. I find this story altogether cheerier than "Twowd" or, for that matter, the third page of the *Daily News:* at least herein it is inferred that we may still touch one another, if only in the instants of our shared obliteration, and if one considers communication a value —every writer must or give up the ship at once—then murder might be a transcendent act.

Individual murder, that is to say. Technochratic, technologically induced murder is another issue and the most likely face of the present, let alone, far let alone, the future.

The Ballad of Slick Sid

This is a song. Everyone has their own way of doing things. A song is mine.

Sid: I am Slick Sid. You asked me to tell you how my life looked and what I think of the situation and when you talk situation you really mean the future. Even a machine knows that. All life is a question of future make-it: some make it fast like Sid over here, others make it slow like the government man but everybody living makes it one way or the other.

The only checkout is the F.T. But not for Sid, not yet.

SHERRY ON THE BACK SEAT: LOVE

The Mars shot lays down the pipe, two, *three* and I go *up*, hovering like a rocket wasted. Sherry backs me off, her little hands beating at my chest. "No," she says, and it is all I can do not to swat the little bitch in the face but I am cool. Sid is cool, he knows all the moves; I say, "*Now*, Sherry. We are celebrating the landing on Mars. We have conquered Mars and we must be happy."

"I didn't think you believed in stuff like that," she says . . . and in the back seat, the rotting upholstery crumbling around us, the dead wires of the turbo-hydramatic drive pushing from the rusting floorboards, I must explain to her just as I explain to you that some make it to the future fast and some make it slow but all alive are making it, and that to stop the future is like death . . .

Or worse.

"I don't like sex," little Sherry says and bounces. "Not at times like this." But Sid is insistent and I talk to her quietly of passion and need until finally . . .

As I knew she would.

But it is no good at all as I am moaning and crying into her shoulder while somewhere over us the hatchway of the rocket opens on Mars and men scuttle on that planet like roaches.

Sherry turns on the radio for bulletins which is how we hear this, but I do not care about Mars—nor, for the moment, even about Sherry. I am concerned with my own uncool but urgent need as I plunge into the future.

MAKING IT IN THE BACK ROOM DREAMING LIKE A DOVE

At an easy session, nothing special, just spiralling, Jug says that he is going to take the final trip and shoot death. He is very serious: sweat and seriousness come off Jug's face like the idiocy which haunts Sherry's. "I will meet the master," he says and takes it on, really deadly: four cc's of the stuff into the vial and only then do we begin to protest; but mildly because no one in the serenity group has yet seen a final trip before them. "You're too young, Jug," the leader says and points out that the final trip must come through enlightenment, but never from spite which is the only emotion which Jug, that dullard, understands. "Crap," he answers and without arguing further takes in the needle, drives it through and faints over his arm as if it were a plank of wood. *"Cool!"* Jug says, his features receding and dies in front of us.

We conclude in our discussion that this is a brave and even a remarkable thing; we also come to the assessment that the act must be inextricably bound to the actor and hence nothing which Jug does can suggest the moment of ultimate serenity. This is how the leader puts it. "Inextricably bound to the actor." So we go on our way, feeling bad about Jug but maybe a little envious, too, and the session ends with helpers coming in for the corpse. But that night and for many nights thereafter I find myself dreaming of the final trip and waking up to stare at the ceiling, quivering with my need and fear.

"I don't want to die," I say to the ceiling. "Not yet." But all along I know that this is not quite the point and from looking at the other members of the group I sense that they are going through the same thing. But there is no way to discuss it and no one else F.T.'s either, so after a while we forget about it . . .

As the future overtakes us.

TALKING TO THE ELDERS, KEEPING MY COOL

On the day the first three men are lost on Mars my old man calls me in for a talk and asks me what I am going to do with my life. I explain that I am now doing it and he says that all is make-it, but some bewilderment in his eyes suggests that he does not understand what I am truly saying. So for a little while I lay the truth on him, just enough to keep him active and interested. "Cats on Mars are going to die all over the place," I tell him among other things, and at last he leaves.

"I respect you Sid," he says at the door, but he is by then out of my life. So I do not have to listen to any more of this garbage, being locked into my continuing apperception which, as the serenity group teaches, enables me to truly meld with the future.

HITTING FOR THE BIG RIDE: I AIN'T NO FOOL

Sherry tells me that we must reach some kind of adjustment in our relationship, that she can no longer continue in this way. I have been getting her for three days now and must move to a different level. Other stuff. "Are you ready to make a commitment, Slick Sid?" she says (I make her call me that) and she does things to me with her mouth. But I am no longer interested. I have already had my fill and then too I have a slight overload of Jug's stuff trickling in me which has anesthetized me at the fringes. He willed it to me. "We've got to feel *something*," she says. "You don't feel, Slick Sid."

"Heavy," I say and take her out then in the Buick eleven miles out on the flats, doing one hundred ten on the turns: then put it flat into a guardrail at the peak. It is fifty-fifty that the restraints open after twelve rusting years but the fact that I am singing this out to you is proof that they did. Sherry screams when she gets out of the wrecked Bolt but when I point out that I am only trying to give her some of the feeling she asked for she becomes quiet and I realize that things are ended. Back through the flats and into the project before search time and I leave her there to consider her destiny as I lock down the Bolt and race the dose toward sleep.

Sleep is the fast way into the future.

AIN'T GONNA MAKE IT TILL SEVENTY-THREE

In the night I have an astronautic experience, a spacedream. I feel that I am on Mars, part of the landing crew in fact, sifting my way through artifacts and ruins in a meditative way while the sands drill their way into my helmet, closing off respiration. Before I real-

ize what has happened I am choking, and before I can save myself
I am dead; in that death within the dream I meet a Martian.

He is the last Martian in fact, a tall gangly creature with crushed
legs and a stomach pod. "Exactly what do you think you're doing
on my planet?" he asks and I answer that I am doing what men always do, that is, I am exploring. "Exploring for what?" the Martian
says and I shrug and say that I hardly know.

"I'm kind of a drug expert," I say. "I'm researching the ancient
Martian hallucinatives." The Martian nods solemnly and says that
he could have expected this; hallucinatives killed his own race.

"At a certain point of technology," he says, "life becomes unen-
durable for many; drugs overtake the culture. We survived but one
hundred Earth-years past the introduction of drugs." I ask him how
he can say that drugs destroyed his culture if he himself concedes
that after a certain point such are inevitable.

The Martian has no answer to this; his limbs instead begin to
sway and pulse, and grunting threateningly he hurls himself upon
me . . .

But Slick Sid has too many moves for any damaged Last Martian; I sidestep and kick him squarely in the center of his pod. He
cries and disintegrates, the petals of his being falling on me like
ash. I rise from this death, I rise from the dream, and find myself
lying in bed with a simple overload, no part of the future.

HOPE I DON'T MAKE IT TILL FIFTY-THREE

On the day that the sixth and seventh explorers on the planet
Mars are sucked into the sands never to be heard of again I am
visited after-hours by a slender cat who says he is from the government and wants to talk about Jug. There is some indication, the
government says, that the death was foul-play and this his final trip
was not deliberate.

This government man does not seem to be entirely comfortable
with Sid. I attempt to put him at ease by demonstrating certain
moves and turns, dimly remembered from Jug, at which I am quite
capable. "Slick Sid," he says, when I insist that he call me by that
name, "We were told to see Slick Sid, that you know something
about the subject issue." This is the way that many of them still
talk.

"Slick Sid's the tag," I say, "but I'm going to gag," and so I do this: I say absolutely nothing while the slender cat raps on for ten or fifteen minutes in increasing disgust.

"We are going to get *into* these serenity groups," he says, finally. "We are going to *explode* this situation. It is only a matter of time before we put you kids under very strict controls. You have gone too far—*there is no trip in death.*"

"Says you," says Sid, raising a finger. "You are in death."

"You are eighteen years old," the government man says, looking at some papers, refusing to lift his head which is the way that they show you they are angry. "You know *absolutely nothing. None* of you know anything except how to destroy and take on names for yourself, but I am here to tell you that you are *completely misguided* and we are going to *get after you people* before 1998."

And I say to him, Slick Sid says to him with a giggle, finally opening up to this cat because he is the government and after all what man, even at the age of eighteen, does not like to meet his government. "Man, you do not understand anything. Man, you so far out of this that you are not even going in. Get this now, cat: *we are the government.* We are out on the main strip and you cats just the sideshow. We are your future."

WHY EVEN BOTHER WITH FORTY-TWO

In the machines they tell us about the Kenny cats and how they were always getting assassinated and then pull a trick question on us, a real fakeout: *which Kenny was forty-two when assassinated and tragically cut short?* I take the stylus to the special box where you can print answers if you want and write: "Forty-two, that cat was ancient! do you understand? No one gets cut short at forty-two, particularly a Kenny cat who always got mixed up with the wrong people anyway." With a smile I put the answer through, thinking that it is a joke on the machine because the programming will not know to make of this one at all.

But it is serious, too. It is as serious as Slick Sid can be, because if you were a Kenny cat and took all of that stuff seriously as we are told the Kenny cats did, how could you make it to forty-two and not be *grateful* to have an end to all that crap? To say nothing of forty-six or whatever the older was—forty-six and thunder in the head. I would be better off *dead* then believing any of that stuff; the Kenny cats should have killed themselves for shame is what they should. Slick Sid knows better than any Kenny cat. The time is now: it is always the time right this minute and the only tragic thing about the Kenny cats is that we got to hear about them when instead we ought to be learning more and more about the future.

IF THE FINAL TRIP CAN BE FOR YOU

The night the ninth and tenth Martian explorers wander off and are never seen again, therefore bringing the conquest of Mars to a halt, I dream again, and in this dream I see Jug. There is no overload this time; I have gone to the sack with wet head and clear spirits and all that I seek is the darkness. Nevertheless, there is Jug, looking about the same as he did before he started on out but just a shade more rugged because death is not so good for the complexion.

"Hello you old Slick Sid," he says and gives me the signs, but it is a weary, washed-out Jug who appears before me; some element of vitality is gone forever and he does not give the signs with the old brass, sliding instead to the floor and leaning an elbow on knee, chin on hand, to talk. "It is not so good," he says, "this Final Trip. It is not what you think to be Slick Sid. But it is full of thoughts and colors. I thought that all of it would stop but this is not the case; instead it seems to go on and on and on maybe forever."

"Who asked you?" I say. "Who wants your opinions? Get out of here!" but Jug gives me only the sweetest and saddest of grins and says, "I can't change the rules, Slick Sid. You called me down from your own desires and now you must listen to me. This Final Trip is not what serenity said it would be: it is something else, so you'd better forget it."

"Who said I was thinking of it?" I say but Jug only gives me this smile again and then stands, uncoiling himself in parts. He becomes translucent. "I just thought you would like to know," he says. "That's all I wanted to tell you," he whispers, and he is gone.

I wake from this dream cursing and shouting, wishing that I could get my hands on Jug to squeeze the life out, but I remember that he is dead and am ashamed of himself. I will *not* think of the F.T.

The F.T. can wait: it will come when I say it will and when it is done it will always be done. Dead once is dead forever, but for now I pick and choose among all the fruits of possibility from the magnificent flourishing tree of the future.

SLICK SID IS GOING ALL THE WAY

Sherry meets me in the elevator after group and says that she cannot forget me. "It can't end this way," she says. "I'm ready for a relationship, and *you* owe me something. You can't turn it off." She is momentarily at least, desirable: soft, open and accessible; and so I say, "Relationship? I'll show you a relationship."

I slip her inside to my cubicle. It would be a rape if she were not cooperating but cooperative she is; I rise above her in the last moments, thinking that I could kill her for kicks; I reach my fingers down behind her eyes to rip her face like a mask.

But just as I am literally about to do it, the juices fail and I am on the comedown; I fall against her sobbing. I realize that what I thought was murder was only climax and I am ashamed, because this means that I am not yet ready for murder.

After this she talks and talks: wants to establish new ground-rules, even offers to jag down with me, but I do not listen; I shut her off with the curtains in my head until finally she leaves the room crying, saying she will get back at me for all of this.

I see our mark on the sheets: it has the aspect of a face: it is the face of Jug as he appeared in the dream, mocking deep from the F.T. I rip the sheets off the bed and try to wash him away with lye, but he will not vanish. The sheet disintegrates and finally I am left holding Jug's little face in my hands, his eyes winking at me and only then, deep from that nest, does he give me the Word.

It is the Future.

SLICK SID GOT NOTHING MORE TO SAY

At the hour when all contact is lost with the men on Mars and the telescopes pinned to that planet show small dots which suggest flame, at that very hour, Slick Sid finishes off these notes and prepares to take his next step. Slick Sid is prepared: he has waited for this so long. Now he knows exactly what to do.

He sings out his song. He promised to give a picture for you of how he felt and what he did and even a machine should find it helpful. I will drop it in your receiver-slot as you requested, the last thing.

Then I will end the future.

AFTERWORD TO THE BALLAD OF SLICK SID

This story is a kind of subterranean success. It was commissioned for an anthology of originals about "young people in the future" but was rejected because of the sexuality (fair enough I suppose since it—the anthology that is—was meant to be for younger readers) and wound up in the *Infinity Four* anthology instead. *Swank* picked it up for reprint and it became—no one has ever noticed this—the skeleton for my Bobbs-Merrill novel, *Guernica Night*, which although not a commercial success at least was reviewed, as a literary work, by Joyce Carol Oates in the New York *Times Book Review*.

In short, "The Ballad of Slick Sid" comes as close to being entirely successful as virtually any story published within the category of science fiction . . . and yet I know that of the forty thousand people in the town where I live no more than two or three would have ever read it. And ninety-five out of a hundred attendees at a science fiction convention would react similarly blankly. It is only one story out of two thousand published in 1972 by one science fiction writer out of five hundred . . . and science fiction itself is but a marginal category of commercial literature with a far smaller (although noisier) readership than that for Gothics.

Small wonder considering the negligible impression even the best of us can make upon the culture why almost all science fiction writers succumb to despair by mid-career. We are talking, after all, of a huge nation, 225 million people, nine tenths of whose adults have never read a book past compulsory education. We are talking of a nation in which the best-selling novels of them all, *Valley of the Dolls*, say, or *Jaws*, might reach 10 million people whereas any prime-time television situation comedy reaches four times that number; a presidential speech might double that. We are dealing with a category-within-a-minority here; if a science fiction novel sells over 75,000 copies it is doing well for the genre. But what is 75,000 out of a nation of 225 million?

One person out of three thousand. That is what it is.

Still, we go on, we try to do our work and I did earn $275 for the two prior sales of this story which, for an hour, hour and a half's work, isn't too bad, I guess. Believe me, if it *had* reached 10 million people, they wouldn't have paid me much more.

Notes Leading Down to
the Events at Bedlam
8/18/189—

Gentlemen:

So here I sit, pen in hand, and I will try to comply with your request, that is to write an explanation of my condition and why I think I am here to the best of my ability although I do not know if I am capable of doing this or what purposes it will serve even if this dismal task were accomplished. Gentlemen! Gentlemen! You are so *solemn* with your posturings and rubbings of hands, your mumbling of strange words like *dementia* which I can barely understand and I do not know how I can reach past this solemnity to strike to the core of truth because I am not myself a solemn man; I am a man, you will find it hard to believe this, known until fairly recently for the merriment of his disposition, his *joie de vivre*, his *je ne sais quoi* which insouciantly carried him larking through all the passageways of life. And no more now, no more.

I know that you have discussed all of this with my wife, Wilhemina. This memoir may well be her idea and not yours. I tell you, I tell you at the outset, do not believe a word she says, gentlemen. There is no credibility in her. She merely wishes to know how well I know her secrets.

Nevertheless, I will write this memoir or at least a brief set of notes leading toward a memoir. There are so few matters to occupy my valueless time in these rather grim surroundings and I know that my failure to cooperate will only make my confinement more indefinite than it is already. Also these notes are sure to amuse me. Also I appreciate what one of you called your "new view of madness," madness as being caused by external facets of one's history and not necessarily being a mere investiture of demons. I know that I am not mad even though you take me for this but if I do not cooperate with your proposed "cure" by explaining to you how and why I feel I am in these rather dismal environs you will conclude, will you not, that the demons are inviolable and I will be here through eternity.

(Do not listen to a word my wife says. She is treacherous, deceitful, filled with hypocrisy and as the cause of these events will lie to protect herself. Dismiss her, gentlemen!)

At least if I am here through eternity I will be separate from Wilhemina; this the only good to be wrenched from the horrible pass to which I have come. I know that in your naïveté and innocent, stumbling lust, you cannot understand why I would feel this way, for Wilhemina is a lovely woman, twenty-four years old at this time and at that tantalizing point where the frivolities of the girl and the true, darker sensuality of the woman merge to a depth of temptation. Without your solemnity in her presence where would you be? At her veritable knees, gentlemen, you do not need to apologize. This is simple truth.

I met and married Wilhemina, the daughter of friends of my business partner, in the fall of 189–, just seven scant months ago although it now seems that a different man must have made this tragic error. Beautiful she was and mysterious in the way of all beautiful women, nor was I ever able to find out much of her background. "I am a mystery to everyone," she said, "often enough even to myself, just believe in me," and I believed in her, gentlemen, I took her from her parents without dowry and in my large if cheerless unfurnished apartment and after a wedding trip to Spain about which I can only seem to recall a series of rooms and carriages swept by heat and lust, groveling and connection (I have no recollection whatsoever of landscape) we began our life together. Soon I found that she was an adopted child who had wandered into her parents' lives through ways remarkable and devious in 187– and never a word about her background, but there was no more information to be derived from this couple, an ancient and embittered pair who had attended our wedding in ecstasy and had then left their dwellings for a long trip to Scotland, no return date posted, no forwarding address yielded. My partner at this time also found obscure business in the North which caused him to place the firm in my hands for an indefinite period and the last I had heard of him, the police were unable to ascertain his activities or location since he had checked out of a small hotel in the Netherlands four months ago.

Nevertheless business prospered. The elixir of the gods is being paid for in the most mundane (but most profligate) of coin and the winery at that time had been expanded to take in not only a large number of new distillers but a kind of subpartner whose competence with accounts was stunning and who left me virtually unlimited free time to pursue my new life with my twenty-four-year-old bride, who opened up layers of knowledge for me, night after night . . . until I became a man quite dazzled, fascinated and entrapped.

I had waited until middle life to marry. As is common with so many men of my class I believed that I should not marry until I had reached a position of financial and professional stability and although I was fully forty-seven years old when I met and married Wilhemina—I blush to confess this, gentlemen, but complete frankness was demanded in these memoirs and I am beyond self-delusion *no matter what your diagnosis*—I was greatly inexperienced in matters of the flesh, having channeled my energies to the establishment of a business and finding substantiation, so to speak, in life.

Now I know what had been stolen from me in small pieces throughout all those empty years but even in the early months with Wilhemina I did not know it then. I thought that joy forestalled was joy twice gained, and I would now find in the last twenty years of my life a magnitude of joy well eclipsing the deprivations of the first forty-seven years, and Wilhemina, I do say, assisted me in this insane endeavor. (Now, you see, I know it was insane; one can never atone for what has been lost.)

I was very much possessed by her. Gentlemen, I was very much possessed by her. Even at this moment I feel that necessity, the desire to drive myself against her, to touch her, to entwine myself with her in the night . . . I cannot go on. A certain delicacy must infuse these memoirs, owing to the conventions of the day, and conventions to one side, to be explicit about what happens to us in private has always struck me as evil and disgusting. What we do with ourselves or with one another alone is none of anyone's business. You will forgive me; I know of the more modern researchers who feel that sexuality is a legitimate area of discussion but I will have nothing to do with their bizarre ideas. You will forgive me. You will forgive me, gentlemen. Solemn as all of you might be with your beards and heavy coats, even an alienist must have known passion in his time and I like to think that outside of these walls, far from the needs of the patients, outside these walls as I say and in private as I was once in private with my young wife . . . you commit secret acts out of honesty and passion. And that you understand. And that you understand.

In the fifth month of our marriage after a long and tumultuous night with Wilhemina I awoke at one of those off-hours of the morning where time itself seems shuffled and dispersed: two o'clock, four o'clock, perhaps five-fifteen. It does not matter the time; I awakened with that peculiar and startled awareness which so many of us know only at those strange hours when something within us throws off the cloak of sleep to confront the unspeakable . . . and found, as I turned instinctively to my dear wife for comfort, that lying next to me in the bed was not her but a beast, a beast of such awful description—

—A beast neither human nor inhuman, skin like scales, the tint like no color in the universe, features that were neither hers nor those of any animal I have seen: the whole cold, cold, emitting a cold breath like fog which engulfed me and as I retreated from the beast in horror it moved, apparently in its own sleep, nearer to me, and we *touched*. I touched the skin and scales of the beast, my body galvanized to an intensity I had never before known, literally contracted and I must have screamed then.

I must have screamed, something peculiar and terrible pouring from me, a vaulting, a congelation of self, leaping from the sheets, groaning and gasping, and the beast screamed too, a sound less a shriek than a cry, and then as I uncovered my eyes (for being human means that in all of our perversity we wish to confront the unspeakable even as we flee it) I saw the beast shudder, waves and rivulets running, and it assumed again the shape of Wilhemina—

—Wilhemina reaching toward me from the bed as I cowed in a corner. Wilhemina uttering soothing words. Wilhemina extending comfort and moving toward me and, gentlemen, I could not stand it, you must believe this, I could not stand it as my wife came upon me, her eyes lit with desire and pain, I feared that her touch was that of the beast and I would have fled the room, seizing what clothing I needed from a closet, and run across the moors like a lunatic (this the only time, admittedly, that I did approach lunacy; otherwise your diagnosis is false) but my limbs did not have the strength to move me and then she came upon me, put her hands on mine and it was the familiar, sweet, dark touch of her flesh against mine. "Come," she said. "Come back into the bed. What's wrong with you? Why are you cowering like that?"

I allowed her to lead me shaking back to the sheets. I did not have the strength of a child, gentlemen, or its diction, being able only to sputter incoherent sounds which may have made me sound bestial myself. "Great God," I was finally able to say or some similar religious expletive, "God help me," and made another effort to leave the bed but Wilhemina, now shorn of her bedclothing, clambered over me like the night and held me fluttering, mouth against neck, gently biting, and I did not have the strength to move or to resist as she spoke to me.

And speak to me she did as we lay wrapped that way in the bed. She said something like this, I must have seen her Condition. I must have seen her Symptom, she said, she had had it all her life, it did not happen very often, there was no explanation for it, she had never seen it herself because she was *not* herself when it happened, but a few times, when there had been poor luck she had been seen by others: her parents, who might have seen her in her sleep.

(She will deny all of this when you bring the point to her, gentlemen. She is cunning in ways I could not have understood. She will say that I have lied out of dementia but I do not care for I know what I have seen and where I have been now and what I am in a way which you never will.)

Some might have seen her in the dark, she said, but it meant nothing. I was barely able to listen. I can hardly recount it now. Her explanation as placed against what I had seen was like a solitary weak flower in a storm. What did it matter? What could it measure? And shrinking, retreating, I fell from her, without the strength now to flee, but feeling my skin beginning to glaze under her touch. It was uncontrollable, she said sadly. She did not even know what happened to her during these periods of sleep. Could I tell her? The others had only babbled. Would I explain? Could I give her details? She could not obtain medical counsel on her own, of course, because she would be institutionalized for dementia (I trust, gentlemen, that you note the irony of this!), but perhaps if I, a credible, established businessman not to say her husband, were to attend to the doctors and—

I stayed with her. That was my fundamental error although not the cause of my condition as you will see. She was my wife, I loved her (and love her, God help me, yet), what I had seen was so incredible that in retrospect it diminished to the easy, fuzzy representation of nightmare like the masks of children on All Hallows Eve and the only condition I placed was that we did not speak of it again and that no recollection of that first night be shared.

(Why *did* I not leave her? Why did I not abrogate the marriage as a man of my position and influence could well have done with legal ease? Why did I not evict her from my quarters without settlement? I could have done this. It would have been accomplished with facility. I told myself that the reason I would not evict her was that she was my wife and what we had known together was irreplaceable; that I might have been hallucinating despite her confirmation of her "condition," that the "condition" itself might not reappear due to the Love of a Good Man . . . oh, I told myself many things. You will see through the center of this, gentlemen, as you claim erroneously to see through so much else . . . although never Wilhemina. Deny, deny. She will deny all.)

And life passed placidly enough for some days or weeks. No recurrence of the "condition." No indication that it had ever happened. A total, blissful denial. Until I awoke once again in that bellows hour of the night, body tensed as if for culmination or collapse, and found beside me—

—Ah, but this time it was not nearly so bad. I had been this way once before, you see, also I could gauge my own reaction more closely and look with objective interest upon the beast which lay like a human in the bed, breathing in palpitation, scales fluttering like feathers, and I found that I was able to confront it straight on without hysteria. Anything, I learned, *anything* could be confronted if you were willing to face it and it was only when the beast's horrid "eyes" opened and it looked at me with a stare both luminescent and somehow pained—

—that I screamed and the thing shuddered. Wilhemina returned in an instant (the transition was so quick as to be almost unnoticeable) and clutched me to her saying impossible, this was impossible, the "condition" was a phenomenon which occurred only once in a while and now it had appeared twice within a short time and how terrible, terrible this must be for you, Gerald, her fingers floating up and down my body, horror in the touch but horror turning once again into its kind companion lust . . . and so I allowed myself to be taken by and to take her, the two of us grasping in the darkness and it was not so bad, gentlemen, not so bad at all and we said nothing more, did not remark upon what had happened the next day or the next but the night after that—

—awakening yet again, just three days later I saw the beast and the beast, two of its eyes open, was looking at me, had obviously been looking at me for a long time, a woe and acceptance in that dreaming gaze which I cannot describe, and then, grumbling and gasping, it closed the gap between us, put its "hands" upon me, the skin glinting like a dead animal under the moon and that touch, only that touch must have restored my voice. Is it true that I screamed? No, I did not scream, I fairly died—

—and Wilhemina returned and I fell into her as if she were the earth, her return the only reassurance that the horror beside me was not the exact quotient of my past and future life, the life after death too, and she whispered to me words of comfort yet again but I did not want to hear them. The "condition" could not possibly recur, she said, perhaps if it did she would seek assistance. She could not live this way. She saw in my eyes the horror she had induced. And I took her and took her and nothing more of this and the next day between us without comment as it had always been and the next night—

—the beast was upon me, wrapped against me, I could find the smell now, a harsh scent like teak and vomit intermingled, pulled up through my nostrils, pleadings in the grumblings of the beast as it wrapped me in and I could not scream, being held so tightly until at last, released, I shouted and blessed Wilhemina—

—reappeared against me and I took her and there was no difference in the taking as between her and the beast. This is what I came to understand, gentlemen, with my eyes closed, fulminating against her. It was not one but the other, the two together, my dear wife, the beast, have not one but both because this was what had been created and this was what I had married and my confusion was great, oh gentlemen, it was great as was my horror but underneath, beneath the horror, another perception was growing and it is of this perception which I think you now want me to speak so we will get at the roots of this and hasten my cure. She brought me here under false pretenses. It is not me but *she* who is mad, not me but she who needs treatment, not she but me you must attend, night after night the clutchings and the shifting in the bed beside me, the straining acuteness, the knowledge of what I had married—

—but you wanted the perception, gentlemen, so I give you the perception. I give you this: the realization that it was not annulment of beast I wanted after that first horrid moment of confrontation, not the death of the beast but its continuation, the intermingling if you will and that in wanting the one, my wife, I wanted the other, the beast, and it had always been this way, this was why, the real reason, I had waited so long to marry, knowing unconsciously what was within me, the desires of the fiend. Now I will never know, the two of them so mingled together. I am losing control: *it was not her I wanted but the other.*

I must have had intimations before our marriage, I must have suspected this but I wanted I wanted I wanted I can no longer control this put the leeches on me or the ropes if you will put me in a cage in the square and batter on the bars. I will not continue with this yea though I be in Bedlam for fifty years more dying a shrunken old man than to continue these notes do not listen to her she is treacherous and cunning will say anything you wish to hear, listen to me, no do not listen to me.

For I have gauged and measured now my madness and know myself to be madder by far than even the least solemn of you oh God the *scent* of it coming against me in the night—

AFTERWORD TO NOTES LEADING DOWN TO THE EVENTS AT BEDLAM

This story, commissioned for the first of a number of Roger Elwood anthologies on "strange beasts and creatures" is a fairly adept pastiche of the arch but unsettling baroque style of the eighteenth-century horror story, not much more than that, but Elwood reacted with enthusiasm almost uncontrolled, telling lots of people (who dutifully told me) that I was "the new Lovecraft." I sincerely hope not; with all due respect to the departed Howard Phillips I find nothing enviable about his life, little about his career, and nothing of his personality.

Rereading the piece I can see another of the sources of its power: it is a lovely equation of sex and death than which there is no better fusion in the American popular culture of the 1970s. I did not consciously mean to do this, which means only that the story has the greater force for all of this: the unconscious has a clearer idea of its purposes (to say nothing of its origin) than the conscious mind. I have written little with the conviction of the last page or so of this story; this could open up large areas of self-investigation but gladly and gracefully and eternally, I hope, I will pass up the opportunity.

Seeking Assistance

I

Well, in my stumbling way. I look for help, beg what favors I may, otherwise try to stay within myself. The world, perhaps, is too much with me. For diversion, however, to fill the interstices, I collect injustices.

Not only do I collect: injustice is a fine cocktail but a poor meal, roiling the blood as it does, damaging the complexion, doing complex things to the digestion otherwise indifferent. To collect must be to seek excretion. To witness is to sanction, to respond then to move to a higher, better plane. I have worked this out for myself.

In New York a radio announcer makes a foul pun on the name of a forgotten writer. I go to the typewriter, prepare the envelope and stamp it first (this assuring I will go through with the act), then content. *Dear X: It is the lowest of all criticism to make fun of a person's name.* Months elapse but X, devastated or indifferent, does not reply. For a while I listen to his program waiting for him to make fun of *my* name (I am also a forgotten writer) but no luck. Eventually I realize that he will not respond, that there is nothing he can say. Meanwhile, fortunately, there are other outrages to busy me. A feminist calls the male orgasm bestial. I write her a scurrilous letter. Someone in California insults my Collected Works. I write *fuck you.* A municipal scandal is defended editorially in the local paper: the writer says thay all do it. *Dear Y: You do it; I do not.* The letter languishes unpublished; yet I do not falter in my righteousness.

And still more. Injustice is not only within the public domain. My elder daughter's substitute teacher refuses to allow her to go to the bathroom. I confront the principal. My wife refuses sex (at least with me) saying that my constant rages drive her to distraction. I rage at her. A car-pool lady forgets to pick up my younger child at this address even though specific instructions were furnished and, humiliatingly, I am forced to drive her to Wonder Waffles myself.

In five brisk one-line paragraphs I deal with the car-pool lady, who I have passed several times in the supermarket unrecognized, she in a housecoat and curlers, crying and absently fingering bread. I suspect menopausal shock: allowances ought to be made. But allowances bespeak compromise, acceptance, collaboration. Give the world a little nod of assent and the next time it will clean you out in an alley. One must be at ready. Constant ready. This is not to say that I enjoy my work. I do it sadly, lacking pleasure.

II

My wife says, "Presidents are criminals. Vietnam falls; millions dead or devastated. Innocents die in prison, felons take full pardons. What does it matter if the car-pool lady did not come? The Mafia control everything. Why do you listen to the radio? You cannot clean up the world personally."

The woman is right. (Even though she will use sex as a weapon, not a charming habit.) Still, she sees nothing at all. Vietnam is overseas, the Mafia is invisible whereas the car-pool lady is part of my life. One cannot deal with felonious heads of state yet the car-pool lady weeps in Pantry Pride. The demon that moves within the one lurks near the stained heart of the other. One must do what one can; one must try to resolve what is within one's means. The two million Vietnamese dead can gain nothing from me but if I can scour the corruption in circumstance which promises similar, more private, evil . . . *Hey, Y: Your latest statement is incredibly dumb even for you.* Herzog dealt with the dead; my communications are saved for the living. The dead are beyond us. For a time. Technology has not yet found a way to make them a market. When this final breakthrough is accomplished there will be time enough to deal with the dead.

III

At night I hover birdlike over my wife, who is, of course, not cooperating. Her eyes are distracted, small waves of concentration which mimic frenzy weave their embattled way across her cheekbones. It is hopeless in the extreme and yet I have physical needs which must be met if my life and career will continue. One cannot carry more than a single, fine obsession at any given time.

Concentration in her expression, distraction in her movement.

Surely there is paradox and at some quiet, pastoral moment I will have to give this consideration: for now it is merely essential that I finish. Moan. Groan. Snaffle. Terminus. Terminatus est. *Terminatus est in Deo, Kyrie eleison* I mumble and depart from her gracefully. One breast trails underneath my elbow semi-attached, breaks moist contact like a petal falling from the inner surfaces of a flower. I lie to one side of her rotating ceilingward, staring at crosshatches, considering my fate.

"You don't think," she says.

I think.

IV

While the television news discusses gang rape my daughters fall into vicious battle. The elder wants her place on the couch but the younger feels that she is displaced and kicks back wildly, striking the elder in the eye. Tears and screams: underneath in a huddle of attention my wife and I consider dispatches from victims. There is, after all, very little to be done about children at this stage of their lives. The situation is hopeless. One must cultivate patience and accept one's inability to change matters.

V

Oh B, oh B: Have you no compassion? No concern? These are not people you discuss, not within your cold mind you have made them statistics. But you delude yourself for they are human just as you and I, they bleed and sweat, they cannot be reduced to the level of abstraction. The machinery of contemporary technology has given us opportunities unparalleled to reduce people to the level of abstractions. I accept the dilemma this poses for the conscience-stricken, the opportunity for the conscienceless. But the revolution awaits.

VI

The car-pool lady and I have begun a discreet affair. Outside of her stained housecoat she is not unattractive nor does she weep (the stains must depress her) and she is only thirty-eight. How our affair began is still mysterious to me and I am not sure that there is logical explanation or justification. After all in this quiet, working-class neighborhood discovery would be disastrous and her husband, who labors nearby, often comes home early or for lunch. Risk however heightens the conversation of our blood: I move within her feeling thin, poised, dartlike and attentive to her cool innards. In the damp touch of her palms I feel the invocation of blessedness.

Seen this way the car-pool lady is not lacking in quality. It was cruel of me to so despise her without knowing her pain as I do now and as she does mine. She disagrees however that anything may be done about the rectification of injustice; she feels that writing letters is disagreeable, even hopeless, and that it would be better to turn these energies toward personal salvation. I cannot say that she is wrong and later, inflamed by her advice, I penetrate her deeply, thin genitals firm, firm voice shrieking thinly.

VII

My serious work fails again of acceptance. Unquestionably my career has reached an abyss as has the question of age: older is no longer better. Like many men of my age and modest creative gifts I am seemingly condemned to spending the rest of my working life doing as I have without possibility of wider acceptance. Also the rejections are incomprehending. I feel that my work is not only being turned away, it is being turned away without having been noticed. Even my protests have a curiously insubstantial feel as they are stuffed into envelopes: they seem to disintegrate in my hand, vanished before they have departed. Often I have the feeling of functioning in a vacuum then, although thanks to the car-pool lady, whom I now see twice a week in a regularized way, I intimate that the vacuum does not pertain to my personal life but is more generalized.

VIII

Today my left hand vanished.

IX

In the evening a caller to a local radio talk show makes a filthy comment about someone I respect. Reaching hastily for the telephone (I have bandaged the stump of the other hand in a makeshift but serviceable fashion; furthermore no one here has noticed my disability, we have not looked at one another in years) I dial numbers shakily, wait through the gasping sounds of wire and finally hear the host on seven-second delay. Radio off. "Swine," I say, "swine, does no one care?" I seem to have more in mind but my throat is choked by little burbles and shrieks and I can say no more. Sobbing as well. After a time the host rings off and I am left with the dead phone against my lips, my lips pursed against the blank holes in a kiss, my tongue casually flicking over the darkness. I turn on the radio but my moment has long passed.

X

M: This must stop. It cannot continue. It is completely unfair that we live in conditions like this. What are we, beasts? Can we not measure our humanity in ways other than self-loathing?

XI

The car-pool lady says that our affair must continue, otherwise she will kill herself. (I have been thinking of getting out.) She does not seem disturbed by the absence of my left hand until I wave the stump before her and then she says that it hardly matters. She has lived without legs for years.

Only then, looking down at her, at the expanse of blanket below her waist where legs should be, do I see that this is true. Prostheses, she says. Detachable and adjustable.

XII

Daughters, oh daughters: you must stop this it is too much already and I cannot bear

XIII

My right foot is shriveled and I have developed, in compensation, a rather fetching limp. Messages of support flood the President for his courageous recent actions. We are shown, on evening news, the stacks of letters on his desk.

AFTERWORD TO SEEKING ASSISTANCE

This one, for a cynical professional with 4 million published words of fiction behind him, is pretty much untransmuted; the line between persona and first person, in fact, is so thin that much of the story's energy or tension derives from the technical attempt to keep some separation visible. A less hi-falutin' English 303B way of putting it is that "Seeking Assistance" is a self-indulgent story. So it is. What the hell. In 4 million published words of fiction you deserve to get your own voice in print just once.

Although I did just barely: it took a round of rejections and I had to cut it severely in order to sell it to Ed Ferman, who had kindly said he would take a second look if I couldn't sell it. Published in the April 1976 issue of *Fantasy & Science Fiction* (eight years exactly after my first appearance in the market of all the markets that is closest to my heart) along with a bitter essay it was meant to be my farewell to the practice of science fiction. It probably is. (I reserve the right to realize as much as I can on the body of published work, however; a writer cannot be underpaid or underread on what he has created.) There has been many a chuckle along the way, however, just as there are a few chuckles in this story, and I thank you all, most graciously, for putting up with me.

Redundancy

I

The President appears on television in a Ford commercial. "This is an excellent car," the President says, slamming a door to show the solidity of the body, tapping his fingers on the roof to reveal the gleam. "I think that you'll be very happy with it. See your Ford dealer today and find out what kind of a deal can be made for you. The First Lady and I have been very happy with our Ford." He smiles, the car twirls on a turntable, lights flick, music rises and the station returns to its regular showing of the late night movie starring the late Senator Spessard L. Holland (of Florida) in an impressionistic documentary of the abuses of the welfare system.

II

I dream that I am masturbating but when I awake I find that my wife is on top of me clutching me in the dark and we seem to be fornicating instead. It is strange, strange and complex to be linked so with my wife at the end of a simple dream of adolescence but regret, loss, nostalgia will get me nowhere and so I reach for her eagerly, forcing myself through the motions of generation. At the end of our coupling I think that she is praising me but then I awake from all of this, realizing that all of it was but a double-dream and get up to have some coffee before phoning my mistress to arrange a date.

III

I meet a beggar on the street who curses me and demands money. "We have had quite enough of this submissiveness," the beggar says, "the invisibility of the socially deviate is at an end; we are in a genuine revolution of group. Give me everything you've got before I kill you," he says, producing a worn but deadly knife and putting it against my stomach. Nodding, I give him three one dollar bills, all of my credit cards and my car keys whose identity tag gives my blood type and the name of a relative to phone in case I am pulled out of a fatal automobile accident. "That's fine," the beggar says, appropriating my goods and putting away his knife. "I'm sorry to use methods like these but we are in an era of militancy now and the old methods, as you are well aware, simply do not work." He turns and proceeds toward Fifty-third Street but before he can move more than a very few paces I move up behind him and removing my gun from its secret shoulder holster, press it into his spine. He turns to me astonished. "I'm quite sorry," I say, "but the old rules of the game simply do not work," and I show him my card from Victims United which, as everyone knows, was formed in the spring of 197– in the basement of a church on lower Broadway and since then has spread through most of the major sectors of the country, growing by leaps and bounds, so to speak, as it gives pride and dignity for the first time to a group of people who have been abused as much, perhaps, as any sector of the society. "I only demand my rights," I say to the beggar as I shoot him through the heart, then reappropriate my goods as he falls away from me like a leaf, hitting the pavement with a thin metallic sound. As I move my head from side to side, watching to see if any or all of this has been observed by passers-by, two policemen clamber from a passing patrol car and seize me roughly, thrust me kicking into the rear seat of the car which looks like a yellow gelatinous maw. "We can't have this kind of thing going on," they say, as they beat me into unconsciousness in the surprisingly roomy back seat, meanwhile using their free hands to give me the well-known and frightening sign of their organization, *Authorities Unlimited*, "we can't be flouted like this; you have to give us some pride and dignity, we must defend our right to defend your rights," and darkness overwhelms me, I seem to have fainted although the blows which still fall upon me now feel like caresses and it is hard to believe that the members of *Authorities Unlimited*—which, as all of us know, is not a revolutionary organization—would treat me like this.

IV

The Secretary of Defense and the Chairman of the Joint Chiefs of Staff hold a press conference in the Marble Room during which they announce that they have been oppressed too long and will now do their own thing. That night the first reports of massacre are carried by couriers from the West and when I awaken it is to news that five million members of various organizations have been exterminated for the public good by tanks, armaments, bombs and twenty-ton howitzers for the mopping-up operation. Another press conference is called for the next day and the Chairman of the Joint Chiefs states that for the first time he has turned the corner of the reality-basis; by acting out his desires and enacting repressions he has become a total human being. "You have got to do it," he says. "Do it in the streets, do it with bombs, do it with grenades and ten divisions but above all you must do it." The Secretary of Defense is not present at this latter conference; it is rumored that he is undergoing an identity-crisis as a result of these actions for which he had not been yet fully structured.

V

The President, on videotape, appears on another late program, this time on behalf of the Pontiac Motor Division. "You'll trust this one," he says, slamming the hood of a Grand Prix emphatically, his little eyes winking in the excessive lights. "It has wide-track ride and corners like a stallion but the performance is as smooth and dependable as you can wish. You ought to see your dealer for a test drive tomorrow," he says, waving at the screen and at this moment, not for the first time, I feel a certain lagging in trust. It does not stand to reason that the President could recommend Ford and Pontiac who are, of course competitors, equally . . . but then again there is the so-called credibility gap and in the country as it has become at the present time, it is perhaps best not to trust anyone completely.

AFTERWORD TO REDUNDANCY

I wrote this story in twenty minutes in October of 1972 when McGovern was fast fading, the Water was far from the Gate and Gerald Ford was not even the faintest gleam in the orb of one

Richard Milhous Nixon. It was rejected by *Esquire* and lay forgotten by all in my agent's cupboard until 8/75 when a gifted lady then in his employ, Cherry Weiner, found it and sold it to a men's magazine. I had so forgotten the story (and had so misplaced the carbon) that I did not read it until publication in January of 1976 when its surrealistic lunacy assumed the shape of a really grotesque predictiveness. Who was to know? I had come back from Shea Chevrolet and an $85 repair bill for a heater and merely wanted another fast exercise in the absurd.

As the reader might suspect, this kind of story is much easier for a competent writer than the writer would ever care to admit. I did thirty or forty in this light schematic vein over the years and sold more than three quarters of them at an hourly wage rate that would astonish even a Teamster. Here is a demonstration of a writer floating on the top of his talent, doing what is easy within the narrowest range, attempting almost nothing, succeeding without strain. Left to my own devices and a better market I would have, twenty years ago, spent a career doing nothing more ambitious than pieces of this sort. The collapse of the market for shorter fiction, however, militated against a career of such pieces; in our time only Donald Barthelme has been able to do it. Unlike Barthelme—who really might be quite gifted if he ever tried to find out—I was forced to go into the world of portions and outlines and *struggle*. I am not bitter about this.

Leviticus: In the Ark

I

Conditions are difficult and services are delayed. Conditions have been difficult for some time, services have been delayed more often than being prompt, but never has it weighed upon Leviticus as it does now. Part of this has to do with his own situation: cramped in the ark, Torahs jammed into his left ear and right kneecap, heavy talmudic bindings wedged uncomfortably under his buttocks, he is past the moments of quiet meditation that for so long have sustained him. Now he is in great pain, his body is shrieking for release; he has a vivid image of himself bursting from the ark, the doors sliding open, his arms outstretched, his beard flapping in the strange breezes of the synagogue as he cries denunciation. *I can no longer bear this position.* There must be some Yiddish equivalent for this. Very well, he will cry it in Yiddish.

No, he will do nothing of the sort. He will remain within the ark, six by four, jammed amidst the holy writings. At times he is sure that he has spent several weeks within, at others, all sense of time eludes him; perhaps it has been only a matter of hours . . . well, make it a few days since he has been in here. It does not matter. A minute is as a century in the Eye of God, he remembers—or did it go the other way?—and vague murmurs that he can hear through the not fully soundproofed walls of his chamber inform him that the service is about to begin. In due course, just before the adoration begins, they will fling open the doors of the ark and he will be able to gaze upon them for a few moments, breathe the somewhat less dense air of the synagogue, endure past many moments of this sort because of his sudden, shuddering renewal of contact with the congregation, but, ah God! . . . it is difficult. Too much has been demanded of him; he is suffering deeply.

Leviticus turns within the limited confines of his position, tries to find a more comfortable point of accommodation. Soon the service will begin. After the ritual chants and prayers, after the sermon and the hymn, will come the adoration. At the adoration the opening of the ark. He will stretch. He will stand. He will stretch out a hand and greet them. He will cast light upon their eyes and upon the mountains: that they shall remember and do all his commandments and be holy unto him.

He wonders if his situation has made him megalomaniac.

II

Two weeks before, just at the point when Leviticus' point of commitment to the ark loomed before him, he had appeared in the rabbi's cubicle and made a plea for dispensation. "I am a sick man," he had said, "I do not think that I will be able to stand the confinement. Also, and I must be quite honest with you, rabbi, I doubt my religious faith and commitment. I am not sure that I can function as that embodiment of ritual which placement in the ark symbolizes." This was not quite true; at least, the issue of religious faith had not occurred to Leviticus in either way; he was not committed to the religion, not quite against it either, it did not matter enough . . . but he had gathered from particularly reliable reports going through the congregation that one of the best ways of getting out of the ark was to plead a lack of faith. Perhaps he had gotten it wrong. The rabbi looked at him for a long time, and finally, drawing his robes tightly around him, retreating to the wall, looked at Leviticus as if he were a repulsed object. "Then perhaps your stay in the ark will do you some good," he had said; "it will enable you to find time for meditation and prayer. Also, religious belief has nothing to do with the role of the tenant. Does the wine in the goblet conceive of the nature of the sacrament it represents? In the same way, the tenant is merely the symbol."

"I haven't been feeling well," Leviticus mumbled. "I've been having chest pains. I've been having seizures of doubt. Cramps in the lower back; I don't think that I can—"

"Yes you can," the rabbi said with a dreadful expression, *"and yes you will,"* and had sent Leviticus out into the cold and casting light of the settlement, beginning to come to terms with the realization that he could not, could not under any circumstances, escape the obligation thrust upon him. Perhaps he had been foolish to have thought that he could. Perhaps he should not have paid credence to the rumors. He returned to his cubicle in a foul temper, set the traps to *privacy* and sullenly put through the tape of the *Union Prayer Book, Revised Edition: For the High Holy Days.* If you really were going to have to do something like this, he guessed that a little bit of hard background wouldn't hurt. But it made no sense. The writings simply made no sense. He shut off the tapes and for a long time gave no further thought to any of this, until the morning, when, in absolute disbelief, he found the elders in his unit, implacable in their costume, come to take him to the ark. *Tallis* and *tefillim.*

III

In the ark, Leviticus ponders his condition while the services go on outside. He has taken to self-pity during his confinement; he has a tendency to snivel a little. It is really not fair for him, a disbelieving man but one who has never made his disbelief a point of contention, to be thrown into such a position, kept there for such an extended period of time. Ritual is important, and he for one is not to say that the enactment of certain rote practices does not lend reassurance, may indeed be a metaphor for some kind of reality which he cannot apprehend . . . but is it right that all of this should be at his expense? He has never entered into disputation with the elders on their standards of belief; why should they force theirs upon him?

A huge volume of the Talmud jabs his buttocks, its cover a painful little concentrated point of pain, and cursing, Leviticus bolts from it, rams his head against the beam forming half of the ceiling of the ark, bends, reaches, seizes the volume, and with all his force hurls it three feet into the flat wall opposite. He has hoped for a really satisfying concussion, some mark of his contempt that will be heard outside of the ark, will impress and disconcert the congregation, but there simply has not been room enough to generate impact; the volume falls softly, turgidly across a knee, and he slaps at it in fury, little puffs of dust coming from the cover, inflaming his sinuses. He curses again, wondering if this apostasy, committed within the very place in which, according to what he understands, the spirit of God dwells, will be sufficient to end his period of torture, release him from this one kind of bondage into at least another, but nothing whatsoever happens.

He could have expected that, he thinks. If the tenant of the ark is indeed symbol rather than substance, then it would not matter what he did here or what he thought; only his presence would matter. And fling volumes of the Talmud, scrape at the Torahs, snivel away as he will, he is nevertheless in residence. Nothing that he can do will make any difference at all; his presence here is the only testament that they will need.

Step by tormenting step Leviticus has been down this path of reasoning-after-apostasy a hundred times during his confinement. Fortunately for him, these are emotional outbursts which he forgets almost upon completion, so that he has no memory of them when he starts upon the next; and this sense of discovery—the renewal of his rage, so to speak, every time afresh—has thus sustained him in the absence of more real benefits and will sustain him yet. Also, during the long night hours when only he is in the temple, he is able to have long, imagined dialogues with God, which to no little degree also sustain him, even if his visualization of God is a narrow and parochial one.

IV

The first time that the doors had been flung open during the adoration and all of the congregation had looked in upon him, Leviticus had become filled with shame, but that quickly passed when he realized that no one really thought anything of it and that the attention of the elders and the congregation was not upon him but upon the sacred scripts that one by one the elders withdrew, brought to the podium, and read with wavering voice and fingers while Leviticus, hunched over naked in an uncomfortable fetal position, could not have been there at all, for all the difference it made. He could have bolted from the ark, flung open his arms, shrieked to the congregation, "Look at me, look at me, don't you see what you're doing!" but he had not; he had been held back in part by fear, another part by constraint, still a third part from the realization that no one in the ark had ever done it. He had never seen it happen; back through all the generations that he was able to seek through accrued knowledge, the gesture was without precedent. The tenant of the ark had huddled quietly throughout the term of his confinement, had kept himself in perfect restraint when exposed; why should this not continue? Tradition and the awesome power of the elders had held him in check. He could not interrupt the flow of the services. He could deal with the predictable, which was a term of confinement and then release, just like everyone who had preceded him, but what he could not control was any conception of the unknown. If he made a spectacle of himself during the adoration, there was no saying what might happen then. The elders might take vengeance upon him. They might turn away from the thought of vengeance and simply declare that his confinement be extended for an indefinite period for apostasy. It was very hard to tell exactly *what* they would do. This fear of the unknown, Leviticus had decided through his nights of pondering and imaginary dialogue, was probably what had enabled the situation to go on as long as it had.

It was hard to say exactly when he had reached the decision that he could no longer accept his position, his condition, his fate, wait out the time of his confinement, entertain the mercy of the elders, and return to the congregation. It was hard to tell at exactly what point he had realized that he could not do this; there was no clear point of epiphany, no moment at which—unlike a religious conversion—he could see himself as having gone outside the diagram of possibility, unutterably changed. All that he knew was that the decision had slowly crept into him, perhaps when he was sleeping, and without a clear point of definition, had reached absolute firmness: he would confront them at the adoration now. He would force them to look at him. He would show them what he, and by implication they, had become: so trapped within a misunderstood tradition, so wedged within the suffocating confines of the ark that they had lost any overriding sense of purpose, the ability to perceive wholly the madness that they and the elders had perpetuated. He would force them to understand this as the sum point of their lives, and when it was over, he would bolt from the synagogue naked, screaming, back to his cubicle, where he would reassemble his clothing and make final escape from the complex . . . and leave *them*, not him, to decide what they would now make of the shattered ruins of their lives.

The long period of confinement, self-examination, withdrawal, and physical privation had, perhaps, made Leviticus somewhat unstable.

V

Just before the time when the elders had appeared and had taken him away, Leviticus had made his last appeal, not to them, certainly not to the rabbi, but to Stala, who had shared to a certain point his anguish and fear of entrapment. "I don't see why I have to go there," he said to her, lying tight in the instant after fornication. "It's stupid. It's sheer mysticism. And besides that, it hasn't any relevance."

"But you must go," she said, putting a hand on his cheek. "You have been asked, and you *must*." She was not stupid, he thought, merely someone who had never had to question assumptions, as he was now being forced to. "It is ordained. It won't be that bad; you're supposed to learn a lot."

"*You* go."

She gave a little gasping intake of breath and rolled from him. "You know that's impossible," she said. "Women can't go."

"In the reform tradition they can."

"But we're not in the reform tradition," she said; "this is the high Orthodox."

"I tend to think of it more in the line of being progressive."

"You know, Leviticus," she said, sitting, breathing unevenly—he could see her breasts hanging from her in the darkness like little scrolls, *like little scrolls,* oh, his confinement was very much on his mind, he could see—"it's just ridiculous that you should say something like that to me, that you should even *suggest* it. We're talking about our tradition now, and our tradition is very clear on this point, and it's impossible for a woman to go. Even if she wanted, she just couldn't—"

"All right," he said, "all right."

"No," Stala said, "no I won't stop discussing this, *you* were the one to raise it, Leviticus, not me, and I just won't have any of it. I didn't think you were that kind of person. I thought that you accepted the traditions, that you believed in them; in fact, it was an encouragement to me to think, to really think, that I had found someone who believed in a pure, solid unshaken way, and I was really *proud* of you, even prouder when I found that you had been selected, but now you've changed everything. I'm beginning to be afraid that the only reason you believed in the traditions was because they weren't causing you any trouble and you didn't have to sacrifice yourself personally, but as soon as you became involved, you moved away from them." She was standing now, moving toward her robe, which had been tossed in the fluorescence at the far end of his cubicle; looking toward it during intercourse, he had thought that the sight of it was the most tender and affecting thing he had ever known, that she had cast her garments aside for him, that she had committed herself trustfully in nakedness against him for the night, and all of this despite the fact that he was undergoing what he took to be the positive humiliation of the confinement; now, as she flung it angrily on herself, he wondered if he had been wrong, if that casting aside had been a gesture less tender than fierce, whether or not she might have been—and he could hardly bear this thought, but one must after all, press on—perversely excited by images of how he would look naked and drawn in upon himself in the ark, his genitals clamped between his thighs, talmudic statements by the rabbis Hill and Ben Bag Bag his only companions in the many long nights to come. He did not want to think of it, did not want to see her in this new perspective, and so leaped to his feet, fleet as a hart, and said, "But it's not fair. I tell you, it isn't fair."

"Of course it isn't fair. That's why it's so beautiful."

"Well, how would *you* like it? How would *you* like to be confined in—"

"Leviticus," she said, "I don't want to talk to you about this any more. Leviticus," she added, "I think I was wrong about you, you've hurt me very much. Leviticus," she concluded, "if you don't leave me right now, this moment, I'll go to the elders and tell them exactly what you're saying and thinking, and you know what will happen to you *then*," and he had let her go, nothing else to do, the shutter of his cubicle coming open, the passage of her body halving the light from the hall, then the light exposed again, and she was gone; he closed the shutter, he was alone in his cubicle again.

"It *isn't* fair," he said aloud. "She wouldn't like it so much if this was Reform and *she* were faced with the possibility of going in there someday," but this gave him little comfort; in fact, it gave him no comfort at all. It seemed to lead him right back to where he had started—futile, amazed protest at the injustice and folly of what was being done for him—and he had gone into an unhappy sleep thinking that something, something would have to be done

about this; perhaps he could take the case out of the congregation.
If the ordinators were led to understand what kind of rites were
being committed in the name of high Orthodoxy, they would take a
strong position against this, seal up the complex, probably scatter
the congregation throughout a hundred other complexes . . . and it
was this which had given him ease, tossed him into a long murmur-
ing sleep replete with satisfaction that he had finally found a way
to deal with this (because he knew instinctively that the ordinators
would *not* like this), but the next morning, cunningly, almost as if
they had been informed by Stala (perhaps they had), the elders
had come to take him to the ark, and that had been the end of that
line of thought. He supposed that he could still do it, complain to
the ordinators—that was, after his confinement was over—but at
that point it hardly seemed worth it. It hardly seemed worth it at
all. For one thing, he would be out of the ark by then and would
not have to face it for a very, very long time, if ever. So why bother
with the ordinators? He would have to take a more direct position,
take it up with the congregation itself. Surely once they understood
his agony, they could not permit it to continue. Could they?

VI

In the third of his imaginary dialogues with God (whom he pic-
tured as an imposing man, somewhat the dimensions of one of the
elders but much more neatly trimmed and not loaded down with
the paraphernalia with which they conducted themselves) Leviticus said, "I don't believe any of it. Not any part of it at all. It's ridiculous.

"Doubt is another part of faith," God said. "Doubt and belief in-
tertwine; both can be conditions of reverence. There is more divin-
ity in the doubt of a wise man than in the acceptance of fools."

"That's just rhetoric," Leviticus said; "it explains nothing."

"The devices of belief must move within the confines of rhetoric,"
God said. "Rhetoric is the poor machinery of the profound and in-
controvertible. Actually, it's not a matter of doubt. You're just very
uncomfortable."

"That's right. I'm uncomfortable. I don't see why Judaism im-
poses this kind of suffering."

"Religion *is* suffering," God said with a modest little laugh, "and if you think Judaism is difficult upon its participants, you should get a look at some of the *others* sometimes. Animal sacrifice, immolation, the ceremony of tongues. Oh, most terrible! Not that everyone doesn't have a right to their point of view," God added hastily. "Each must reach me, each in his way and through his tradition. Believe me, Leviticus, you haven't got the worst of it."

"I protest. I protest this humiliation."

"It isn't easy for me, either," God pointed out. "I've gone through cycles of repudiation for billions of years. Still, one must go on."

"I've got to get out of here. It's destroying my health; my physical condition is ruined. When am I going to leave?"

"I'm sorry," God said, "that decision is not in my hands."

"But you're omnipotent."

"My omnipotence is only my will working through the diversity of twenty billion other wills. Each is determined, and yet each is free."

"That sounds to me like a lousy excuse," Leviticus said sullenly. "I don't think that makes any sense at all."

"I do the best I can," God said, and after a long, thin pause added sorrowfully, "You don't think that any of this is easy for me either, do you?"

VII

Leviticus has the dim recollection from the historical tapes, none of them well attended to, that before the time of the complexes, before the time of great changes, there had been another kind of existence, one during which none of the great churches, Judaism included, had been doing particularly well in terms of absolute number of participants, relative proportion of the population. Cults had done all right, but cults had had only the most marginal connection to the great churches, and in most cases had repudiated them, leading, in the analyses of certain of the historical tapes, to the holocaust that had followed, and the absolute determination on the part of the Risen, that they would not permit this to happen again, that they would not allow the cults to appropriate all of the energy, the empirical demonstrations, for themselves, but instead would make sure that the religions were reconverted to hard ritual, that the ritual demonstrations following would be strong and convincing enough to keep the cults out of business and through true worship and true belief (although with enough ritual now to satisfy the mass of people that religion could be made visible) stave off yet another holocaust. At least, this was what Leviticus had *gathered* from the tapes, but then, you could never be sure about this, and the tapes were all distributed under the jurisdiction of the elders anyway, and what the elders would do with material to manipulate it to their own purposes was well known.

Look, for one thing, at what they had done to Leviticus.

VIII

"I'll starve in here," he had said to the elders desperately, as they were conveying him down the aisle toward the ark. "I'll deteriorate. I'll go insane from the confinement. If I get ill, no one will be there to help me."

"Food will be given you each day. You will have the Torah and the Talmud, the Feast of Life itself to comfort you and to grant you peace. You will allow the spirit of God to move within you."

"That's ridiculous," Leviticus said. "I told you, I have very little belief in any of this. How can the spirit—?"

"Belief means nothing," the elders said. They seemed to speak in unison, which was impossible, of course (how could they have such a level of shared anticipation of the others' remarks; rather, it was that they spoke one by one, with similar voice quality—*that* would be a more likely explanation of the phenomenon, mysticism having, so far as Leviticus knew, very little relation to rational Judaism). "You are its object, not its subject."

"Aha!" Leviticus said then, frantically raising one finger to forestall them as they began to lead him painfully into the ark, pushing him, tugging, buckling his limbs. "If belief does not matter, if I am merely object rather than subject, *then how can I be tenanted by the spirit?*"

"That," the elders said, finishing the job, patting him into place, one of them extracting a rag to whip the wood of the ark speedily to high gloss, cautiously licking a finger, applying it to the surface to take out an imagined particle of dust, "that is very much your problem and not ours, you see," and closed the doors upon him, leaving him alone with scrolls and Talmud, cloth, and the sound of scrambling birds. In a moment he heard a grinding noise as key was inserted into lock, then a snap as tumblers inverted. They were locking him in.

Well, he had known that. That, at least, was not surprising. Tradition had its roots; the commitment to the ark was supposed to be voluntary—a joyous expression of commitment, that was; the time spent in the ark was supposed to be a time of repentance and great interior satisfaction. . . . But all of that to one side, the elders, balancing off the one against the other, as was their wont, arriving at a careful and highly modulated view of the situation, had ruled in their wisdom that it was best to keep the ark locked at all times, excepting, of course, the adoration. That was the elders for you. They took everything into account, and having done *that*, made the confinement, as they said, his problem.

IX

Now the ritual of the Sabbath evening service is over, and the rabbi is delivering his sermon. Something about the many rivers of Judaism, each of them individual, flowing into that great sea of tradition and belief. The usual material. Leviticus knows that this is the Sabbath service; he can identify it by certain of the prayers and chants, although he has lost all extrinsic sense of time, of course, in the ark. For that matter, he suspects, the elders have lost all extrinsic sense of time as well; it is no more Friday now than Thursday or Saturday, but at a certain arbitrary time after the holocaust, he is given to understand, the days, the months, the years themselves were re-created and assigned, and therefore, if the elders say it is Friday, it is Friday, just as if they say it is the year thirty-seven, it is the year thirty-seven, and not fifty seven hundred something or other, or whatever it was when the holocaust occurred. (In his mind, as a kind of shorthand, he has taken to referring to the holocaust as the H; the H did this; certain things happened to cause the H, but he is not sure that this would make sense to other people, and as a matter of fact wonders whether or not this might not be the sign of a deranged consciousness.) Whatever the elders say it is, it is, although God in the imaginary dialogues has assured him that the elders, in their own fashion, are merely struggling with the poor tools at their command and are no less fallible than he, Leviticus.

He shall take upon himself, in any event, these commandments, and shall bind them for frontlets between his eyes. After the sermon, when the ark is opened for the adoration, he will lunge from it and confront them with what they have become, with what they have made of him, with what together they have made of God. He will do that, and for signposts upon his house as well, that they shall remember and do those commandments and be holy. Holy, holy. Oh, their savior and their hope, they have been worshiping him as their fathers did in ancient days, but enough of this, quite enough; the earth being his dominion and all the beasts and fish thereof, it is high time that some sort of reckoning of the changes be made.

Highly unfair, Leviticus thinks, crouching, awaiting the opening of the ark, but then again, he must (as always) force himself to see all sides of the question: very possibly, if Stala had approved of his position, had granted him sympathy, had agreed with him that what the elders were doing was unjust and unfair . . . well, then, he might have been far more cheerfully disposed to put up with his fate. If only she, if only someone, had seen him as a martyr rather than as a usual part of a very usual process. Everything might have changed, but then again, it might have been the same.

X

The book of Daniel, he recollects, had been very careful and very precise in giving, with numerology and symbol, the exact time when the H would begin. Daniel had been specific; he had alluded to precisely that course of events at which period of time that would signal the coming (or the second coming, depending upon your pursuit); the only trouble with it was that there had been so many conflicting interpretations over thousands of years that for all intents and purposes the predictive value of Daniel for the H had been lost; various interpreters saw too many signs of rising in the East, too many beasts of heaven, stormings of the tabernacle, too many uprisings among the cattle or the chieftains to enable them to get the H down right, once and for all. A lot of them, hence, had been embarrassed; many cults, hinged solely upon their interpretation of Daniel and looking for an apocalyptic date, had gotten themselves overcommitted, and going up on the mountaintops to await the end, had lost most of their membership.

Of course, the H had come, and with it the floods, the falling, the rising and the tumult in the lands, and it was possible that Daniel had gotten it precisely right, after all, if only you could look back on it in retrospect and get it right, but as far as Leviticus was concerned, there was only one overriding message that you might want to take from the tapes if you were interested in this kind of thing: you did not want to pin it down too closely. Better, as the elders did, to kind of leave the issue indeterminate and in flux. Better, as God himself had (imaginarily) pointed out, to say that doubt is merely the reverse coin of belief, both of them motes in the bowels of the Hound of Heaven.

XI

The rabbi, adoring the ever-living God and rendering praise unto him, inserts the key into the ark, the tumblers fall open, the doors creak and gape, and Leviticus finds himself once again staring into the old man's face, his eyes congested with pain as he reaches in trembling toward one of the scrolls, his cheeks dancing in the light, the elders grouped behind him attending carefully; and instantly Leviticus strikes: he reaches out a hand, yanks the rabbi out of the way, and then tumbles from the ark. He had meant to leap but did not realize how shriveled his muscles would be from disuse; what he had intended to be a vault is instead a collapse to the stones under the ark, but yet he is able to move. He is able to move. He pulls himself falteringly to hands and knees, gasping, the rabbi mumbling in the background, the elders looking at him with shocked expressions, too astonished for the instant to move. The instant now is all that he needs. He has not precipitated what he has done in the hope of having a great deal of time.

"Look at me!" Leviticus shrieks, struggling erect, hands hanging, head shaking. "Look at me, look at what I've become, look at what dwells in the heart of the ark!" And indeed, they are looking, all of them, the entire congregation, Stala in the women's section, hand to face, palm open, extended, all of them stunned in the light of his gaze. "Look at me!" he shouts again. "You can't do this to people, do you understand that? You cannot do it!" And the elders come upon him, recovered from their astonishment, to seize him with hands like metal, the rabbi rolling and rolling on the floor, deep into some chant that Leviticus cannot interpret, the congregation gathered now to rush upon him; but too late, it has (as he must at

some level have known) been too late, from the beginning, and as
the rabbi chants, the elders strain, the congregation rushes . . .
time inverts, and the real, the long-expected, the true H with its
true Host begins.

AFTERWORD TO LEVITICUS: IN THE ARK

The character of Leviticus of course is a perfect metaphor for
that of the author, and his condition of entrapment, waiting for the
Magic Incantation which will spill him free from the Holy of
Holies, already is similar to that of the author around the time of
the *Musaf* service on the afternoon of Yom Kippur. Let it be done,
let it be done. Still, rigor and confinement are good for one (or at
least good for *me*) and a little bit of pain never hurt an honest
man. I can't think of anywhere I would rather be than in synagogue
during the High Holy Days.

I have written elsewhere of my curious reluctance, for many
years, to get near the Judaic issue in my fiction, an avoidance the
more inexplicable because I have been writing stories of a religious
theme almost from the beginning and one of my best novels, *The
Confessions of Westchester County*, is seated of all things upon a
scholastic Catholicism. Maybe I felt I had nothing to add to the
monstrous available body of American Jewish fiction, maybe I did
not want to get too close into something that was more central than
I wanted to admit. I am still not sure of this. In any event, starting
in May of 1972 I loosened up just a bit and there is another story of
Judaic theme, of course, earlier in this volume.

Robert Silverberg, co-editor of the original anthology for which
this was written, said that although the sire of "Leviticus" was
Judaic, the dam was Heinlein, which had not previously occurred
to me. He was quite right of course. (Silverberg has been wrong, in
fact, exactly twice in all the years I have known him.) The synagogue of this story, in fact, is the Mars of *Double Star* and Leviticus
is Lorenzo making pilgrimage to the Martians. Since I had long admired that novel—I think it is the best Heinlein ever published and

I am an admirer of much of his work—I was surprised to have to have this brought to my attention.

Leave not, by the way, Heinlein's more recent and slowly weakening work cause readers to miss the point: this man in the forties and fifties was no fool and close to the best writer of them all. He had a perfect sense of how the world, before Hiroshima, worked and a great deal of artistic integrity as well. His best work may well outlast us all.

Rage, Pain, Alienation
and Other Aspects of the
Writing of Science Fiction

The end of Intelligent Writing: Literary Politics In America, By
Richard Kostelanetz. Sheed & Ward, $12.95; New York, 1974; 434
pp. plus bibliography and index.

Kostelanetz's basic theory, articulated over several chapters and
with an occasional awesome specificity, is that a small cabal of
(mostly Jewish) intellectuals now in their fifties and sixties seized
control of the major publishing/critical/review outlets shortly after
World War II, exert something approaching complete control over
those who would have a major career in American letters and *won't
let anyone new in*. Most specifically, Kostelanetz (himself now
thirty-six) claims that almost no American writer under forty has
been able to achieve a wide audience for serious work much less
critical acknowledgement; with the exceptions of Renata Adler,
Joyce Carol Oates and Thomas Pynchon (two women and an
enigma) the youngest American writers of high reputation are
Phillip Roth and Susan Sontag, both over forty.

The cabal, Kostelanetz states, has erased almost all competing
schools—the southern agrarian, the old New England Protestant—
by taking over the careers of a few of its more noted members and
ignoring or suppressing the work of others. The most devastating
weapon available to this cabal—which stretches from the offices of
Random House to those of the *Partisan Review* to the editorships of
many of the mass magazines like *Harper's* to the offices of certain
literary agents to the *New York Review of Books* and the *Sunday
Times Book Review*—is not to attack but to ignore, and its hold
upon the small, tempestuous world which controls access to the ob-
servable literary media is so complete that it can virtually create,
suspend or deny reputations as effortlessly as it can convene a cock-

tail party . . . at which most of the real business is contracted anyway.

The book was rather guiltily and prominently reviewed in most
of the media which Kostelanetz attacks in a kind of unanimity of
two-pronged response: 1) Mr. Kostelanetz is just jealous and envious of those who have succeeded; there is no cabal, just a bunch of
nice, mutually helpful people some with common roots who are always looking for good new writers and good new work, just can't
find enough of it but we're so fair-minded that we're reviewing this
book right here, and 2) anyway, all those mostly unknown writers
who Kostelanetz cites as being starved out of the markets aren't any
good anyway, judging from the excerpts of their work he quotes.
He just wants to promote his coterie which is less talented than
those coteries which have made it, not that there are any coteries at
all, of course. We're all just good friends here.

The book then disappeared into the basements of libraries
(which is where I picked up my copy a year after publication) and
to the remainder tables; it has never been paperbacked to my
knowledge and has had no visible influence upon the course of the
markets to say nothing of the people most concerned with it, those
cited in *The End of Intelligent Writing* as being denied a future.
The unknowns are still unknown, the unpublished still unpublished,
the critically ignored and forgotten (Cecil Dawkins, Leon Rook)
not yet selected for the Modern Library.

I came to this book late because of my almost automatic hostility
toward what I took to be its central thesis (that the author's friends
were being denied, but that if this situation were to reverse itself
they would deny others; in short there was no objection to the system, merely its misapplication in the author's case) and my own
suspicion that, since I am a commercial "pop" writer, Kostelanetz
would regard me as being even a step further down the rung from
the nexus and their excluded; as someone simply not worth men-
tioning or campaigning for at all. I was partially right but mostly
wrong on both of these rather knee-jerk reactions, and I wish that I
had come to this book a long time ago and I recommend it fer-
vently to each and every one of you who buy this magazine for any
reason other than to get through the next hour or so (not an objec-
tionable reason at all; these are the readers who have kept science
fiction alive) because it has a heart of darkness and a true message:
we, meaning those who toil in the wilted vineyards of commercial

fiction, may soon enough be the only ones left to perpetuate the form. If there are any left at all.

This is not quite what I wanted to say here however—nor did I want to spend much time investigating Kostelanetz, who seems to be essentially right although wrongheaded in many ways and in shocking ignorance of science fiction in particular. (For instance he says "Of the periodicals founded in the late sixties by paperback publishers, the best of the lot, Delany and Hacker's *Quark* died much too soon after auspiciously introducing not only several good young writers but a valid new development in s-f that combines modernist literary values with speculative intelligence," an incredible hash of misstatement since *Quark* was not the best of the original anthologies but very likely the worst, was in a part a coterie publication for friends of the editors and collapsed while leaving the market for original anthologies as viable as it ever has been. He also includes several s-f writers in his list of four hundred writers born after 1937 to "watch" but manages to ignore Norman Spinrad while putting in Lawrence Yep, put in Panshin while neglecting Effinger, put in Terry Champagne while ignoring Dozois. Not critical judgment; ignorance is operating here.) No, in truth and upon the occasion of the publication in the same magazine that published my story "Final War" eight years ago to the day and gave me my career of what will be my last science-fiction story . . . actually I wanted to talk about myself.

Bet you never thought I'd get there.

"Seeking Assistance" will not be the last s-f story I will ever publish, I fear; several written earlier remain in the inventories of editors like Silverberg and Elwood. It is, however, in point of chronology the last I will ever write, and publishing it here in the magazine which has been central to my career, under the editorship of the man who, along with his late father Joseph Wolfe has been instrumental in keeping me psychically above ground seems the proper thing to do. I would have it no other way.

Reading *The End of Intelligent Writing* took me back ten years in time. It took me back past my decision in January of 1975 to cease writing science fiction; it took me past 1973 when I won the Campbell Award and was able for a brief period to sell as much s-f as I wanted at higher advances; it took me back twenty-two novels and a hundred and fifty short stories and the struggle to achieve what I am now deserting, to 1965 when my misguided and somewhat tragic career in science fiction began as the result of conscious decision.

Exposed in the early sixties in sub-acute form to the reality which Kostelanetz chapter, by angry chapter documents, I realized by June of 1965 that it would be impossible for me to make a career in what was my field of choice: as a literary writer. The quarterlies were impenetrable, the coteries omnipresent, the competition murderous, the stultifying control of the publishing houses' literary editors absolute. If I was ever going to achieve outlet as a writer of fiction, I saw I would have to go to the commercial markets, the mass or genre markets that is to say, and while partially converting myself to the strictures of category fiction *sneak in* my literary intentions.

Science fiction was what I chose because from the outset science fiction seemed to be that field in which one could sell stories of modest literary intention with the least amount of slanting: one could, if one touched the base of stricture, be paid a living wage for somewhat ambitious work. Historically the field has been open to new writers and approaches in a way that, say, the mystery never has been. Almost from the beginning I was a "success," that is in terms of my original ambition. As a writer who could write a little in a field where almost no one could write at all, as enough of a cynical hack to purposefully manipulate my work and as one who had an excellent understanding of the field by virtue of childhood reading (indispensable to any who would write a lot of this stuff) I was able, I say in all due modesty, to produce a body of work which is without parallel, quantitatively, in the history of the field. In less than seven years I sold the aforementioned number of works, about two million words in all, I won a major award, I even, for a brief period in 1973/4 had the exhilarating experience of *almost* making a living from the writing of s-f alone. (Only almost. And more than half of my published output has been out of the field from the outset.)

But, I discovered, I was *invisible* outside of the confines of the s-f market itself. Of course that was what I had wanted, what had attracted me to the field. Kostelanetz's academic/literary nexus either does not know we exist or patronizes us as pulp hacks for escapist kids; in any case they leave us alone and enable us to be probably the only medium (but less so than in years past) for dangerous, ambitious work. But if you win, you lose; my ambition had turned upon itself. I had beaten the system by getting out of the system, but the system wouldn't be beaten after all because it would not acknowledge that I existed and that made my work meaningless. Also I was getting knifed up pretty good *inside* s-f. Ambitious writers always do; historically the field has silenced or reduced to ineffectiveness its best writers. There is not a single American s-f writer over the age of forty-five, whose work is the equal of what it was a decade ago, if it even exists.

So there I was: devil and the deep blue sea.

Denied as a literary writer, loathed and largely isolated within s-f. Let us sit upon the ground and tell sad stories of the death of kings. Let us shed one tear and no more. Have mercy, friends, I suffered.

But I also decided to get out. Where yet I am not sure; perhaps to the field of the commercial novel, perhaps into something else, perhaps into light manufacturing or the processing of ceramic mix. Who is to say? One way or the other I will work my way through; I always have, this is my problem and not that of my audience (which, although small by s-f standards has been huge by literary standards and surprisingly loyal. Thank you all very much.) I am not to burden you. I come not to discomfit.

I come, folks, only to say, that this is for the last time: I am getting out. Kostelanetz, like all the rest of humanity, is a mixture of the good and the bad; he is right and he is wrong, he is dull and he is brilliant but the argument holds and so does mine. No future here. Perhaps no future for writing in our time. But thank you all very much.

AFTERWORD

December 6, 1975: On this date, the first copies of my 38-story, 160,000 word Pocket Books collection, *The Best of Barry N. Malzberg* are available and in my hands and having them forces, in all fairness, a postscript to this bitter essay.

It is true that I must leave science fiction. As the vise of the seventies comes down upon all of us in every field of the so-called arts, there is almost no room left for the kind of work which I try to do. But it is also true that this collection—which is a major effort of at least intermittent literary intention and execution—would not even exist, nor would the career it capsules, have come to be had it not been for science fiction, which gave me a market, an audience, and a receptivity to my work that I would never have found elsewhere. In this sense I owe my career and large pieces of my personal life as well to science fiction. (Such a career as it has been.)

Where else could an unknown writer whose only virtues (other than a modicum of talent) were energy, prolificity and a gathering professionalism be able to write and sell twenty-three novels and five collections of some literary intention in a period of less than eight years? Even if I had satisfied my original ambitions I would have been dealing with a market which held me back, not only quantitatively but in terms of "artistic" growth. The only limits which s-f imposed upon me (until 8/74 when the bottom fell out) were those framed by my willingness or unwillingness to turn out work of such pretension for what was, inevitably, an audience not intersecting with the academic/literary nexus. That is not a very large sin on the scale of things. Not at all.

I want to make it clear on December 6, 1975: I *love* this field. My debt to it is incalculable. What has happened to writers like myself, Silverberg, Ballard, Disch, is not the fault of the category itself (which allowed us to go as far as we wanted artistically for a while) or necessarily even the audience. The fault, as in most other aspects of America, is in what has happened to squeeze diversity from our culture in the last five years. I was either twenty years too late or twenty years too early for this kind of work: even so—didn't I?—I got the work done.

And some of it, dammit, will live.

Down Here in the
Dream Quarter

For the dream always lay central to the literature, the literature began in dreams. Rip Van Winkle and the horseman of the hollow, the deerslayer moving deathly still through all the forests of the mind, Huck pulling Jim from the terrible river. Sister Carrie in Chicago rocking and rocking away her mortality, eyes closed, the stare inward toward what she might have been, might still become. Hemingway's laughing Indian, the red badge of courage for those who fled the cannon. They came to America in full pursuit, empty for the continent and somewhere between the other our dreams, our machines, our literature, the engines of our power whispered that they were the same.

The land and our pain merged.

But it was in 1926, a hundred and fifty years down the dark way before the dream was labelled, lopped off: a radio engineer named Gernsback owned a publishing house and from his desire to promote scientific careers for teenage boys came the first issue of *Amazing Stories:* it went on sale for the first time fifty years ago this month. *Scientifiction* was Gernsback's term for what he was publishing and he ran reprints of Wells and Verne in the hope that a new and special literature of scientific device would come from Americans . . . a literature which would advance the cause of science lo! even unto the bedrooms of Forest Hills or the midwest and would make those wonders and possibilities not frightening but beautiful. The headless horseman had a name, Irving's dusky and mysterious river ran through factory-lined banks. It had a name and slowly, slowly in the second quarter of the century of print and machines the wheels moved, ah they moved.

Amazing lurched through a few years, failed, was sold to Tek Publications, picked up again. *Astounding* joined it in January of 1930, failed for George Clayton, was picked up by Street & Smith in 1933. Continued. John Campbell succeeded Orlin Tremaine there. Other magazines followed in the mid to late thirties, one of them

Gernsback's own *Wonder Stories*. Letter columns, fandom, conventions. Ray Cumming's golden atom blew up in 1945. Suddenly there were anthologies, hardcover novels, paperback novels, forty other magazines in the nineteen fifties, hundreds more novels, millions of readers. A science-fiction world. Gernsback died forty years after it had begun. Campbell died in 1971. Most of the magazines died. The novels had not. The writers had not. *Amazing* had not. It is fifty years old today; a quarter as old as America, the cerebrum has one quarter the bulk of the old brain. Will s-f live to be a hundred? It is very difficult to say: for one thing, will America make two hundred and fifty? Who is to say? Who can know? We congregate; we have survived. We are the people. We are here. *Let us now praise famous men.*

Let us now praise famous men and our fathers that begat us: Let us praise Gernsback who believed that science was good and knowledge power; let us praise Harry Bates who gave Clayton *Astounding* and wrote *Farewell to the Master* about a kind machine. And F. Orlin Tremaine, Ray Cummings, Clifford Simak, Will F. Jenkins and Jack Williamson, the last three originators who had not one but three careers as they followed the dream where it would. Let us praise John Wood Campbell who called it literature, knew it had to be literature if it would survive and in the intimation both served and shielded us from fate because if it had not been for Campbell science fiction after all might have died at the end of the nineteen thirties or at the latest by the early fifties along with all the other categories of pulp fiction. Remember that if Gernsback was the rock then it was Campbell who was the prophet giving the spirit life, and whatever errors he might have made as time froze upon him, there would have been none of us today without him. We would have been utterly scattered, would not have known the language of our longing.

Remember Harl Vincent, Raymond Z. Gallun, Arthur K. Barnes and all the others who tended the light before Campbell came to shape it. Remember Stanley Weinbaum who would have been only in his early seventies right now and who might have been the best of them all just as he was the best in his own time.

They have wrought great glory by them through his great power from the beginning: And Campbell wrought great glory through them. Name the names who brought the machinery to life. Heinlein who understood it all almost too early, Asimov and del Rey and de Camp and van Vogt—van Vogt who knew that at the center of the century lurked a thing without a face that killed for profit, del Rey who knew of the near, foreign places, de Camp who knew that the future, not only the past, was archaeology, was lived in the interstices of the human condition. And Kuttner, tragic Henry Kuttner and beautiful Catherine Moore whose range knew no apparent limits and who gave us "Gallegher and Fury" and the "Private Eye." Is anybody listening? Is any of this important? Does any of this make a difference? Who writes this kind of crap? Who reads this kind of crap? Ask Sturgeon of "Thunder and Roses" and "Killdozer." Ask Cleve Cartmill who deduced the Bomb and published a 1944 story, "Deadline." The bomb fell. Now many of us began to understand that they might be living in the end of days: that there were very possibly people on the planet at that time who might see the end of humanity.

And they met at Potsdam. The editorship of *Amazing* fell to Raymond Palmer. Gernsback was out of the business; he thought he had found a Better Way. He was publishing *Sexology* now. Groff Conklin, Raymond Healey, Francis McComas appeared with the first great postwar anthologies. *And they all had great power from the beginning.* Phillip Klass. Tom Sherred who noted that the most wonderful of inventions would be seized by governments to corrupt and kill. Judith Merrill. Eric Frank Russell. A. Bertram Chandler. Peter Phillips. Dreams are sacred.

All were honoured in their generations and were the glory of their times: Cyril Kornbluth, Frederick Pohl, Robert Sheckley, Damon Knight, James Blish, Edgar Pangborn, James Gunn, all of these writers who the new magazines, the new audience, the new, quieter horrors of the fifties brought into the field. *All of them were honoured in their generations.* Alfred Bester who won the first Hugo award for *The Demolished Man.* Sturgeon and *More Than Human* for the International Fantasy Award. Sturgeon again. *More Than Human* always. Horace Gold, the first editor of *Galaxy*, perhaps the greatest editor in the history of all fields for the first half of his tenure: ah, Horace, who saw history as spite. Boucher and McComas who desired grace although grace was hard bought in the decade of Ike, the Starfire and Edsel, Army-McCarthy and Levittown. And the Four Coins. Adlai was out of joint. Phillip K.

Dick and *Solar Lottery*. Kris Neville and Katherine MacLean and Roger Aycock and Robert Flint Young. Hubbard, the redhead, scooted off into dianetics, Campbell in mourning took up parapsychology, the Hieronymus and Dean Drives. Raymond Palmer took Shaver to *Other Worlds* and the editorship of *Amazing* came to Howard Browne who gave s-f Mickey Spillane. Still, *Amazing* sold 150,000 copies in those years, fifteen times its initial circulation, maybe more than *Astounding* and *Galaxy* together. Persistence of myth. *Surface Tension. A Case of Conscience. The Issue at Hand.* F. L. Wallace. Slowly and painfully a small group of writers in this decade were struggling toward the realization that it might be art, that work could be done in it to equal the best work anywhere. They got together and talked about it a lot. *The Space Merchants.* "Preferred Risk." "When You're Smiling" and "Time Waits for Winthrop." "Crucifixus Etiam." The awards became institutionalized, the conventions were international. Attendance went over a thousand. Donald Wolheim built Ace Books. *They were the glory of their times.* Walter Miller, Jr. and Jerome Bixby and "The Quest for St. Aquin." *For their light has gone out all over the lands and as if in a shout we praise them. A Canticle for Leibowitz.* A. J. Budrys.

There be of them that have left a name behind them . . . and some there might be which have no memorial: who perished as though they had never been and are become as they had never been born but whose righteousness hath not been forgotten: with their seed shall continually remain a good inheritance. Mark Clifton, Roger Phillips Graham, Cyril M. Kornbluth, P. Schuyler Miller, Henry Kuttner, Charles R. Tanner, Miriam Allen deFord. Will F. Jenkins, Stanley Weinbaum, Malcolm Jameson, James Blish, John W. Campbell, Jr. Time has turned for science fiction as for the century and America: now the field enters the time of its necrology. It was always, here is the pain, such a *young* field, created spontaneously in 1926, its first practitioners starting off so early that in the nineteen fifties most of the elder statesmen had not yet left their forties and because of this, because almost everyone who had ever written science-fiction was still writing it now it was a *happy* field, that happiness joined to an essentially optimistic vision of the future which some of them believed in, of course some of them did not. *Fred Brown. Harl Vincent.* The critics did not know that the lit-

erature of technology and its effects upon man must at the heart
be pessimistic; they did not know (and we did not then know
either) that what is born even in wonder must also die and at
last, slowly, the layers of the field were peeled back in the late
fifties, the sixties revealing the gnarled and damaged heart. The
magazines died, almost all of them, and the specialty presses folded
but the century went on and so in its way did the field, the course
of it more profoundly paralleling the movement of the century,
twin streams to meet at last in 1976, the first year of the last
quarter of the century of machinery and print. *Charles Beaumont*.

And their children are within the covenant. Rogue Moon and the
Death Machine. "The Man Who Lost the Sea," only the second science fiction story (the first was Judith Merrill's "Dead-Center") to
reach the *Best American Short Stories*. Sturgeon of course. A new
editor at Galaxy, another at *Fantasy & Science Fiction*, that latter
the author of "The Golem," "Or All the Seas with Oysters," "No
Fire Burns": Avram Davidson, the finest short fiction writer of them
all. Randall Garrett and Laurence Janifer and "That Sweet Little
Old Lady" in sweet little old *Astounding*. Gordon Dickson and his
legends of the parapsychic military locked by power the deeper
into the devastated heart. *Amazing* fell to the editorship of Cele G.
Lalli, a litterateur of all things, dangerous stuff for the field, never
more dangerous than for Ziff-Davis in the sixties. Thomas M. Disch
and David R. Bunch and Samuel R. Delaney and Roger Zelazny, all
children of the covenant. Middle-period Silverberg. "To See the Invisible Man," the beginning of his gift. Harlan Ellison. New sounds
from Britain, not from the writers like E. C. Tubb, Arthur Clarke,
Eric Frank Russell who had amalgamated themselves into the
American magazines from the first but a different kind of Briton
now, one who had seen dying Empire and talked of it in certain ur-
gencies, certain poignancies which science fiction could absorb if
not yet, perhaps not ever, understand. Brian Aldiss, J. G. Ballard,
Michael Moorcock: Ballard the best writer of the decade: Ballard a
child of the covenant. James Schmitz and the Telzey series, Schmitz
now in his late forties and at the top of his powers, perhaps the best
extrapolist in the history of the field with the possible exception of
Poul Anderson who took Rip and the River into space. Norman
Spinrad. Alexei Panshin. Anne McCaffrey and Kate Wilhelm who
wrote stories that could have appeared in *Dubliners*. Christopher

Anvil and Jack Wodhams and Lawrence Perkins and Mack Reynolds over in *Astounding*. Ziff-Davis folding *Amazing*. Declining sales. Piers Anthony and Sterling Lanier, the Floridians (Joseph Green, too.) *Amazing* fell into limbo as Ziff-Davis looked for a buyer.

Sol Cohen who had helped save *Galaxy* procured *Amazing*, named Joseph Wrosz editor. Hugo Gernsback in his eighties now received a plaque. Johnson winked and McNamara blushed and Westmoreland marched and the Chiefs of Staff danced and they made us a proper fire and the fire was Vietnam. *Flower of American youth*. Damon Knight revived the Milford Conference and the concept of the original anthology. Bad karma for magazines: *Venture* and *Dimension X* and *Worlds of If* and *Vertex* went right down the tube. But *Amazing* held on. James Tiptree Jr. and Gregory Benford and D. G. Compton and Ursula Krober LeGuin and George Alec Effinger and Gardner Dozois and Robert Thurston. Silverberg was proving the point now; in novel after story after novel he was the best writer of science fiction in terms of technical mastery who had ever lived, without any qualification at all he was one of the best American writers, perhaps the best. Tet happened but Eugene McCarthy did not anyway. King and Kennedy were murdered. *The Book of Skulls*, nevertheless, lives. Apollo gave us the Moon and we were delighted to have seen it (Willy Ley was not, he died a month before the landing; why?) but what many of us did not understand until much later is that our dream had always been more of the River, of the Horseman, than of the Moon. The Moon had only been the reflected light by which our dream, moth-stricken, had danced. Campbell cared of the Moon and Ben Bova and G. Harry Stine and many, many more of us in our own way but the Moon had little enough to do with what had sped us into this field . . . and this in a way might have been the knowledge by which the field, in 1969, began slowly to become very sick: our realization that while we thought we had been drafting blueprints it had only been the *unavailability* of the design which had moved us.

Grissom and the others died on board, in fire. Anthony Boucher died. Hugo Gernsback died. Horace Gold moved to California. Harry Harrison, a good writer, became editor of *Amazing*, struggled to bring it from a reprint policy, passed on the burden to an interim editor after a few months. The interim editor gave it up in turn and in October 1968 Ted White became the last captain of the Caine. His accomplishment speaks for itself; it needs little explication, no defense. Alfred Bester came back. Robert Heinlein had never left. George Zebrowski, Pamela Sargent, Jack M. Dann, Gordon Eklund, P. G. Wyal, Christopher Priest, Gene Wolfe. Nixon walked in, had a long, *long* cup of coffee and walked out. Conventions were now running fifty or sixty a year on the continent and attendance in the multiple thousands was not unusual. Harlan Ellison attended many of them. Wrote pretty good too. Watergate. I have no mouth and I must scream.

John Campbell's successor was Ben Bova. Fred Pohl's successor was Ejler Jakobssen was James Patrick Baen. (Palmer and Browne, a long time coming, were a long time gone.) Ed Ferman completed his eighth, ninth, tenth year as editor of *The Magazine of Fantasy & Science Fiction. Dangerous Visions, Again Dangerous Visions.* Joseph Wolfe Ferman died. James Blish died. Phillip K. Dick was interviewed in *Rolling Stone* as "the best living s-f writer." Could be. Why not? Acceleration, more time, time and the river. 1976, the fifty year issue of *Amazing.* We are fifty years old today and what has become of us? What will become of us?

Their seed shall remain forever and their glory shall not be blotted out: Yea and even if we shall live a hundred years they shall not be forgotten, even those whose names I have forgotten, *Mea Culpa, mea maxima* . . . Joe and Jay Haldeman and Mildred Clingerman and Margaret St. Clair and Reginald Bretnor. Jack Vance. Robert S. Richardson, Bill Pronzini, Howard L. Myers, Christopher Youd. Tom Godwin of "The Cold Equations." Eric St. Clair, Hans Santesson *in memoriam.* Jon Stopa, Oliver Saari, Sylvia Jacobs, Charles Dye *in memoriam.* Charles V. de Vet, Charles Fontenay. Brian Stableford, James Sallis, Pamela Zoline. Vonda McIntyre and Joanna Russ. *Their glory shall not be blotted out.* And what is their glory?

What is the glory of Hugo's children, the engines of his desire? What has brought us to this particular magazine to make peculiar and solemn convocation, all thousands of us, celebrating that from which even the devices of Apollo have come?

Well, folks: I do not know. Ahem. Once I thought I did but that was a long time ago and if despair does not destroy conviction then G 45 chronology alone will. I thought at one time that what these people, that what all of us were trying to do was to find some paradigm of the universe, one which we could encompass in our own time and by this manipulation find immortality but this could be a description of all fiction, all dreams, as true of the mystery as of the rocketship. But I do not now think this is the case.

I thought once that piece by piece in the forties and fifties they were trying to Build A Better World only to find ruin in the sixties and in that ruin the shadow of the field's own fall but I think that this misses also. *Their light has gone out on all nations: it has not died.* (Ron Goulart, Ken Bulmer, Horace Fyfe, H. Beam Piper *in memoriam.*) I do not think that they were in it for the money either because there is very little money in science fiction relative to the effort involved although not as little as what starved out its very best in the decades past. No, none of these answers were quite right.

Now I think it has to do with Rip and the River.

Deep in the darkness of our history lies that river, lies sleeping Rip, sounds the clatter of the horseman over the cobbles of what became devastated New York. Deep in the heart of this strange and tormented country, born of exile, theft, pain and murder still lies the dream, two centuries old now and only another form of *kitsch*. Junk for the Franklin Mints and the bicentennial coins and Little Olde Newe Yorke Candye Barse and yet the dream is not all junk, not all of it . . . if it exists at all it does in science fiction. It may live nowhere else. In their pained, distracted, foolish way Hugo's children may be the last custodians of Irving's America, the America of our past which lies as well as the only alternative to the mindless and electrical future.

Their bodies are buried in peace but their name liveth forevermore. My own career in the field ends with this essay. Ends with these lines as I write them. In another magazine now on the stands is my farewell essay: of that and my own difficult career nothing here. *Their names liveth forevermore.* Fifty years and forever, yet into darkness, I am one of Hugo's children.

Me too.

AUTHOR'S BIOGRAPHY

Born 1939, married 1964, one daughter 1966, another 1970. Resident of New York City (with side trips to Fort Dix and Syracuse) until 1971, when I fled to the pastoral serenity of this town of forty thousand souls in Bergen County, just two miles from the Ridgefield Park Oil Dump & Refinery. Author of about seventy published novels, some of them science fiction, and over a hundred and sixty short stories, the majority of them science fiction. *Beyond Apollo* (Random House, 1972) won the first John W. Campbell Memorial Award for year's best science fiction novel. I've been a full-time writer for almost nine years now and a part-time writer for thirty but this collection may be considered my employment application to the world at large. Anybody want a good scenarist? Copywriter? Collection agent?